The Holy Embrace

Mario Brelich

The Holy Embrace

Translated from Italian by John Shepley

T M P

The Marlboro Press / Northwestern
Evanston, Illinois

The Marlboro Press/Northwestern
Northwestern Unviersity Press
Evanston, Illinois 60208-4210

The publication of this volume has been made possible in part by a grant from the National Endowment for the Arts.

Printed in the United States of America

ISBN 0-8101-6029-3

Contents

The Holy Embrace

1. Abraham laughs

WHEN AFTER AN INTERVAL OF FOURTEEN YEARS, THE LORD AP-
peared unexpectedly before him, Abraham felt a gloomy presentiment rising in his heart. In his opinion, there was no reason for
the Lord ever again to intervene personally in the private affairs of
His discoverer and sole follower. Such an epiphany might be reassuring in grave situations, but when everything was going reasonably well, it looked like a threat.

Pricking up his ears to the divine declamation, he gradually
yielded to the hope that he might change his mind, since at first
it was a matter of the usual, all too familiar promises. And even
when the business of circumcision was sprung on him, it still
seemed to Abraham that the painful operation might not be the
agonizing and endless one that he—perhaps needlessly—had
feared.

But when the Lord told him, point-blank and almost in passing, that Sarah would give birth to a son, Abraham for a fraction of a second felt the blood run cold in his veins, but then immediately broke out in a hearty laugh. A particularly hearty laugh, which helped him somewhat to recover himself, and also to chide himself for the imbecility of letting his blood run cold by hearkening to such a stupid idea. For what the Lord had said was truly a stupid idea. It was even unimaginable that anyone should have been able to utter anything so outlandish with a straight face, and in the case of the Lord such a howler was simply incredible since He claimed to read the future like an open book. Was it possible that the present was actually hidden from Him by an impenetrable veil? Or merely that in His peculiar sense of time, tempered by eternity, fourteen years were no longer than a humanly perceived moment? But here was the point: in the imperceptible duration of that divine moment the eighty-five-year-old Abraham had become a ninety-nine-year-old Abraham, and—what was still more painful—Sarah's number of years had risen from seventy-five to eighty-nine! So what might have happened fourteen years ago, or ten years ago, or even only a few years ago, by now was absolutely out of the question. In the absence of proof, Abraham was not a hundred percent sure of his own generative capacities, but that Sarah's womb would no longer be capable of conceiving, of this he was absolutely sure, since it had *ceased to be with Sarah after the manner of women.*

A silly idea is a silly idea, and yet the laugh died in his throat and a cold sweat broke out on his forehead. All of a sudden he realized that to laugh out loud at the Lord was worse than an act of irreverence, and so he fell on his face, huddling as low as he could. But any desire to laugh was also dispelled independently of this thought, so much so that he hated himself for the mere fact of having been able to laugh. For the Lord's words had reopened a wound in his soul that had never completely healed and still ached. The subject He had broached with such a ruthless lack of consideration was the great drama of his life and it brought back to him a swarm of sad, shameful, and humiliating memories that left a bitter taste in his mouth and brought a flood of tears to his eyes.

Besides hating himself, he directed a sullen reproach at the Lord, who not only had reopened the wounds in his soul, but had done so in a manner so indelicate as to border on the impropriety of a joke. Abraham, huddling on the ground, feverishly sought a justification for the Being he himself had discovered. Should one suppose that He hadn't pondered what He'd said? That He'd paid no attention to it? Or that He was unaware of reality? To be able to suppose all this, Abraham would have had to refashion entirely the idea he had formed of the Lord, the idea that had been revealed to him in a flash of intuition and with a clarity impossible to doubt, and confirmed later as well by a goodly number of experiences. But one could imagine anything about the Lord, except that He'd been joking.

By now Abraham's shoulders were shuddering. If the Lord had not been joking, then He'd been speaking seriously, and this meant that everything was about to collapse. At least his masterpiece was about to collapse, that serene and harmonious equilibrium that almost seemed like happiness and which, in the course of these last fourteen years, he had built out of renunciation, humiliation, and compromise—for his personal use, as well as for the greater glory of the Lord. The edifice, whose bricks were made of his ceaseless abnegation, cemented by the tears of his daily submission, all of a sudden seemed fated to fall. And with it the peace and quiet of his domestic life, as well as the splendid future repeatedly promised and just now reconfirmed by the Lord, a future that so far had seemed to rest on Ishmael, his only son, who had also been foretold by the Lord and begotten with the handmaid more as a favor to Him than to himself. What more did He want? What did He still want? In Abraham's opinion, things were going fine the way they were; he was already old, he wanted no changes, he had even come to enjoy the melancholy order of his life, and, most of all, he loved his only son, Ishmael.

All of a sudden he realized that—although he'd been thinking about the Lord without interruption—he had forgotten His presence. He was struck by the profound silence that seemed to emanate from his interlocutor. Was He still there? Or, mortally offended by his disrespectful laugh, had He left him to himself and his worries?

He plucked up his courage and risked a quick look. But raising his eyes wasn't enough, he had also to raise his head. For while he was lying there in fear, his face pressed to the ground, the figure of the Lord had grown stupendously, reaching three times His original height, and now He was standing there erect, His arms folded in patient, almost pitying expectation. Now Abraham realized that his last hopes that it was all a joke—by now he would have preferred it to be only a joke, even if one of questionable taste!—were wholly in vain, and at the same time he knew with deadly certainty that whatever the Lord desired would always and irrevocably happen. By this time his requests had been reduced to the minimum, and he would have been more than content if the Lord at least took no notice of his laughter . . .

He rose to his knees and, with the submissive gesture of someone declaring himself beaten and vanquished, spread his arms. But the Lord did not move. He still stood there motionless, with aloof patience, and it seemed to Abraham that He was waiting for him to say something. With what courage he had left, but with extreme modesty, almost whimpering, he presumed to remind the Lord of Ishmael's existence.

But the Lord was obviously expecting something else. Hearing the name Ishmael, He wrinkled His brow, like a teacher who, having thrown an easy question to a slow pupil, hears him answer like a jackass. Instead of resorting to His own omniscience for something so minor, He let Himself be persuaded by His first impression, which was that His faithful follower hadn't heard or hadn't understood what He had said. But since it was something of which Abraham had necessarily to be aware if he was to collaborate, the Lord took pains to make sure that even the slightest doubt was dispelled from his brain. From the height of His superhuman stature, He bent slightly forward; not thundering this time, as was His habit, but almost whispering, while nevertheless articulating His words, and in particular—to avoid any misunderstanding whatsoever—reducing everything to the simplest terms, He repeated: *"Sarah thy wife shall bear thee a son . . ."*

Abraham, who already for some time had been unable to understand how he could ever have laughed, now went pale and gave himself up to unrestrained trembling; touching his throat as though he were about to suffocate, he gazed at the Lord with his eyes popping out of his head. Whereupon the Lord, His eyes glaring in a burst of anger, bent down still further and—now in His usual manner—thundered in the ear of His faithful follower: *". . . and thou shalt call his name Isaac!"*

And thus He remained, stooping slightly forward, almost as though to observe or savor the effect of His words. Hearing this name uttered, the man, who seen from his interlocutor's supernatural height must have looked like a miserable worm, visibly shook, drew his neck back between his shoulders and groped with both hands on the ground so as not to fall. For "Isaac" meant nothing less than "laughter," and this suggested that his laugh had not escaped the Lord's attention. It was clearly His subtle way of punishing his irreverent behavior. In drawing this conclusion from his experience, Abraham was able on the spot to add to his knowledge of the Lord the observation that it wasn't even possible to fool Him. He accordingly prostrated himself and surrendered to the Lord's discretion.

The Lord felt almost sorry for the little man whom He Himself had put in such a sorry fix, and so, partly out of pity, partly to instill strength and courage in him in view of the grandiose and imminent tasks awaiting him, He spoke some bland and conciliatory words, promising that He would establish His covenant with that troubling son, who merely by being named had aroused such terror, and reasserting that it would be *an everlasting covenant, and with his seed after him . . .* Indeed, to compensate His chosen follower for the troubles that would befall him, He reassured him that He had not been deaf to his moans and that He wished to provide for Ishmael as well by blessing him, making him fruitful, and multiplying him exceedingly. Nevertheless, He added emphatically: *"But my covenant will I establish with Isaac, which Sarah shall bear unto thee at this set time in the next year!"*

Abraham, who until that moment, face down on the ground, had been indulging disconsolately in all these consolations, on hearing these last divine words began spinning like a top, and jumping to his feet, backed away with the heaving chest and wild eyes of someone who has seen a ghost. He felt that he'd been rudely awakened, not from sleep, since he had undoubtedly been awake from the start, but from a hugely mystifying nightmare. Now he felt sufficient presence of mind to clarify a few by no means negligible circumstances with the Lord.

But the Lord had vanished. Abraham stood there by himself, bewildered, dazed, and powerless in the face of the nightmare. Already, in his mystified stupor, he had almost ended by accepting the absurdity that Sarah would bear him a son. But being informed of the time period, that looming deadline, drove the absurdity, never completely accepted, back into the realm of the impossible.

Abraham still did not know that the Lord was capable of performing miracles. But even had he suspected it, the fact remained that he would certainly not lend the Lord a hand in producing the miracle in question. And not only because in his heart he was opposed to the divine plan. Rather it was the simple fact that he wouldn't even be able to broach the subject to Sarah.

II. The discoverer

NO ONE SHOULD HOLD IT AGAINST ABRAHAM FOR FAILING TO understand how the advent of Isaac was important to the Lord. It's all very well too discover the only God, but understanding Him is another matter. To come relatively close to comprehending Him requires historical perspective, something that, *ipso facto*, was denied to Abraham, along with a wealth of experience in which he was lacking, having barely gathered a few first fruits. His relations with the Lord were necessarily limited to "walking together," that is, to seeking His approval and serving His plan, willingly or unwillingly, or even resisting and impeding it. All this is compatible with this wonderful "walking with the Lord," and even an integral part of it.

The most important and—we might say—fundamental step that he could have taken was in discovering, or—to be precise— rediscovering the Lord, by identifying Him with the sole true and living God, creator and ruler of the Universe, an eternal and infinitely powerful Being, compared to whom all the other gods worshipped by his ancestors and kinsmen, and by neighboring peoples, turned out to be nothing more than false and lying idols. The existence and essence of this sole true and living God were so obvious to Abraham as to exclude any doubt whatsoever and automatically determine his regular and religious behavior. Taking his stand on the evidence and on his considerable intuition, he admired and venerated this Lord, worshipped Him, sacrificed to Him animals chosen in accordance with common sense, and faithfully implored His favor. Personal experiences also came to his aid. He had found in the Lord a very austere, almost grim Being, who simultaneously aroused fear and faith; His promises seemed to be both challenges to reasoning calculation and expressions of an inflexible will. Since the Lord had kept His promises and even given Abraham more than he'd expected, Abraham would also have been inclined to call Him good, had not this goodness contained a menacing rigidity that made it almost horrifying. It was Abraham's experience that the Lord was even too powerful to bother about being consistent, and so the discoverer never succeeded in freeing himself from anxiety that His generosity might all of a sudden cease, leaving him once again in trouble. Abraham could not forget the hard times of the famine that had driven him to the land of Egypt, nor the awful trials that had befallen him there, laying, to be sure, the firm foundations of his prosperity but also of his unhappiness. For the Lord had undoubtedly abandoned him that time. But since He had been close to him before and had been so again afterward, for Abraham there was only one explanation for such behavior: the Lord was capricious as well.

It is clear that despite the originality of some of Abraham's observations, his knowledge of the Lord was rather rudimentary, and the image he had formed of Him, while incomparably more flattering than the one later formed by Job, was nevertheless quite paltry, not to say offensive, compared to the idea of God that would be developed by the Doctors of the Church in the course of subsequent millennia. But what can we say? To re-exhume and put back in circulation the sole true and living God, who had been submerged in oblivion, was an enormous human achievement, and one for which Abraham deserves a prominent place among the greatest and most important figures in our history, if not actually the place of honor. To ask that he also be the founder of theology would really be too much.

Nothing could have been further from Abraham's mind than an intention to theologize. Mystical by nature and calling, he arrived at the concept of God thanks to an immediate intuitive vision, and—like all outstanding mystics—he was satisfied with the experience as he had had it, as well as with the practical conclusions that spontaneously flowed from it. Given his direct contact with God, he would have found it quite unnecessary to rack his brains over what He was like in reality or *an sich*. The discovery alone was enough to make him exultant and elated, as is shown besides by old legends.

The Bible tells us nothing about Abraham's youth, but the memory of it has been preserved in the rabbinical texts. According to the tradition, Abraham was a hotheaded young man, restless to the point of fanaticism. Having gained possession of the great truth, he was unable to contain himself, and in his impatience was driven to commit rash acts. Having come to know the sole true and living God, he became intransigent in the presence of idols, and this was a disaster, because it was precisely by keeping a store that sold statuettes of idols that his father, old Terah, made a living and supported his numerous family in Ur of the Chaldees. Helping to run the store was the duty of his firstborn son, to wit, our Abraham. But the elated store clerk's presence did the business more harm than good. Instead of urging the customers to buy, he would frighten them by picking up a statuette and smashing its head on the counter, in order to show that it was just a piece of pottery and had nothing to do with gods. He ended by judging the buying and selling of idols to be incompatible with his discovery. Hotheaded as he was, he became the torment of his family, haranguing them at every moment and exhorting them to give up that accursed shop. One fine day, after Haran, the second of his two younger brothers, had tried for the nth time to make him understand that the store was the single humble basis for the whole family's subsistence, Abraham flew into a rage and set fire to the storeroom full of statuettes. By this rash gesture, he also became the unintentional cause of his brother's death, since Haran, in an effort to save whatever he could, had plunged desperately into the flames, and in his excessive zeal perished along with his beloved idols.

All this we learn from the rabbinical tradition. Without going into the question of the "historicity," in the absolute sense, of the legends and biblical tales, nor that of the "veracity" of the legends as compared to the biblical version, we are glad to include this tradition because it allows us to imagine, on a historical and psychological level as well, what is added mythologically: the reason for Terah's departure from Ur.

Mythologically speaking, Terah's move had been a foregone conclusion from the beginning of time, determined by that kind of destiny that is contained in numbers and to which primordial generations in all mythologies are subject. The specific case of Terah was irrevocably influenced by the fact that he found himself in a position similar to that of Adam or Noah, and sometimes both of them simultaneously. On one side, he was the tenth and last of a series of generations that ended with him; on the other, he was the first of another series of generations of which he was the beginning. There should be no need to recall that these last and first tenths always find themselves in a situation that compels them to leave the place where their ancestors have lived and to move someplace where their descendants will continue to live. The "move" in this case is not purely a matter of space; it is also, and primarily, of a spiritual nature, since the man, by changing his place, finds that his whole position before God, the universe, and his own life has changed as well. The mythical move, whether Adam's removal from Eden, or Noah's upward voyage on the waters of the flood, always ends by setting humanity's march on a new track, and

Adam's son Seth and Noah's son Shem not only found themselves in new physical surroundings, but also in a wholly new spiritual position, with the task of creating *ex novo* a world for future humanity. And this precisely without the resources lost by reason of the move, and with only the ones now discovered, which moreover have at the same time been the primary cause of the compulsory move. This, then, was the case with Abraham, son of Terah the emigrant, simultaneously tenth and first.

As we mentioned, and as anyway everyone knows, neither Adam nor Noah left their original residences on their own initiative, but were forced to do so by God: they were, so to speak, evicted. At first sight, Terah's case would not seem to be identical with theirs. But thanks to the version preserved by the rabbis, we can easily imagine that the destruction of the store that sold statuettes, and the subsequent death of his youngest son, Haran, induced him to leave Ur and, old and tired of living as he was, to try to make a new life for himself elsewhere and forget his grief. And when we stop to think about it, Terah's emigration was the direct result of Abraham's great discovery: the reappearance of the sole true and living God in the history of man. Though its cause was indirect, the move was once again by divine command. This was how Abraham arrived in Haran, close to that land of Canaan where the next phase of humanity's life, in its march toward new positions of the spirit, later began.

Historiography points to religious antipathy and economic oppression on the part of a formerly hospitable empire as the cause for the southward migration of the Semitic nomad tribes, and it is our impression that the legend faithfully mirrors these two principal factors stressed by scholars. It is gratifying when tradition agrees with historiography and psychology, even if such consistency has little or no importance and can be considered as pure and simple coincidence. For us the importance of tradition lies in the very fact that it was once conceived by a people as truth: this in itself is already an essential historical fact and a sufficiently solid basis for our investigations. Thus when we try to probe, for example, the

"Abrahamic moment" in humanity's march—a term we like to use for the historical phase in which man discovered the idea of the sole true and living God—we can rely with complete confidence on the biblical story and the rabbinical legends, without worrying about their "historicity." It follows logically that in this particular case the question as to whether old Terah was really a shopkeeper who sold idols and whose capricious eldest son had actually caused the death of his youngest brother has no importance. What is essential for us is the historical fact that "once upon a time" in the eyes of the Jewish people the collision between the old gods and the new God centered on the figures of Haran and Abraham.

The biblical account, while giving no motivation for it, relates that after Haran's death old Terah *took Abram his son, and Lot the son of Haran his son's son, and Sarai his daughter-in-law, his son Abram's wife; and they went forth with them from Ur of the Chaldees, to go into the land of Canaan; and they came unto Haran, and dwelt there.* One can well imagine that it was a real relief for Abraham, in his increasing impatience with false and lying gods, to leave the land of the Chaldees. But if he found himself uncomfortable in Ur, he was surely no better off in Haran, the religious center of the cult of the moon god Sin and his wife Ningal, who were worshipped with spectacular rites. And in addition to the unbridled idolatry of the population, Abraham had another reason for disliking the place, for if his family had just managed to get by in Ur, they were even worse off in Haran. If we decide to exclude the trade in idols as having too legendary a flavor, we have no clue as to the profession exercised by Abraham with his family in Ur: whether they were really engaged in commerce or handicraft, typically urban occupations, or had remained faithful to the occupation of their ancestors, raising livestock. In any case, Abraham in Haran started raising sheep. Had it not been for Terah's advanced age, the little tribe of shepherds would not have been tied to the city; Abraham's nomad soul roamed eagerly over Canaan's endless expanses of verdant grazing land, which enticed him with the promise of ample food for his modest flocks and freedom from the hell of idolatry.

The dream of God's discoverer was to devote himself intensely, in those nearby yet inaccessible plains, to his discovery, toward which he had felt driven from the beginning by a mystical rapture. To worship this Being that he had divined and conceived as pure spirit, to merge the best part of himself, his spirit, with Him in unsurpassed orgiastic unity, to possess Him completely and be possessed by Him—this was what he had craved ever since his arrival in Haran.

If Abraham was never able to achieve a mystical union with the Lord, whom he had after all discovered for this very purpose, it was largely due to his repeated meetings and personal contacts with Him. The first divine apparition can already be said to have left him disappointed, since he would never have imagined that such a god could materialize in apparitions, especially in human form, and moreover in the shape of a venerable middle-aged man, bearded and dressed like a simple shepherd. This god, of course, inspired considerable respect, but not loving outbursts and mystical rapture. From the beginning, this god had not seemed to care about being worshipped or loved, but occupied Himself exclusively with His discoverer and in particular with his future. And when this Lord had promised him point-blank that He would make of him *a great nation* and would treat other nations in the manner in which they treated Abraham—and especially after the second apparition, during which this god had also promised him the rich land that had enchanted him at first sight—a strange idea had begun forming in Abraham's head about the Being he had discovered, namely, that all the Lord would be good for—and this would be His mission—would be to protect him and make him rich and powerful. It was painful to realize that this god was not suitable to be worshipped in loving ecstasy; on the other hand, the disappointment was largely compensated by the discovery of those of His aspects that guaranteed practical advantages, even though they lay outside the confines of his great intuition. Besides, the Lord, apart from these greater and lesser disparities, corresponded more or less to the image that His discoverer had formed of Him, and the same outer appearance in which he made Himself visible fully confirmed the qualities glimpsed in the discovery: strength, iron will, and unlimited power. Thus Abraham ended by being convinced that he could wholly entrust himself and his future to this attentive god, who almost seemed unable to find proper words to express His gratitude at having been discovered.

The promptings of this extraordinary god made it imperative that Abraham decide to leave Haran and set out for the plains of Canaan. Although his heretofore cherished idea of great mystical abandonment had lost its allure, he was all the more seduced by the possibility of getting rich and becoming the founder and respected leader of a great people. Now nothing could keep him from setting out. While up until that moment he had kept in mind his father's advanced age, all of a sudden he deemed him not so old as to be unable to be alone (indeed, the old man was only 145, fairly old, but not too much, since he was to live another sixty years in his solitude in Haran!). The objections of his beautiful wife and the worries of young Lot counted for nothing, and Abraham squelched them by declaring that things would go much better in the land of Canaan, and in any case no worse than they had gone in Haran. And this was an incontrovertible argument.

Actually, for a long period of time, this argument was all he had to console him. The land, so enticing when viewed from afar, did not welcome him with open arms, and because of one of its frequent droughts, Abraham was forced to migrate still farther south to find pasturage for his meager flocks. Now he no longer dared to say that things were going no worse than they'd gone in Haran, preferring to state cautiously that even in Haran things hadn't gone much better. But verbal subtleties did not prevent him from finding himself, along with his family, shepherds, and flocks, faced with the terror of famine.

These times were also critical for his relations with the Lord. Abraham arrived at the hasty conclusion that the Lord had abandoned him just when his fortunes were at their lowest. And note that Abraham did not say this in the metaphorical sense, as an ordinary mortal might express himself in his hour of need, but in the literal sense of the word. He had believed—and according to his best conviction he had every right to believe—that the Lord, who had already appeared to him twice without being asked, promising him everything under the sun, would turn up again now that His faithful follower really needed Him, and at least make a down payment on his future riches so that he wouldn't die of hunger. But the Lord remained deaf to the most desperate appeals, and poor Abraham, left to his own devices, could do nothing but follow the example of other nomad tribes and seek refuge in the powerful land of Egypt.

Egypt was the supreme test of Abraham's faith. It would be rash to say that God Himself had put him to the test, but the fact is that Abraham was offered a unique opportunity to prove his faith. He suffered the tragic moment of the believer: he would have liked to doubt the validity of his discovery but realized he was unable to. The existence of the sole true and living God was so overwhelmingly obvious to him as to leave him with not even a doubt—despite the Lord's frightful deafness and total eclipse—about whether or not to worship Him, pray to Him, or offer Him sacrifices. At most, Abraham could expand his fund of knowledge of the Lord with the observation that not only was He not an ideal object for loving impulses, but was also essentially different from the way He had hitherto shown Himself. For now it had turned out that the Lord had other things in mind besides helping Abraham, and that he, on the other hand, did not have the power to summon Him in every circumstance in which he might need Him. He still did not have in his hands any decisive proof that would cast doubt on the Lord's honesty and make him lose faith in His promises, but he could not help observing that in His generosity—assuming it wasn't simply boasting—there were large gaps that He was in no hurry to fill. Abraham found himself faced for the first time with the horror that derived from the singleness of the single God. Sarah and Lot prayed with almost ostentatious fervor to the idols they had smuggled from Chaldea, while he directed his prayers to the canvas of his tent or the empty air, beyond which he heard only the Lord's indifference. Thus Abraham also discovered the tragedy of the monotheist: there was no one to appeal to against the Lord!

It was only later and little by little that Abraham came to realize that, in the final analysis, it had been the horror and disgrace of Egypt that had laid the foundations for his comfortable life, and that thus it had been in that period of desolation that one of the most important of the Lord's promises had started on its way to fulfillment. In keeping with this discovery, he had immediately to rectify his previous opinions on the subject of the Lord, which had been suggested to him less by common sense than by hunger and despair. In reality, the Lord had not abandoned him, since it is wrong to call it abandonment when someone withdraws who has previously taken measures that are to our advantage. The Lord had promised to make him rich and had certainly arranged it all in such a way that at the moment of leaving Egypt, the land of his ordeal, he really was rich. But he might have pointed out to the Lord that He had never mentioned the circumstances in which He would make him rich, nor the price he would have to pay. Having realized all this, Abraham began to understand that it would be his responsibility, and not the Lord's, to deal with his wife.

When, after the separation with Lot, the Lord finally deigned to appear again, He behaved as though His follower's family disasters were no concern of His. He didn't even think it necessary to justify Himself for the trials and tribulations that He had put Abraham through. From the height of His inaccessibility, He gazed at him with a total lack of compassion, while His attitude seemed to say, "What I promised has become reality. You're rich and you're going to get richer. You see, I keep My promises." And after this silent yet eloquent preamble, He began to utter explicit words: *"Lift up now thine eyes, and look from the place where thou art northward, and southward, and eastward, and westward. For all the land which thou seest, to thee will I give it, and to thy seed forever."* Abraham didn't doubt it for a moment, for by this time he understood that all sorts of things could be expected from such a god, and now having set out on the road to fortune, he by no means excluded the possibility that he would get even richer—much, much richer.

There was one point, however, in this divine speech that disheartened him. The Lord, who from the beginning of their contacts had never failed to stress that He would make him the progenitor of a great nation, had now gone further and supplied details about his descendants: *"I will make thy seed as the dust of the earth,"* He had said, *"so that if a man can number the dust of the earth, then shall thy seed also be numbered"*—which, in plain language, meant an awful lot of descendants. And the Lord had declared all this with the most natural self-assuredness, as though becoming the progenitor of so many offspring were the simplest and most obvious thing in this world. But this was precisely what disheartened Abraham: after all these years of marriage and in the middle of his life's journey, he found himself without even a single child. And after his relations with Sarah had deteriorated badly due to the Egyptian mishap, the question had become an acutely painful one. But the Lord seemed unmindful of the difficulties of his conjugal life.

But from that moment on, Abraham no longer had any doubts that the Lord was with him, despite the fact—fortunately in diametrically opposed circumstances, and even for a much longer period of time—that what had once happened during the months of testing in Egypt was later repeated: God had indeed abandoned him. But what a difference! This time the abandonment was purely physical in nature, in that the Lord did not put in an appearance for many long years, but Abraham had the pleasurable sensation that in all his acts his hand was being guided by God. He lived in a kind of giddy whirl of his own success and was convinced that nothing could impede his rise. By now he was not only rich, but respected and feared. By now he fought with kings and fraternized with kings, and the number of servants born in his household was large enough to form a small army. And once he had joined his own slender forces with those of four allied kings and inflicted a stunning defeat on the combined armies of five enemy kings, freeing Lot, along with his family and goods, from captivity, others also realized that he had extraordinary good fortune and began to entertain the idea that he was being helped precisely by that mysterious Lord he worshipped.

If Abraham had hitherto had any doubts (which he didn't) about the validity of his discovery, it was in this very period of time that an exceptional occasion arose that would have thoroughly convinced him that the god who had been revealed to him in a flash of intuition and with undeniable clarity was not simply a fixation of his own resulting from visions and hallucinations, as people—including his own consort, the beautiful Sarah—tried to insinuate and even said explicitly. The exceptional occasion was an exceptional meeting. One day Abraham made the acquaintance of a very authoritative person to whom the sole true and living God, creator of heaven and earth, omnipotent sovereign of the universe, was just as much a reality as for him.

In the presence of Melchizedek, priest-king of Salem, Abraham had the irritating sensation of being a vulgar *parvenu*, because His Majesty, when important feasts were held, made offerings of bread and wine to the sole true and living God, and he did so in a routine fashion devoid of any emotion, his ancestors having done the same thing since time immemorial. It was with aristocratic detachment that Melchizedek always spoke of the Lord, whose existence seemed to him a matter of ordinary administration, no more curious that any phenomenon of daily life, and he showed not the least surprise at the fact that Abraham venerated the same Lord; the only thing that amazed him was the frantic way in which the leader of the nomad tribe conducted his religious worship.

The polite welcome, by no means the enthusiastic one he had expected, caused Abraham some difficult days, and feeling he had been humiliated, he gave in to a deep sense of depression. In this state of mind, he felt exactly like someone who—as we say nowadays—realizes all of a sudden that he has "discovered America." For while on the one hand it was extremely comforting to persuade himself that the Lord was not simply his own fixation, on the other it was disappointing to learn that he had not been His first discoverer, and not a little worrisome not to be able to consider Him his private property. Envy gnawed at his heart, and he racked his brains in an effort to demonstrate at least to himself that the king of Salem's experience of the Lord was far from being genuine like his own, and in any case was much inferior in value. The problem seemed to him immensely important. For who and what was there to guarantee that the purpose of divine existence was to help Abraham and not, for instance, Melchizedek? It was truly agonizing to imagine that any newcomer might assure himself the Lord's favors by the simple act of discovering Him and offering Him sacrifices. In Abraham's view, the Lord ought to remain the prerogative of himself and his progeny!

After much mental effort he finally found his irrefutable arguments, and for expounding them with a certain authority the above-mentioned battle came at the right time. For the king of Salem, Abraham's resounding victory was the work of the sole true and living God, who in a manifest way had hastened to back up His follower. Abraham understood that his stock was rising and that the time had come to register the patent on his great discovery. In the course of a friendly banquet, he astonished and almost quashed his royal host by revealing to him—as he had never dared to do before—that he often entertained the sole true and living God, and that the Lord had already several times deigned to pay him a visit in human and superhuman form. Melchizedek found this hard to believe, since they were dealing with a Being of pure spirit, but he couldn't completely withhold credence, since this Being was also omnipotent. Abraham even went on to tell him about the divine promises and the down payments that had been made on them. Melchizedek listened with growing astonishment—now he was the one to envy the stranger—and delicately began to question him on how to induce the Almighty to cooperate more actively and fruitfully with him and his people as well. The king's probings served Abraham as a pretext to tell him something that had been weighing on him for some time and, in his opinion, was one more proof of the superiority of his own experience with the Lord. "There may perhaps be a way, my royal friend," replied Abraham, with ill-concealed arrogance, "but you people have never tried it. I confess that your sacrifice has bothered me from the beginning. You have tried to persuade me, but tacitly I've always refused to offer bread and wine to the Lord. Anyone who truly knows Him, who knows Him personally the way I do, would consider such an offering almost detrimental. So that you can correct your idea of Him, I'll let you in on a secret: God is carnivorous!"

That the Lord was owed a sacrifice of animals was one of Abraham's prime convictions. The ancient legend of the first sacrifice, in which God had accepted Abel's sheep and disdainfully rejected Cain's cereals, had been handed down in his family from father to son. He was only worried by the fact that as a result of their wanderings and their contacts with other peoples in the course of the millennia, his ancestors had not only lost any precise idea of the sole God, but also the memory of the divine tastes, which meant that Abraham, in reinstating the institution of sacrifice, had had to use his own judgment in choosing the sacrificial victims, and always with the painful impression that they were not to the Lord's liking. But the Lord had never declared Himself on the subject; to tell the truth, He had not even asked for a sacrifice. It would have been a great relief to Abraham were He to communicate His gastronomical preferences. Indeed, he could not get it out of his head that the Lord would treat him still better if he were able to treat Him better. After all, from a certain standpoint, the Lord was still in his debt.

Among the Lord's debts, Abraham did not really count those promises involving a more distant future. From the beginning he had been convinced—although he kept getting richer, increasingly so and potentially to the utmost limit of what was possible—that he would not live long enough to be able to make sure, for example, whether the land of Canaan had come into his descendants' possession or not, and therefore to this aspect he displayed the greatest indifference. Of course, such indifference bordered on selfishness, but on the other hand it was also marked by a kind of benevolent indulgence as far as the Lord was concerned. In his heart Abraham, without realizing it, tended to excuse the Lord from expending His energies in huge efforts to keep such long-range promises, exhorting Him privately to concentrate on keeping promises closer in time.

Indeed, he did not feel disposed to dwell on those of the Lord's promises that directly concerned the present but whose fulfillment seemed to be postponed simply because they also referred, in more spectacular dimensions, to the future. Abraham could not understand why the prospect of becoming the progenitor of a great nation should in the meantime exclude or delay his becoming the father of a son, at least of an only son. In line with his selfish way of reasoning, this primarily interested him from the standpoint of the present: he ardently wished for a son, not so much as a link in a chain between himself and his immense progeny, as for the simple and quite understandable motive of having an heir to whom he could leave his name, his wealth, and the general reputation that he had achieved for himself. With childish cunning he tried to interest the Lord in this question, pointing out to Him that, in the absence any offspring, it would be difficult to become the progenitor of a posterity as numerous as the dust of the earth. But since the Lord had not put in an appearance for many long years, there was nothing for Abraham to do but pray, though always with the painful impression that his prayers did not go beyond the walls of his tent, or, what was worse, rebounded against the Lord's apathetic deafness. And since otherwise everything kept sailing smoothly along, Abraham could permit himself the luxury of yielding from time to time to the bitterest despondency.

He was precisely in one of these moments of depression when the Lord, after an interval of seven or eight years, unexpectedly reappeared to him. The Lord, for reasons He had carefully considered, would have liked this encounter to be an exceptionally solemn one, and had thus renounced the paltry guise of the nomadic divinity in which He had so far shown Himself, in favor of a supernatural appearance that allowed Him to take on a luminous and suggestive form. He had not foreseen that His discoverer and sole follower would be in such a glum mood, hadn't foreseen it or didn't notice it. Anyway He paid no attention to it, and in His usual fashion began to assure Abraham of His favor and promise him great rewards. That was all Abraham needed! Losing all self-control, he burst out in a string of reproofs, upbraiding the Lord to His face that all His gifts and rewards weren't worth a hill of beans, since he, Abraham, was still without offspring and all his worldly goods would be inherited by the sons of his servants.

The Lord was hurt, having frankly expected a quite different welcome. But He was also perplexed by the very fact that His follower had scolded Him with such bitter vehemence. For the first time His eyes were opened to the strange reality that Abraham as yet had no children, while according to the best testimony of His omniscience he was supposed to become the progenitor of countless generations. The Lord was certain that an error on His own part was to be excluded, if only for the qualities inherent in His divine essence, and that He could therefore trust blindly in His own prescience. When He realized this, His luminous face darkened in a fit of rage, and in the indignant tone of someone who has suffered an undeserved affront, He thundered in His discoverer's ear that his heir would not be the son of a servant but *shall come forth out of thine own bowels!* The images that sprang from His prescience gradually took on more precise outlines and He clearly remembered having compared the multitude of His follower's progeny to the numberless dust of the earth. Suddenly seized by one of His frequent rhetorical outbursts—for the Lord considered rhetoric one of the most effective means of persuasion in His dealings with men—He felt the urge to invite the little man, still sputtering and red in the face with emotion, to come out of the cave in which they found themselves and try to count the dust, or at least the dust of that piece of earth that his gaze could encompass. But in a flash of inspiration, a much more compelling poetic metaphor came to His mind. With a violent shove He flung Abraham out of the cave into the open air and with an inimitable gesture of triumph pointed to the sky: ". . . *tell the stars, if thou be able to number them!*"

No one would dare to doubt that the Lord is a gifted stage director, but this scene—perhaps because it was improvised—should be considered one of the most serious oversights of His career. For when Abraham raised his eyes to the sky, he couldn't see a single star, since it was still daylight and the sun remained well above the western horizon. But the wonder was that the Lord gave no sign of embarrassment, obviously because He saw the stars all the same and also had some idea of their infinite number. To Abraham, however, the new poetic image may also have implied a drastic reduction in the promised progeny, because if the dust of the earth was clearly infinite, the same could not be said for the number of stars, which even at night, when you could see them, barely amounted to a thousand or so. Fortunately Abraham felt both too confused and too tired to argue, and so when, at the Lord's prompting, he raised his eyes to the sky and failed to see even one star, he didn't bat an eyelash. Whether the stars were there or not, he was now well aware of what the Lord meant by telling him to count them. The main thing, even now, was that the Lord was promising him innumerable descendants, this time including, however, a son born from his bowels.

We ought not to scold Abraham if the divine generosity did not immediately succeed in dispelling his black mood, and if his distrust, after so many bitter experiences, did not instantly dissolve. The Lord, warming to His theme, spoke again of the promised land, but Abraham was too exhausted to be moved by rich future prospects; he had waited too long to be satisfied with relations based on trust and patience: now he wanted certainty. He therefore took the liberty of arresting the avalanche of divine words and asked for a sign.

The sign he received was not exactly an answer to his problems, but it was undoubtedly a sign. Its meaning and importance, namely, that the Lord had concluded an everlasting covenant with him, must have unfolded in his mind only at a later stage; for the moment the sign, chaotic, overpowering, annihilating, did nothing but confuse and cloud his reason. Everything that happened proceeded slowly and turned into a nightmare.

When the Lord, in an unusually low voice, ordered him to take *an heifer of three years old, and a she goat of three years old, and a ram of three years old, and a turtledove, and a young pigeon*, Abraham realized that a great thing was happening, a huge wish of his was about to be granted. The Lord, finally, was asking him for something and moreover specifying the sort of offering He preferred! Beside himself with emotion, he ran to his stables, took the largest of the animals that had been demanded, and as he led them toward the site of the apparition, he blushed in recalling his previous sacrifices, which must have left the Lord dissatisfied; at the same time, however, he had to laugh, thinking of Melchizedek's grotesque offering! He had been right in supposing that the Lord liked meat. But never would he have imagined that He had such a huge appetite!

The agitation that had seized him from the beginning was now growing, also because, the Lord being in the mood to be specific, Abraham hoped for further clarification of his promised paternity. He therefore breathlessly slaughtered the animals, *divided them in the midst*, and with hands trembling in this feverish state, *laid each piece one against another*, separating what was due to God from what was due to man. Although he had performed these operations with precision, he could feel his ideas getting more and more muddled; all of a sudden he began wildly gesticulating, almost crushed by the realization that although the victims for the sacrifice were there already, the wood and fire were missing. (And he would remember this strange coincidence many years later, when the Lord was to demand another sacrifice of him, and his unsuspecting son would point out to him that, yes, the wood and fire were there, but the victim was missing!)

He had still not found a solution when from above certain *fowls came down upon the carcases* and with fearful persistence and greed tried to take possession of what should have had a more sacred destination. Abraham, huffing and puffing, attacked them furiously with a club, but oddly enough, while human intervention usually made vultures change their minds, these kept coming back. Abraham, no longer thinking of the Lord, who stood waiting in silence a few paces away, or remembering that he was expecting a specific and important answer, gave himself up entirely to the struggle, which in its maddening futility seemed more and more like a horrible nightmare. He ended by hoping that it actually was a dream, since it would have been a real relief to take the horror of reality for a dream.

In this uncertain state between dream and reality he finally succeeded in his efforts, and with threatening squawks the vultures dispersed to the four winds. But their sudden disappearance, instead of giving him comfort, increased in him the terror of the nightmare, since what would have been quite natural in reality seemed to him most unnatural in the ambiguity of the dream. An indescribable anxiety constricted his throat, he would have liked to cry out, but was only able to utter faint moans, and even these were stilled on his lips at the powerful sound of a voice that came—as he immediately understood—from the Lord. He no longer saw Him, he heard only His voice, shrill and distinct this time, but no less frightening. The Lord, in keeping with the intrinsic logic of nightmares, gave him the expected answer in an unexpected form: by announcing the four centuries of captivity in Egypt that lay in store for his descendants, the Lord indirectly confirmed his destiny as the progenitor of a great people, and thus necessarily as the father of a son. The powerful voice reaffirmed moreover that his progeny would take possession of the land of Canaan, but only in a second stage, after the four centuries of slavery in Egypt.

Oddly enough, Abraham was not particularly bothered by the sad fate awaiting his future progeny, since he was too upset by the fact that he still heard the Lord's voice but was no longer able to see Him; in His place rose a whirling fog which, as it thickened, dimmed the last rays of the sunset. The sun had already fallen below the horizon, but the sunset was not followed by night and not even by dusk, rather the whole world was enveloped in an unnatural dull and suffocating gloom. Abraham suddenly realized that all this was the result of the dense haze that now surmounted the clouds and seemed as substantial as a stone wall. This stone wall, however, was marked by a continual and inexplicable rippling: everything rippled like an enormous cloak moved by the wind. At this point Abraham discovered that the wall of stone was simply the cloak of the Lord, whose figure in the meantime had grown to frightful proportions, while His head touched the vault of the sky. Then Abraham again tried to cry out, but something began to happen that drew his attention, and his astonishment diminished his anxiety. Before his dazzled eyes there rose, from nothingness, *a smoking furnace*, with above it, arranged in good order, the victims cut in two, and simultaneously, from somewhere or other, appeared a fiery tongue that, like *a burning lamp*, began to skip over the pyre, setting fire to the pieces of flesh. And all around rose the nauseating stench of scorched raw meat.

The heavenly voice, absolutely indifferent to all these marvelous phenomena, made itself heard again, and having now become stronger, clearer, more crystalline, began to define with extreme precision the geographical borders of the promised land and to enumerate the peoples who inhabited it. The *Kenites*, the *Kenizzites*, the *Kadmonites*. The *Hittites*, the *Perizzites*, and the *Rephaims*. The Lord's voice took on increasing vigor, and with nightmarish logic slowly pronounced these names of peoples in a well-articulated manner, almost beating time, separating one from another by solemn pauses and raising the tone from one name to another. The *Amorites* and *Canaanites* were shouted, the *Girgashites* were howled, and when the thundering name of the *Jebusites* came, it seemed to Abraham that the sky was falling on him and the earth collapsing . . .

But now, finally, the cry of salvation burst from his throat. He came to, lying on the ground, panting and bathed in sweat. It was the dead of night and the stars—which had not shown themselves when they were supposed to be counted—twinkled at him with benevolent indifference. Of the Lord there was no longer a trace, nor of the fiery tongue, and not even of the sacrificial meal. While Abraham had been in the grip of his tortured dream, the Lord had eaten everything. Including the portion that should have gone to his faithful follower . . .

One would have to be a fanatic like Abraham to see the results of this encounter in a positive light. Anyone else would have noted that the Lord's promises, though monumental and dumbfounding, were invariably orchestrated according to a long-range plan and that—what was more serious—their realization was attended by very sad, even tragic events. Since Abraham knew from personal experience, albeit limited to a few months, what a forced stay in Egypt meant, the idea of spending four hundred years there in slavery should have given him pause. Instead, thanks to his particular nature, he evaluated the terrifying encounter quite differently. What mattered to him was the sealed covenant and the fact of having learned at last what he should sacrifice to the Lord, who, satisfied with his veneration, would give him and his descendants riches and power. Never, even for a moment, did the idea cross his mind that it might be appropriate to die without a son.

On the contrary, Abraham did his utmost to have one as soon as possible. And here is another merit to be ascribed to his religious genius: he truly could not have known that the Lord's promises were not a result of His exuberant goodness of heart, but simply statements in advance of events already accomplished and fulfilled in the future, small fragments, premeditatedly revealed, of the content of divine prescience. Abraham, so inexperienced in theological notions, understood by his genius that a promise of the Lord for him meant a command that had to be carried out at all costs. It is due entirely to this intuition of incalculable importance that our hero was able to accept his wife's advice to take Hagar, and with the Egyptian handmaid's assistance smooth the path toward the fulfillment of the divine promises.

Everything helped to make him believe that the expedient suggested by Sarah had met with the Lord's approval. For surely it was a sign of divine grace that Abraham succeeded in impregnating Hagar, and it was a sign of special grace that he was able to do so in such a short time, thus relieving himself of the need to keep going to bed with the servant woman. Everything seemed to proceed so much in accordance with the divine will that Abraham had no misgivings that he was acting against it when, to please his adored wife, he drove Hagar into the desert with the ardently desired child in her womb, virtually exposing both of them to certain death. But that this child was even more ardently desired by the Lord, He Himself seemed to have affirmed unequivocally when He personally intervened to save the forsaken woman from a horrible end by ordering her to return home, humble herself before her mistress, and henceforth behave like a good and modest handmaid. All this led Abraham to suppose that the Lord's favor was with Ishmael and that his wise solution had harmoniously fitted in with the divine plan.

The further course of his life also seemed to support this conviction, namely, that the Lord was content with His discoverer and only follower. He had made it possible for him not only to increase his possessions and his prestige for another fourteen years, but had also allowed him to enjoy a lasting truce within the bosom of his family, in the cool shade of the terebinths of Mamre, where he had settled down for good. He felt he had accomplished his mission in life; in his judgment, he had nothing more to do but train young Ishmael in uprightness and the fear of God, in order to make him the Lord's second follower and entrust to him eventually the task of dealing with Him. An indirect confirmation that everything had gone according to the Lord's pleasure was the very fact that He hadn't appeared to him again, and indeed Abraham was inclined to exclude the idea that He would appear again: there was truly no need for it!

The illustrious discoverer of the sole true and living God would never have imagined that in the torment and bewilderment of his nightmare he had totally misunderstood his great Discovery's promise. For the Lord, who makes use of His prescience almost exclusively to recall great events in the future, did not even take into account the incidental existence of a certain Ishmael: from the beginning He had foretold Isaac, promised Isaac, and wanted Isaac, even at the very moment when the worthy Abraham, in the intoxication of his own wretched zeal, successfully begot Ishmael.

III. Love's mystique

THOUGH WE MAY NOW UNDERSTAND MORE OR LESS WHY ABRA-
ham judged the promised advent of Isaac superfluous—and, as we
have learned, he already knew the Lord well enough to accept His
promises as orders to be carried out—our curiosity as to why he
also considered it absurd remains to be satisfied.

Having examined Abraham's relations with the Lord, we must
now, if we are to eliminate this rightful curiosity of ours, take a
look at those with his wife, Sarah, the other protagonist in the
human and divine event that here concerns us. We will therefore
have to familiarize ourselves with the story of a troubled marriage,
of which the Lord seemed not to be aware, or apparently failed to
take into consideration.

As we've already mentioned, the real obstacle—what the Bible
modestly paraphrases by saying that "it ceased to be with Sarah
after the manner of women"—was what bothered Abraham the

least. Hitherto the law of nature, created and established by the Lord Himself, had not allowed a woman, once she had passed menopause, to be able to conceive and later give birth. Abraham was well aware that his wife had not menstruated for many years, and so, by a simple syllogism, he deduced that she could no longer have children: there was thus every reason for his memorable, irreverent outburst of laughter. Since, however, the Lord had throttled the laughter in his throat and had actually repeated the promise twice, Abraham had ended by realizing that in the eyes of the Lord nothing was impossible, and that in His hands even the laws of nature would be transformed into obedient devices. In the end, he was left without any doubt about the possibility that Sarah, despite the utter dryness of her womb, would be able to give birth.

But if the Lord did not know the impossible, Abraham knew it all too well, since he knew reality. Now we can imagine that among our readers there will be some who, having reached this point, will give a knowing wink: sure, the reality was that Abraham was ninety-nine years old and his better half eighty-nine! Hiding behind the pretext of the impossible was all too convenient for him! To spite such readers, we urge and virtually demand that they change their mistaken notion of Sarah and henceforth imagine her, from the beginning of our story to the end, as an extraordinarily beautiful woman—except, perhaps, for a few cruel moments of discouragement to which women are inevitably subject at a certain age. And we also insist on the word "end" because, with the proofs at hand, we maintain that Abraham's spouse must have exercised a notable fascination on men despite her considerable years. First of all, one must obviously keep in mind the biblical concept of time, which prolongs not only the duration of human life, but also proportionately the period of youth, maturity, and old age; hence, to be appreciated at their proper value, the years of the patriarchal era have to be "translated" into the terms of our time, which reduces the individual life to such short duration. Sarah's old age is reduced to the recent cessation of her menstrual periods, and by no means depends on the awesome number of her years, which would correspond to about fifty had she had the misfortune to be our contemporary—and let him who has never seen a beautiful and fascinating woman of that age cast the first stone! Around such women hovers the intoxicating aroma of a marvelous flower that instead of wilting seems to yield to a slow process of self-embalmment. Sarah must have been one of these women, and we have no trouble believing it, since as a young woman she was not only beautiful but extremely so, even according to the biblical version, while the rabbinical tradition actually records her as being the most lovely creature in the world, endowed with a perfect figure and a divine face, and compares her to Eve, to whom—according to the same legends—God had given two thirds of all the beauty in the universe. Certainly we, in judging the two Eves, would give the prize to Sarah, for the primordial woman— let us place her firmly in prehistory, in the biblical dawn—would to our modern taste leave much to be desired, while we must keep in mind that Sarah had brought refinement and cosmetics with her from Babylonia, and was the consort of a rich and prominent man. In short, she was a woman who had never had difficulty in caring for her beautiful body, nor in dressing it in the finest and most costly garments, or adorning it with the most precious jewels. Thus this beautiful woman, though no longer young, but far from the point of being considered old, whose charm made one forget the first signs of the corrosive action of time, that incipient withering that rendered her beauty even more seductive, this extraordinary woman was most certainly well groomed and of a dazzling elegance as well. But all that is needed to corroborate our thesis is the biblically reliable episode according to which the ninety-year-old Sarah was sufficiently lovely and desirable to be carried off to the harem of the young king Abimelech.

We must therefore reject any frivolous insinuation by malicious persons who would like to think that Abraham found it a horrid and repugnant task to make some effort with his wife to promote the realization of the divine promise. At the same time we must exclude the notion that Abraham himself should be judged to be in such poor condition as to make his eventual paternity impossible. In this connection, one need only remember that after Sarah's death—and certainly not immediately after, but well past the age of 137—he remarried and with his second wife produced no less than six sons. And what's more, the old rascal also kept concubines who produced other sons for him (and the Bible doesn't even say how many daughters!). As we see, what had been so difficult for him with Sarah and in his youth became his simplest and most agreeable pastime in his old age.

No defect of male potency in Abraham, no lack of feminine charm in Sarah. What then? To understand the situation we must tell the story of our two protagonists' troubled married life.

Before setting out to reconstruct this life, we honestly ask our readers not to expect a historically authentic explanation, even within the limits allowed by the legendary nature of the subject. We will not adduce any facts of a scientific kind that might help to throw new light on it all: our sources remain invariably the well-known biblical episode and the less known but still accessible legends of the rabbinical tradition. Actually all we plan to do is to set forth in a proper manner these particulars of history and fable, and thus, to the extent possible, wring from them whatever elements are capable of reconciling the apparent discrepancies, cementing the fleeting connections, and filling those gaps that seem to abound in the material itself. We should like moreover to emphasize strongly that we do not intend to ascribe any scientific value either to our method of research or to the eventual results we hope to achieve. We refrain from such an attitude because we are well aware of the limits of our competence in the strictly scientific field, and also because we are convinced that by assuming the attitude of the scholar, we would also put ourselves at a disadvantage with respect to the objectives we've set for ourselves. We expect to arrive at conclusions that scholars would not permit themselves to express, even if they were to divine them on their own.

Apart from the particulars, we will in our task obviously make abundant use of our imagination and intuition, though we're aware that these sources are suspect for most readers, who, by now alarmed, will be prone from this moment on to question the validity of our already hybrid literary genre. All we can do, with a gesture of resignation, is to offer a choice: skeptics should either stop reading, or having gone along with us this far, accompany us to the end. In our own defense, we confess that the dilemma for us was either to leave this wonderful and lively tale buried under the avalanche of words in the Holy Scriptures, where it would be condemned never to be read with proper attention, or else to unearth it in all its drama, highlighting its hidden meanings and using it as a key to penetrate the deeper meaning of one of the most decisive moments in humanity's march, the re-entry of the sole true and living God into the consciousness of man. For us the answer to this dilemma was clear, and so we beseech the kind reader to forgive us if for the purposes of our undertaking we cannot help but have recourse to our imagination and intuition.

To lessen, however, the distrust of some, we're happy to observe that intuition does not necessarily mean plucking our ideas out of thin air, and that imagination is not necessarily the same as giving oneself over to fantasies, if the writer's sense of responsibility stands guard. We guarantee that our imagination, bold as it may appear from time to time, will never stray into the arbitrary or carry us off into the realm of the unlikely and illogical; and as for our intuition, we don't mind stating that it remains tied, albeit sometimes by an undefinable or barely perceptible connection, to the facts, with which moreover it never comes into conflict. These are the criteria that make the use of the two above-mentioned sources of literary inspiration acceptable; greater severity than this no one should ask of us.

In fact, we fear that we've gone too far in offering the reader such a conspicuous quantity of guarantees, since now we must confess that it is not even the fictional reconstruction of the troubled story of Abraham and Sarah that constitutes the main goal of our efforts: it too, no more nor less than our excursions into the field of scholarship, has only an instrumental value. And even this follows from the hybrid nature of our literary genre, where everything is only an illuminating framework around the generally elusive relations that exist between *matters human and divine.* To call attention to and arouse interest in these relations is really the only purpose we take to heart. To gain pardon for the dryness of our one true objective, we'll also do our best, whenever possible, to entertain our readers, by whom we hope in the end to be absolved.

The story of Abraham and Sarah, like any love story, had a trite beginning: boy met girl . . . In this particular case, we can fill in the picture by adding that the boy was a hothead and fanatic, while the girl was extraordinarily beautiful. Neither the Bible nor the rabbinical tradition tells how the two young people met and fell in love. There is reason to suppose that what happened was that trivial miracle of love, the same fatal lightning bolt that later would strike Abraham's son Isaac at the sight of Rebecca, and still later the same Abraham's grandson Jacob at the sight of Rachel. Somehow or other, love at first sight was hereditary in this family, and we would even be reluctant to exclude the idea that once again Abraham was the precursor; anyway our hypothesis is not particularly daring if we keep in mind the tender maiden's dazzling beauty. It is much less certain whether Sarah also experienced the sweet giddiness of a *coup de foudre,* since in those times, when even the firstborn son's choice was severely subject to tribal standards, the sentiments of marriageable girls carried no weight whatsoever. In all honesty, therefore, we cannot deduce anything about the young woman's feelings toward her future husband.

But is there anything we can say with certainty and with at least fair precision about the young Sarah? Unfortunately nothing or almost nothing. And if this is the situation, it is due in part to the conciseness of the biblical account, but above all to our hero's lies, which for all their terseness are scrupulously reported by the holy text. Abraham lies explicitly when he tells Pharaoh's messengers that Sarah is his sister. Some decades later he comes out with the same lie to the messengers of King Abimelech, but when the scandal explodes and the king accuses him of cowardice, Abraham to the great surprise of the onlookers (and also to posterity) declares with a straight face that he hasn't lied at all, since Sarah really is his sister, the daughter of his father, though not of his mother. In modern terms one would therefore call Sarah his half-sister.

Abraham's surprising statement was certainly not enough to make Abimelech change his opinion of the stranger, whom in any case he judged to be base and cowardly. It was really irrelevant that the woman was *also* his sister, when she was *also* his wife: the deceit involved the essential. And, in truth, not even today are we in a position to clarify whether in those two unpleasant episodes of his life Abraham was a coward and liar, or *only* a coward. If we rely solely on the biblical text, the question will forever remain open.

There are other clues, however, to suggest that Abraham—this worthy, honest, and virtuous man, lacking only that minimum of natural courage with which men in general are endowed from birth—lied on both occasions. The rabbinical tradition seems unaware that Sarah was his half-sister, and this silence is an indirect proof of our hero's untruthfulness. The legend speaks instead of another and much more provocative bond of kinship, which is closely connected with a passage from the Holy Scriptures and—if Abraham had in fact lied, a possibility that the Bible neither confirms nor denies—does not even conflict with the biblical version.

According to the legend, Sarah would have been Abraham's niece, daughter of the younger of his two brothers, the prematurely deceased Haran, and thus the sister of Lot, who was also Haran's child. Actually the Bible states explicitly only that Nahor, the elder of Abraham's two younger brothers, married a daughter of his younger brother, namely, *Milcah, the daughter of Haran, the father of Milcah, and the father of Iscah.* For purposes of brevity, the Bible might just as well have said that Nahor's wife was Milcah, daughter of Haran, and in this way it would better have satisfied our desire for clarity and perhaps also for truth. From this standpoint, the exaggerated precision of the biblical statement is even counterproductive, for though it may be no more than a piece of circumstantial information, it looks like a riddle and prods the imagination to solve it. Objectively speaking, one cannot deduce anything from the biblical passage except that, in addition to Milcah, the deceased Haran had another daughter named Iscah.

Since this Iscah does not reappear in any context in the rest of the biblical story, we could say it was gratuitous at the very least to inform us of her existence. We can offer, however, another argument as a starting point for devotees of riddles. Granted that from the standpoint of historical truth, the mention of Iscah in the biblical text seems superfluous, even detrimental, but we still cannot say that the introduction of her name into the canonical text of the Holy Scriptures is the result of pure chance or the caprice of the editors. Were we to say this, we would have to add that all the personal names appearing in long strings in the Bible, but with no organic function or significance in the biblical story, have turned up there gratuitously. The reality is that all these names, even the most obscure ones, are not listed for the purpose of filling the gaps between the important names, but indicate persons who—at least for the tradition—really existed, and whose lives and exploits were known, preserved, and handed down, both before and after the compilation of the five books of Moses. It is thus reasonable to suppose that Iscah figures more rightly in the episode of Abraham than Pontius Pilate in the Credo.

There were legends about this Iscah and they were not speculations, as one might suppose, around a mysterious and insignificant name preserved by the Bible out of love for excessive precision. Quite the opposite, for though Iscah is barely mentioned in the sacred text, such numerous and widespread oral traditions circulated around her that the compilers of the Bible, if for no other reason perhaps than not to be accused of carelessness, could not wholly ignore her and had at least to mention her in their summary, which had been drawn up on the basis of particular criteria. And the tradition would have it that Iscah and Sarah were the same person.

We have every reason to believe that the Sarah-Iscah identity was intentionally muted, or rather suppressed, in the canonical text, and not simply invented by the imagination of posterity at the prompting of an idle or insignificant name. This does not, however, keep the sentence from the Bible quoted above, which is guilty of excessive precision, from easily lending itself to teasing riddles and spontaneously suggesting plausible solutions. The close proximity of three female names in the same sentence may suggest whimsical and convincing combinations: indeed, if Milcah, wife of Nahor, was the daughter of Haran, the father of Milcah and Iscah, there is an irresistible temptation to identify Iscah, the other daughter of Haran, father of Milcah and Iscah, with Abraham's wife, to wit, Sarah. Nor should we be put off by the difference in names, since even in its own time this did nothing to stop the spread and credibility of the legend. The name Sarai, which means "princess" (and this is the one by which Abraham's spouse is called at first), may already seem at first sight the pet name or nickname of the woman to whom the less pretentious name of Iscah was given at birth. When later, in one of those by no means rare moments when He was in the mood to rename His creatures, God solemnly changed Sarai to Sarah, which also means "princess," we are tempted to attribute the divine gesture not to a lack of imagination, but to the specific intention of legalizing the name that before had not rightfully belonged to His chosen one's wife, and to bestow recognition on what so far had been only an arbitrarily usurped title (incidentally, we remind the reader that the Lord at a certain point also changed Abram to Abraham, but for the sake of simplicity we have been using their more familiar names).

There may be a number of reasons why the Bible remains silent on the Sarah-Iscah identity. The Bible was not edited into its canonical form with the intention of making it an encyclopedia of myths and legends; quite the contrary, it already had a rationalizing tendency and was trying to sift the various oral traditions in order to choose the specific version that would become the canonical one. The choice was guided by well-defined criteria, including obviously that of giving the greatest emphasis to the omnipotence of God. Already from this standpoint the Sarah-Iscah identity— which moreover would have introduced an element of confusion into the canonized tradition—had to be rejected, for had it been accepted, it would have diminished the importance of the divine miracle. A Sarah who was the daughter of Haran could hardly have been almost the same age as her Uncle Abraham, between them there would have had to be a difference in age of thirty to forty years, in which case Abraham would have had no reason to laugh at the Lord's words. Or else he himself would have had to be a decrepit old man, a circumstance not in keeping with other elements accepted by the sacred text. But apart from all this, other traditions certainly existed in which the two old people's ages had been fixed since time immemorial, and clearly, in the whole series of legends that had arisen around the figure of Abraham, the accent fell most strongly on the advanced age of this Jewish Philemon and Baucis couple. The concern of the editors of the canonical text was therefore not to point out that Sarah and Iscah were the same person, but that Sarah was old.

Far too many possible combinations of elements blossom around Sarah, her origins, her kinship connections, and her youth, for us to learn anything exact about her. The Arabic tradition, which confirms the sibling relationship between Sarah and Lot, thus making her Haran's daughter, lays it on thicker by handing down an even more fantastic version. According to this version, Abraham's wife would have been of royal origin, being the daughter of the king of Haran and his wife, in her turn the daughter of King Kutba of Babylonia. The name Iscah does not appear at all in this legend; rather we find the name Sarai, which thus seems rightfully to belong to our heroine. But one can only wonder how the hotheaded former store clerk, having turned up in Haran with his whole ragtag family reduced to the utmost poverty, actually managed to marry the king's daughter.

Nothing forces us, however, to consider a myth or a legendary tradition as historical reality, and we can very well do without that historical and psychological "verisimilitude" that so often appears in purely imaginary ancient stories. Far be it from us to look in a mass of gossip for a single suggestion that can be accepted or passed off as "historical truth." This would be a mistaken effort and would deservedly draw down on us the scorn and contempt of even the most naïve of our readers. But let no one think that the tradition— even if fantastic, incredible, or absurd in whole or in part—is to be totally rejected and cannot be more useful for our purposes than an insignificant historical fact of undisputed authenticity. The incomparable value of the tradition consists for us not so much in what it says as in what it doesn't say, for the simple reason that nothing and nobody can express in simple words its essence and innermost truth: these can only be grasped through hints, divined in mysterious ways, suggested, illuminated. None of the legends relating to Sarah states explicitly what is common to most of them and especially fascinates us: the close ties that exist, both for her origins and the circumstances of her life, between Sarah and idolatry, between Sarah and the cult of the moon god. From this standpoint, to be the daughter of the king of Haran, or the daughter of that Haran who died trying to save the idols from the fury of a brother obsessed by the new God, is one and the same, since both have the same precise meaning. And that Abraham's wife was originally called Iscah or by some other name is likewise a matter of indifference, since with the name *Sarai* we are once more back in the realm of idolatry. For Sarai, not only means "princess," but was the customary sobriquet of Ningal, consort of the moon god Sin.

This subdued murmur of traditions, which in the hands of scholars has also given rise to scientific theories, is primarily useful to us in creating an atmosphere around the figure of Sarah, of whose origins and youth the Bible preserves no record. Thanks to the tradition, we now have a certain right to imagine that the young Sarah and the young Abraham belonged to two different worlds, destined moreover to clash; and if the future was to smile on Abraham's world, Sarah could be proud of the past and present of hers. Obviously the tradition has its reasons when it underscores the points of divergence and conflict between the two spouses, or rather between the two protagonists of this crucial moment in the history of humankind. Thus to suppose that there was a substantial difference between the mentality of the man and his wife seems to us entirely called for, and from there it is simply a short step to extending the conflict to their characters, tastes, and ambitions. By attributing, for example, a high lineage to Sarah, the legend, not unlike a fairy tale, implies all the fabulous requisites of elevated rank, from beauty and regal behavior to civilized and religious culture and refined taste, everything that gives Sarah a conspicuous, albeit only apparent, superiority over the uncouth Abraham, who, except for his fanatical faith, cannot boast of any eminent quality. Whether she was the daughter of the king of Haran or the daughter of Haran, defender of idols, Sarah must always have looked down her nose at her husband's restless infatuations, as well as at his God, who for her was surely not something obvious that had sprung from great intuition, but merely a fixation of her spouse's, something that at first she had taken notice of with smiling commiseration, pondering it later with vexation, aversion, and more than once with sincere hatred.

We don't really know how it was that two such different worlds met, but we would not go wrong in supposing that in addition to Sarah's extraordinary beauty, it was that apparent superiority of hers that fascinated Abraham. The discoverer of God, at the height of his capacities, also discovered his goddess, a divine creature in every respect, the earthly incarnation of Ningal, the princess. In the blinding glare of the *coup de foudre*, he knew that this was a woman he would be able to *adore* all the way to the grave.

Our natural honesty once more compels us to advise our less perceptive readers that as our story proceeds we rely with growing confidence on our intuition, and—albeit with due prudence—on our imagination. Actually no document says that Abraham worshipped Sarah; nor do the Bible and other legendary traditions suggest to less sensitive ears that there was anything exceptional about Abraham's love for his better half. Anyone adhering to the letter of the texts would even be persuaded that Abraham must have behaved with monstrous indifference toward his extraordinarily beautiful wife, having handed her over without hesitation to Pharaoh, and to the accompaniment of words so crude and humiliating that it cost him even less to repeat the same monstrous gesture some decades later with the aged Sarah.

Against these arguments we would like to marshal others that show, directly or indirectly, how despite everything Abraham loved Sarah all the way to the grave, and as far as the grave is concerned, no one need have the slightest doubt: the purchase of the cave of Machpelah, for the specific purpose of providing a worthy burial for the body of the 127-year-old Sarah, was a gesture of loving piety duly emphasized by the Bible. Thus Abraham expressed his devotion to the remains of the woman whom, when she was still young and wondrously beautiful, he had smuggled across frontiers hidden in a large wicker basket to protect her from the avid gaze of foreigners. Despite the fact that she was barren, Abraham did not take other wives, as he could have done, and did not keep concubines during their marriage, while as for Hagar, he accepted her only at Sarah's direct instigation and for the exclusive purpose of begetting an heir, in this way producing progeny for his wife as well. Sarah's word was always sacred and decisive for him, and her wish carried more weight in his eyes than a command from the Lord Himself. The Bible attests that Abraham had no hesitation in letting Sarah expel the servant woman who carried in her womb the heir promised by God, and the only explanation for such compliance has to be Abraham's almost servile haste to gratify his wife's wishes. And he even allowed Hagar and her adolescent son to be driven out a second time—albeit unwillingly but without protest—in order to soothe his aged consort's injured pride. And in conclusion we offer the most important and decisive argument: he would have to have had conjugal relations with her even beyond the critical age, if he ended by fulfilling God's command and bringing Isaac, the true heir, into the world. In our opinion, these facts—which would seem to be in glaring contradiction with our hero's pusillanimity and the chilling indifference with which he yielded his beloved spouse to other men—would remain totally incompatible with each other if they did not merge in a quite exceptional love that we would go so far as to call "adoration" on Abraham's part, and which we would even complement, on Sarah's, with the expression "hunger for worship."

Let us admit that this is simply our intuition, nourished less by the facts under consideration than by almost imperceptible hints and by the atmosphere surrounding the conflicting and not easily reconciled testimony of tradition. For us, Sarah's extraordinary beauty, stressed by all the legends, even by the canonical version in the Holy Scriptures, is not an element that can be overlooked in approaching the figure of our heroine and bringing it to life. The "princess" whose name was the sobriquet of Ningal, and who in her dazed admiration of her own beauty sometimes indulged in the fantasy of being identical with Ningal, could scarcely have minded being the object of veneration such as was paid to the goddess, and being like her adored and idolized. And it's not hard to imagine that the man who had discovered God, and whose soul was greedy for mystical effusions, desperately adored this wonderful woman who, at the height of his ecstasy, seemed to him a divine being. It is easy for us to imagine all this, and if we succeed in making our readers imagine it too, this will only speak in favor of our intuition.

There is no doubt that the marriage between Abraham and Sarah was one of the worst imaginable. But if we are able for once to discard the popular belief according to which the purpose of matrimony is the couple's mutual happiness and to accept rather that it is one of the various snares set by our destiny to make us enjoy and suffer what our deeper instincts require, even against our more obvious wishes, then we can say that beneath the appearance of an unhappy marriage the union of our two protagonists was one of the happiest.

For a long period of time the apparent unhappiness was harder on Sarah than on Abraham. For to be adored is a less satisfactory emotion than to adore, also because the one who adores necessarily focuses his adoration on a single person, while generally the one adored is not satisfied with the intensity of a single person's emotions, but also wants quantity and dreams of the intense adoration of many—if possible of everyone. Even had Sarah felt for Abraham an emotion that might have seemed like love, she must have felt from the beginning that she had made a huge sacrifice by renouncing the adoration of the whole world in exchange for the exultations of a single person. Sarah never had the slightest doubt that, thanks to her extraordinary beauty, everyone might have adored her, and that it was thus an immense favor on her part to permit Abraham to do so. Her only consolation for such a waste of munificence came from the idea that sooner or later she would have had to marry someone or other and that her reservations would have been the same in any case. It therefore took Sarah a long time to realize her husband's truly exceptional capacity for adoration; only much later did she learn to appreciate it.

But the apparent unhappiness did not spare Abraham either. It cost him no small pain to realize that Sarah loved herself and her own beauty first of all, and that she loved him only because, and to the degree to which, the object of their respective emotions was the same: Sarah and her beauty. Such a discovery should have had the effect of throwing cold water on the amorous ardor of a young husband, but in Abraham's case it was like pouring oil on fire. He did not give up, and discovering latent energies in himself, decided at all costs to win his wife's love. In keeping with his nature, he expressed his proposal in singular terms, saying he would become worthy of her love! In no way, however, would he have been able to stop worshipping his woman.

Thus real happiness masked by apparent unhappiness began to make headway in Abraham's heart and mind. In fact, "to adore" means much more than an emotion or *habitus* guaranteeing a permanent state of ecstasy. To adore is already a form of life and a solution, the acme of religious life itself since it requires uninterrupted readiness and an extreme tension that knows no letup. It may also be the most intense and indestructible kind of happiness, since it carries its own source and its goal within itself. Egotism and disinterestedness, those two fundamental tendencies of the psyche without which no human attitude can be considered authentic, find themselves in perfect equilibrium in the act of adoration, for they devour and annihilate each other in the incandescence of ecstasy. Strange as it may seem, adoration is essentially selfish, for it pays no attention to the reactions of its object, being content with its mere existence. For the adorer, to adore a beautiful and fascinating woman is an emotion so self-sufficient that whether the object of the adoration repays him with her favors, or begrudges or even withholds her favors altogether, no longer has any importance so long as she lets herself be adored. A soul sufficiently lofty can even bear it if the object of its adoration extends to others the favors denied to itself: masochistic abnegation is likewise a quality of this strange psychological type.

But adoration, that singular manifestation of the human psyche, which by eliminating or consuming every other sentiment, settles on a single object with absolute egotism, and at the same time absolute abnegation, cannot be reduced to the realm of sexuality. Overflowing love that yearns to possess, but first of all to give itself completely, can very well be directed toward beings that are either sexually indifferent or not considered from that standpoint, for example, children or animals, but it can also have as its object things or ideas, and—last but not least*—God, the Being to be adored *par excellence*. All these objects of the mystical fervor of adoration have in common the characteristic of remaining—either by their essence or their nature—absolutely indifferent in the face of adoration (for example, things and ideas), or they react to it capriciously (like children and animals), or arbitrarily and uncontrollably (like God), but in no case with emotional manifestations heated to the level of those of the adorer. At most, they accept the adoration, but they may also reject it; sometimes they are polite,

* In English in original.

but they may also react insensitively, and not even when they are in a generous mood do they give themselves completely. They grant only a crumb of themselves, but only so long as it pleases them and with many reservations. The obvious result of all this is that the psychological type of the adorer, whether he knows it or not, requires the object of his adoration to treat him badly, and certainly enjoys less the rare pleasure of possession than the suffering of unfulfilled desire or the intoxication of vague hope.

One would have every reason to think that having discovered the sole true and living God, Abraham lavished the incandescent flood of his adoration on Him. But, in truth, it didn't happen that way. As we've already mentioned, his immense need to adore may have been one of the sources of inspiration for the great intuition by which he had grasped the Lord's existence and essence, but there are no available documents to show that he was successful in achieving the pleasure of mystical union with the Being he had discovered, as he may still have hoped at the time when he enjoyed smashing idols in his father's store. His relations with the Lord had been oriented from the start toward rigid objectivity, they had unfolded and developed through a series of covenants, agreements, and commercial transactions, and the Lord never presented Himself to him in any light that might encourage His follower's loving transports. In all probability the fact that the Lord did not let Himself be adored, and based His relations with Abraham strictly on business speculation, formed a substantial part of His plan: how could He have allowed the born mystic Abraham, at that early critical stage, to indulge in completely useless ecstasies when He needed his other indispensable qualities? From the beginning of time the Lord had considered Abraham as the future progenitor of a great people, and He subordinated His relations with him almost exclusively to this preconceived idea. And from this standpoint, the Lord undoubtedly thought it more useful for Abraham to give vent to his amorous longings in the nuptial bed.

Thus it was—perhaps by divine will—that Abraham, the discoverer, had no way to adore with a mystic's rapture the God he had discovered, but had to discharge all his reserves of adoration on his adorable wife. Of course, the erotic factor, which is not only a structural element of the worshipper's attitude but also its root, could enter into a more exciting and emotional combination with his religious thirst alongside the beautiful woman than in front of the bearded old man in whose form the Lord usually appeared. The conspicuous masculinity of the materialized God deprived Abraham of any wish to establish sexual relations with Him, which would actually have seemed to him homosexual. For his loving effusions he unhesitatingly preferred the alluring femininity of his beautiful wife.

Obviously beauty alone, however exceptional, would not be enough to provoke mystical reactions. But, as the reader has already been warned, it was Sarah's character that provoked the rest. This extraordinarily beautiful woman concentrated in herself all the requisites of an object of adoration. An unmoved mover, like God Himself, she was able to arouse her husband's erotic-religious desires while at the same time letting him know that allowing him to adore her was always the sign of her magnanimity. And her reactions to Abraham's worshipful attitude were no less capricious than those of God, and sometimes entirely negative. For her the transition from pure worship to the acts of conjugal love was something mortifying and unbearable, if only for the fact that it imposed specific duties on her that were absolutely incompatible with the position of an adored being. Unaccustomed to give and take, she considered marital intimacy from the start as something secondary and incidental, irksome and humiliating, the consequence of Abraham's vulgar and obscene whims, and in any case as showing a lack of respect on her husband's part. In these situations, Abraham was transformed in her eyes from a comical adorer into a real pig, who behaved rudely, used words and gestures injurious to her dignity, and treated her unceremoniously, as though she were not a princess and goddess incarnate but an ordinary woman. Not only that, but at the end he had a certain triumphant expression on his face, as though he'd won some sort of victory over her! Yes, in these situations Abraham became truly odious, and in Sarah the suspicion arose that in reality his adoration was nothing but cunning flattery, and that he fawned upon her beauty and womanly charms for the sole purpose of befuddling her and disposing her to tolerate his foul plans. Then Sarah's resistance stiffened, and she held out even longer in order to observe more carefully how adoration and lust were independent and autonomous in her husband, two qualities that, in her opinion, should have nothing to do with each other, if indeed they weren't mutually exclusive.

No doubt Sarah was an ideal model as an object of adoration, true grist for Abraham's mill, even though, especially in the early days of the marriage, he often succumbed to melancholy because of the apparent unhappiness of their union. In his moments of despair, it seemed to him impossible to endure a whole life alongside a frigid woman who didn't love him, or who was frigid precisely because she didn't love him. But little by little, as he advanced along the path of mysticism, he realized that the happiness he had yearned for would be entirely superficial, even illusory and deceptive, compared to the one that had been revealed to him thanks to his apparent unhappiness. He began to persuade himself, and ended by believing, that he would not have been capable of adoring his wife with such intensity had she requited his adoration with equal fervor. He thus arrived at the conclusion that his marital life could not be called a disaster as long as he himself was so madly in love. Would there be any merit, any sense of awe, in his love, if he loved only on condition that Sarah become different from what she was? And if she were different, would he be able to love her as he did? His wife's coldness, which she politely tried to disguise as reserve, had a more incendiary effect on his senses than any languid wantonness, and when at last he was able to hold the desired body in his arms, he no longer felt like a husband exercising his rights, but a young lover who, after a long siege, was inducing his virginal beloved to sin or actually raping her.

Everything would have been quite different if Sarah—like an ordinary wife—had docilely submitted to her husband's wishes.

Then Abraham, even had he been able to persist in his erotic obsession, would most likely have become a libertine, but never a mystic of love. Instead, in his particular situation, he concentrated all the mysticism that God had not allowed him to lavish on Him, and all the eroticism that Sarah had not allowed him to satisfy, in an incomparable attitude of adoration wholly oriented toward the divine figure of his wife. Perhaps Abraham was not far from the truth when, in the course of his mystical raptures, he conceived the bold theory that the Lord had given him Sarah as a substitute in the roles He did not care to play. This was one more reason for his exultant filial gratitude, the most intense emotion that Abraham was capable of feeling for the Lord: he was intoxicated by the idea that it was by the will of God that he could and should adore his wife as a goddess, and make her the object of a divine cult. Thus Abraham, while instinctively able to divide his profound religious feelings to the proper degree between his Lord and his lady, without either of them having reason to complain, only deepened his strange happiness from day to day. Even the growing resistance with which his wife greeted his overtures made him swell with happiness.

Don Juan would have had every reason to envy Abraham! This beggar of love succeeded in deriving numerous and ineffable satisfactions from his apparently miserable relations with Sarah. For instance, she persuaded herself every so often to view his adoring attitude from a favorable angle, and unexpectedly fell prey to a kind of shame for the deplorable way she had treated him. On these rare occasions, she let her heart be invaded by tender commiseration, set her lips in a compassionate smile, and with a great effort even went so far as to stroke her husband's face, which became flushed with emotion. In these moments of grace, Abraham felt he was in seventh heaven, because not only was it easy for him to bend his wife to his will, but the hope blossomed in him that her heart was also about to yield. These were the most intoxicating moments of ecstasy, but no sooner were they over than disappointment left him with a bitter taste in his mouth. Reduced to a shred, he had once more to climb the difficult ladder of mystical elevation from the lowest rung.

Of course, Abraham was spurred by the ambition to possess the object of his adoration body and soul, skin and bone; but as a good mystic, and in order to preclude the realization of such a coveted fulfillment, he had chosen for his adoration an object that was to remain steadfastly inaccessible. While consciously doing his utmost to conquer not only Sarah's body but her heart and soul as well, he always instinctively managed to create obstacles to the achievement of his goal. In the depths of his soul he knew the truth that all his efforts and hopes seemed unaware of: that the complete and final conquest of Sarah would be for him the worst of all disasters.

Inadvertently we have reached the point where we would like to call the tireless adoration that Abraham paid his wife "love's mystique." Should anyone chide us that, with the excuse of relying on our intuition, we've let our imagination flit about unchecked, we might surprise him by saying that for some time now it has been less a matter of intuition and imagination than of a hypothesis in the strict sense. And this may be a timely declaration. For one can insist that intuition and imagination take their cue from facts, but a hypothesis can be considered to be in order so long as it satisfies the condition of not contradicting the facts; for the rest, it can be based on anything, even on intuition and imagination. On the other hand, however, we make greater demands of a hypothesis: once it is formulated, it should lead to some result worth the trouble of examining.

Well, this hypothesis of ours about Abraham's erotic mysticism, though unsupported by any document, certainly does not conflict with the facts; on the contrary, it sometimes seems that the facts, in one way or another, depend on it and wouldn't even make sense without it. Thanks to it, the scattered fragments of fact would be recomposed into a single mosaic, and their contradictions, which previously clashed and offended us in a jarring way, would harmoniously sort themselves out. We don't see how anyone can raise doubts about the right of such a useful and fruitful hypothesis to exist. This cherished hypothesis of ours will be a great help in presenting the monstrous episode of the Egyptian misadventure in its proper perspective.

Erotic mysticism will also have played a part in the fact that Abraham didn't have to be told twice to leave Haran and set out with his family and his lean flocks toward the unknown Canaan. While he would have willingly left the land of idols without even being asked, he was now fortified by the promises made to him by the Lord, and no one would have been able to hold him back, not even the "princess," who put up a dogged resistance. The idea of wandering in the desert in search of pastureland, living under improvised tents, and exposing herself to the hardships and un-certainties of nomadic life certainly did not appeal to Sarah. Her soul did not overflow with faith in the mysterious Lord whose promises intoxicated her husband. But Abraham, secure in him-self, swept aside the opposition of his wife and of young Lot, who had timidly seconded her. To cut short their objections and win them over, our hero harped on the dreariness of their lives, and tried to minimize the risks to which they would be exposed, insisting with prudent modesty that things couldn't get much worse than they already were. But actually he was trusting blindly in the Lord's promises, while on the other hand, he had a secret reason of his own for believing that the risks were worth taking: it was not simply a matter of getting rich, becoming powerful, and gaining great prestige among people; there was also the possibility of offering himself to Sarah as a new man, worthy of her love!

This reasoning was flawless from the standpoint of judicious logic, but—alas—not from that of a mystic's more instinctive requirements. As we know, matters took an ugly turn and Abra-ham exposed his adored wife to many grave trials, sufferings, and physical and moral humiliations that not only threatened to alien-ate what was left of her good will, but even to make him lose forever the hope of her love, and lose her as well.

The peregrinations on Canaanite soil did not begin under the best auspices, since the pastures did not prove to be as rich as they had looked from afar. Abraham had to go all the way to the locality of Sichem, near the grove of Moreh, and there sure enough he received the encouragement of the Lord, who appeared to him for the second time and suddenly promised the land where he now found himself to his descendants. It was a promise that came at the right moment and lifted him out of his despondency, a considerable promise in any case, even though the land in question had so far been disappointing, with its sparse pastures scorched by the sun and untouched by rain. The sad panorama of the promised land looked no different even after the divine appearance, and Abraham was forced to resume his march, farther and farther southward in search of forage for his starving flocks. Arriving between Bethel and Hai, and judging the situation desperate, he felt an urgent need to consult the Lord—who so far had stubbornly insisted on talking only about the future—and have a thorough discussion with Him about the problems of the present as well. But now, for the first time, he was obliged to admit that it was not enough, indeed did no good at all, to build an altar to the Lord and call out His name. In his state of desperation, he had to acknowledge that to discover the Lord still didn't mean to have Him at your disposal whenever you liked, not even in cases of urgent need. Having been lured on by the Lord, here he was in a strange land, reduced to utter poverty, and the Lord was in no hurry to tell him what he should do.

One result was the poisoning of the family atmosphere. For as long as it gave them satisfaction, Sarah and Lot took their revenge by upbraiding Abraham for his mistakes and the awful fulfillment of their pessimistic predictions, but now they began to yield to despair, terror, and rage. In their opinion, they had been on the road to ruin from the start, every step forward had confirmed it, and Sarah became truly furious when, on their arrival in Sichem, she saw that Abraham had, for no reason at all, plunged headlong into unbridled optimism. Then, as though she had only been waiting for an opportunity and an excuse, all the hostile feelings that from the beginning of their marriage had been building up inside her against this good-for-nothing and eccentric husband of hers erupted at once. She had never received from him any of the things she had dreamed of while dancing at feasts of the moon god: the setting for her divine beauty—of which only the starry firmament might have been worthy—had been and still was modest poverty, from which Abraham made little effort to emerge. And now the way out that the fool had chosen was that she, the "princess," earthly personification of Ningal, be dragged along behind the emaciated flocks, dressed in rags, barefoot, herself emaciated, and terrified by the prospect of starvation! If she was really the daughter of Haran, father of Milcah and Iscah, she now recalled more and more frequently that this wretched husband of hers had even been the cause of her father's death. Despair over her own fate took the form of a profound contempt for Abraham, bordering on hatred, and which she had difficulty in disguising, especially in the marriage bed: her husband's overtures filled her with irrepressible physical disgust.

Abraham, in his unbridled optimism, seemed aware of nothing. On the contrary, intoxicated by the promises of the Lord, who had destined the land of Canaan for his descendants, he paid no attention to his wife's dejected state and began to apply himself with much diligence to the procreation of at least his first descendant. To guarantee the immense progeny seemed to him something that could no longer be postponed, and he wasted no more time in trying to overcome Sarah's hardened refusal by the usual worshipful siege; without mincing words, he boldly invoked a husband's rights and a wife's duties. The result of this approach was that Sarah now denied herself to him unequivocally, and when Abraham demanded an explanation of her behavior, she supplied it with ruthless frankness. It was a terrible blow to Abraham, who to avoid having to come to terms with it, consoled himself with the hope that once circumstances had returned to normal, Sarah would return to normal as well.

But, in truth, the idea of normal circumstances was more elusive than a mirage. The lean flocks were reduced to a few gaunt sheep and the little tribe of shepherds found itself faced with the terror of starvation. Abraham, physically and spiritually depressed, in a state of grave nervous exhaustion, morally shattered, abandoned by God and rejected by Sarah, followed the example of other nomad tribes and took refuge in Egypt. But before he had even set foot on Egyptian soil, he heard something that produced an upheaval in his already tormented soul.

During their arduous march toward the land of salvation, Abraham and his people encountered other nomad tribes, who found themselves in the same situation and for whom there was nothing unusual about seeking refuge in Egypt. Abraham's shepherds turned to them for advice and were accordingly informed of the habits and customs of the country that was about to receive them. These nomads, experts on the subject of Egypt, told them that the sovereign and notables of the great empire had the bad habit of restocking their harems with women from the small tribes who came seeking refuge. If Abraham's shepherds were worried at hearing such news, Abraham himself was all the more so: he thought he would go out of his mind. From the very first moment, he was certain that his extraordinarily beautiful Sarah would be snatched away from him, and if this should happen, he would not survive. Meanwhile, as he gathered every bit of information on the subject with masochistic avidity, he marched resolutely toward Egypt with his people and sheep, haunted by the idea that he was not on his way to salvation but to the gallows. All of his haggard followers were aware of the danger, and all were prepared to confront it, some trusting to luck, others comforting themselves with the hope of eventually gaining some benefit from this difficult state of affairs. But Sarah knew nothing; Abraham forbade everyone to reveal the situation to her and he himself could not bring himself to tell her. For how on earth would he have been able to say to her that in all certainty she would end up among Pharaoh's concubines, while he himself, from one day to the next, one hour to the next, kept marching with absolute determination toward the land of dishonor?

A crazy idea sprang up in his deranged mind: he would keep Sarah hidden from the gaze of foreigners for the entire period of their forced stay in Egypt, even if it should last forever. With the excuse that no one could know what to expect, he persuaded his lovely wife to get into a wicker basket until they had safely crossed the frontier. It was a blow to Sarah's pride to have to accept such an expedient, but later when Abraham tried to get her to go on living in the basket, she rebelled. She also considered her husband's refusal to let her emerge from their tent incompatible with her dignity, and assured him that she wouldn't put up with such a humiliating situation for long. So Abraham finally decided to explain to her that it was possible to imagine much more humiliating situations, and even less compatible with the pride of a princess . . .

The most that we can try to do is to understand our hero and make him credible, but not to rehabilitate him. The fact is that Abraham, one of the greatest figures in the history of humanity, behaved in Egypt like one of the most cowardly, for it was there, trembling in fear for his own life and without offering the least resistance, indeed paving the way with a lie, that he handed his adored wife over to Pharaoh, and not only derived a profit from this execrable gesture, but even went so far as to tell the adored wife that this had been precisely his purpose. Such an accumulation of dastardly acts would seem excessive even in a Shakespearean villain, and far from finding any excuse for him, we are well aware of the difficulties to be overcome in trying to comprehend him. In truth, our Abraham has no excuse: in one way or another, he should have faced the situation as a man, and if worse came to worst he should have unsheathed his sword and yielded only to superior force rather than persuading his beloved wife to lie, and thus denying her the ultimate possibility of being left in peace. This lie is the most astonishing thing in the whole story, since it is clear that if Abraham had not lied, no one would have taken Sarah away from him or harmed even a hair on his own head.

Abraham has no excuse, but if it is true that the great tragedy of his life was born from a misunderstanding, that will serve him forever as an extenuating circumstance. In fact, his conviction that Sarah would be dragged away, and he himself killed on her account, was absolutely unfounded. The only way he might have saved the beautiful woman from humiliation, and himself from the painful consequences that would later ruin his whole life, would have been to declare *sic et simpliciter* that Sarah was his legitimate spouse. That everything would have gone smoothly is shown by the furious remonstrances of Pharaoh, whose sincerity and trustworthiness are supported by the no less furious remonstrances with which King Abimelech of Gerar would later, and for the same reason, confound the liar. Both of them declared unequivocally that they had taken Sarah away only because Abraham had passed her off as his sister, and they would have refrained from doing so had he frankly admitted that the woman was his wife.

The fact that he incurred this misunderstanding, persisted in it, and thereby disgraced himself to the utmost can only be ascribed to his exhausted state of mind, terror, and clouded reason. First of all, he let himself be confused and overwhelmed by the alarming report, while unable to make the slightest effort to ponder it with reasonable objectivity. He may have heard it said that the scouts for the Egyptian lords did not listen to reason and ruthlessly abducted any woman they chose. He may also have heard that their menfolk might be compensated with a modest dowry if they offered no resistance, but were beaten and even killed if they protested. In any case, even assuming that he might have collected more precise information on the subject, he could not have known that the observers posted around the refugee encampment had specific instructions that in investigating the supply of available women, they were to verify each one's family situation before arranging for her transfer to the harems of the Egyptian lords. The observers were under orders not to touch the married women, no matter how beautiful they were, while they had a free hand with regard to any other female refugee, from the adolescent to the attractive widow. Abraham could not have known that Pharaoh, for political and military reasons, was anxious to preserve the friendship of the nomadic peoples and therefore sought to avoid any friction or complications. Pharaoh knew that while the abduction of their wives would lead to resentment among the refugees, the decorous installation of their daughters or sisters in the harems of the nobility, not to mention his own, would be seen by them as a great honor. Furthermore, they were paid a small dowry, which constituted a kind of first aid for their impoverished economies, a small capital with which to rebuild a life before resuming their wanderings.

We'd like to hope that Abraham had no inkling of all this. But we can well imagine that even if he did, he would never have been convinced, since in his eyes Sarah was so desirable as to justify the infringement of even the most explicit rules. Indeed, what obstacle would Sarah's family situation be for Pharaoh? He need only have Abraham killed, and Sarah, no longer a wife but a widow, would be ripe for abduction! In any case, there was not a shadow of doubt in Abraham's disturbed mind that his most beautiful and adored wife would somehow end up as Pharaoh's concubine. In his state of physical and moral deterioration, he was incapable of logical thought, and this is another extenuating circumstance, though still not a justification for him. For one must admit that Abraham, even though he hadn't understood the real situation, should have behaved in a manner consistent with the misunderstanding, by unsheathing his sword in defense of his adored wife and not yielding except to force, even if it meant taking a few blows. But this is not what happened. We know that Abraham told an execrable lie that not only swept away every obstacle facing the scouts, who were happy to have caught such a beautiful prey, but at the same time kept them from harming a single hair on his head.

In our desperate attempt to mitigate our hero's cowardice, we

adduce one more possibility not to be discarded *ab ovo*, if only
because there had to be a psychological process whereby Abraham
arrived at the fatal lie. To give him one more chance of salvation,
we are willing to suppose that there had been a moment when
Abraham would have been ready to defend his adored wife, and
even at the cost of his own life. We would like to think that when
he realized that the presence of the beautiful woman, who kept
rebelling at the need to stay hidden, had caught the attention of
the tireless observers, and understood that the end had come, he
decided finally to reveal to his Sarah the danger they were in.
Squirming miserably at her feet and piteously whining, he restated
his immense love for her, assuring her that without her his life
would lose all meaning. If Sarah at that moment had given in to
terror, if she had become desperate and wept along with him,
perhaps Abraham would have unsheathed his sword and hurled
himself on the Egyptians even before they came to take the woman
away. But Sarah, bitterly noting to herself that such an outcome
would be a worthy and logical conclusion to the tribulations to
which her husband's madness had exposed her, remained haughtily
unmoved. "Instead of sniveling," she said with icy reasonableness,
"it would be better if you thought of doing something about me."
To which Abraham, pathetically: "What can I do, my little goddess? I shall resist to my last drop of blood and die at your tiny
adorable feet! That's what I'll do!" "And what good will that do
me?" said Sarah with a withering little smirk. "If fate wills that in
one way or another I'm to end up in Pharaoh's harem, there's no
point in you getting yourself killed. If that's how it is, better if you
be the one to shut yourself up in the wicker basket from now on."

Abraham's blood ran cold. Unable to say a word, he staggered
out of the tent. He realized it was all over. He realized that it no
longer mattered whether they took Sarah away or not: the main
thing was that he had lost Sarah forever. He realized that the
alternative of dying in defense of Sarah or as a result of her loss had
now become moot, since his life had already collapsed. What he
had feared for years, what he had foreseen for months, had now

instantly become reality. Sarah, who for some time had been more inaccessible and untouchable than the Lord Himself, not only no longer loved him, not only rejected him, but at this point looked on him with such disgust that never again would she allow him to adore her . . . And this was the end—of everything.

Anyone can see that the realization of Sarah's irrevocable loss constituted an incomparably more deadly blow for Abraham than would be the case for any other husband discovering his wife's emotional alienation. This matter, which can turn into a sentimental drama or a tragedy of passion, or even into a loss of faith in the ideals of life, could not for anyone else mean a professional failure as it did for Abraham. The collapse of the task for which he had been born was total. It was not enough that the Lord had withdrawn from him, leaving him to be consumed by doubts, but now Sarah too had abandoned him, depriving him once and for all of the possibility for his mystical-erotic raptures. His God and his goddess had turned out to be no less false and lying than the idols that as a youth he had been in the habit of contemptuously destroying. Abraham was forced to realize that his life and the meaning of his life had been built on mere illusions. By now it was a question of something more than the well-known and always depressing experience undergone by all mystics when *gratia occultat*. Abraham lost not only the strength for his mystical ecstasies and religious veneration, but their very object and goals.

In his indescribable state of physical and moral depression, Abraham could feel himself going crazy, noting that by discovering the Lord and marrying Sarah, he had made the two most solemn blunders in his life. Or rather—and neither was this an idea to be excluded, though it was unlikely to mitigate his despair—that he had not been able to handle these two marvelous revelations of his life in a suitable way, being not a "true mystic" but the lowest kind of charlatan. From the stifling void that had arisen in and around him, the failure of his presumed vocation stared at him with a sardonic grin.

This was the great crisis of Abraham's spiritual path, no different in kind from the sort that drives so many great and unhappy geniuses of thought, art, or science to madness or suicide. The patient reader would be more prepared to believe that we are dealing with the same psychological situation if we could report that Abraham, having reached the lowest rung of despair, had fallen on his sword or hanged himself from the first nail. But we must keep in mind that, in such cases, making an end of it or surviving both seem equally to mean that one is done for, and thus Abraham's crisis could have been genuine even without ending in suicide. One of the most convincing proofs of our thesis is the fact that poor Abraham did what failed geniuses usually do in such a predicament: before deciding whether or not to do away with themselves, they set out to destroy by vandalism the traces of their mistaken work. Abraham threw his adored wife into Pharaoh's arms, in the same way that a painter in a frenzy slashes his own canvases, the scientist disavows his own theories, and the writer abjures his *opera omnia*.

To destroy the living testimony of our failed or mistaken aspirations, the very thing that in the course of an entire life we have considered to be the peak of our creative forces and have coddled with loving pride, is a suicide, or rather a form of annihilation more complete than the suppression of our psychophysical reality. By killing his own creation, the creator kills himself—that "him" in himself that "mattered"—and what follows is death, a more awful death in that it does not involve the death of the body.

The unbridled wish to annihilate his work physically and himself morally was the manifestation and result of Abraham's spiritual collapse as a creative genius. This was why he threw Sarah into Pharaoh's arms, not only without striking a blow, but also in such a monstrous way. For if handing her over—the woman who had already abandoned him in body and soul, and who was the living symbol of the mistaken direction of his whole existence—could be for Abraham the same gesture as that of an artist destroying his own masterpieces, the fact of having yielded her in such a monstrous way even reminds us of the self-inflicted wound of one who—*pars pro toto*—cut off his ear. Unless we accept the idea that Abraham, with his execrable gesture, wanted to drain his bitter cup to its last dregs and keep anything from his hateful past from being saved for the yawning void of his future—not even a crumb of his dignity and honor, even in Sarah's memory!—we would be incapable of imagining how, and especially why, he uttered the notorious words of farewell that would cover him with infamy for thousands and thousands of years: *"Say, I pray thee, thou art my sister: that it may be well with me for thy sake; and my soul shall live because of thee."*

Unfortunately there can be no doubt that these horrible and repellent words were actually uttered, or in any case have been forcibly stamped on the tradition, which to us is the same thing. When Abraham reached the point of being ready to surrender his wife to a form of base and humiliating life, while revealing to her shamelessly, indeed with horrifying sadism, the supposed reason for his gesture, at that point he was already submerged up to his neck in his own inferno, to which he had condemned himself to go on living amid the most exquisite tortures. He could not imagine the horrible void that awaited him except by bringing to it all his own baseness and squalor, nor could he ease the path that led there except by trampling in the mud all the moral and empirical values in which he had once believed and that had disappointed him: only thus was he able to give himself up, with the utmost self-hatred, to the nothingness that would be his lot for the rest of his life.

In the sensual torment of perdition he may have deluded himself that the man who had been condemned to survive would necessarily be the opposite of the man who had failed, and that his future life would likewise have to be the opposite of the one that had collapsed for good. He espoused an ideal that seemed attractive to him by virtue of its very repugnance: a life without reverence and without ecstasy, with no desires and no unattainable goals, the normal life of every simple mortal, modeled on that of other nomadic tribal chiefs, completely devoted to taking care of his property and increasing it, with at his side a good wife who would give him sons, love and respect him, yes, respect him for his as yet unexpressed qualities, seeing him as wise and shrewd, capable and tough, and, if need be, cunning and even wicked as well! To make his own depravity more onerous to himself, he forced himself to toy with this repugnant ideal, perhaps also because, in his heart, he feared from the beginning that he would never be able to accept it. Besides, it gave him a certain satisfaction to coddle something that was the absolute negation of everything he had now come to hate.

It was sensually tormenting to rehearse the role he had chosen for himself for the future. It gave him a feeling of intoxicating giddiness to think that life all of a sudden had taken on such a simple appearance, due solely to the fact that he had changed his ideas about it by getting rid of certain principles, prejudices, ambitions, and unsustainable ideals. They must have been quite heavy burdens if he now felt so lightened. In this curious state of giddiness Abraham conceived the scene of the dress rehearsal.

To introduce his wife to Pharaoh's men as his sister was a diabolically simple idea, and Abraham foresaw that it wouldn't cost him much trouble to get Sarah to accept it; in the nagging paroxysm of self-liquidation he also found the strength to tell her. What he found more arduous was the task of getting his tattered retinue of shepherds and servants to swallow this surprising news, without thereby compromising his own honor. He took particular pleasure in worrying about his honor, knowing that at the same time he was plotting the vilest gesture of his life. But the refinement of pleasure consisted particularly in all the nastiness he had put into meticulously working out the strategy of his plan. How he hated and despised himself when, with grim unctuousness, he declared to his assembled people that the moment had come to reveal to them the truth, or more precisely, the *whole* truth regarding his ties of kinship with *their* lady! He said that the fact that their lady (who, moreover, did not share the same tent with him and had given him no children) was his wife (which therefore, since it was not even confirmed by appearance, might well be a fiction) had less to do with the whole truth than that other fact (and this was surely a fact of the genuine kind, even though they would not actually be able to check it) that she was the *sister* of that Milcah whose father, Haran, father therefore of Milcah and father of her *sister*, was his *brother*, but at the same time also the *brother* of Nahor who had taken as his wife the said Milcah—daughter of Haran, *sister* of Sarah—who for that very reason was Nahor's wife, but *not his wife*. Thus he spoke to his astonished and tattered people, playing cleverly on the ambiguity of the relative pronoun, and solemnly concluding: "That is the whole truth, from which it is by no means clear that your lady is *also* my wife; on the contrary, it almost seems that she's not. I ask you not to talk about this matter with anyone, especially with anyone who asks you about it. But if it can't be avoided, tell them the whole truth, so that—and the Almighty forbid!—should *your* lady be taken away by Pharaoh's men, I would receive in exchange a modest dowry, the indispensable foundation on which to build my and *your* future well-being and my and *your* happiness, once we are ready to resume our normal way of life!" This final sally, whose purpose was only to ensure the complicity of his people, gave one more boost to his mind, which was sliding down the slope of self-destruction, and in this state of inspired giddiness he even decided to repeat it to Sarah.

The editors of the Bible report Abraham's monstrous words with hair-raising terseness, with no comment, no attempt to find some excuse for our hero, who—we must not forget—was above all one of their heroes, and by no means the least important. For our part, we've done all we can to understand this moment, the most horrible moment in his long life, and make it understandable to others, and now it will be up to the kind reader, so called, to say whether understanding can also mean forgiving. In any case, we can be quite sure that with the notorious words addressed to Sarah he gave himself the *coup de grâce*. But can't we at least hope that by demonstrating his vileness beyond all measure, he actually only meant to make the path toward the humiliating life that awaited her less difficult for Sarah, by giving her the sad consolation that the fire could be no worse than the frying pan? The labyrinth of the human psyche is full of twisted alleyways.

So Sarah was led away by Pharaoh's men. The shepherds, in line with the instructions they had received and mindful of the reward, had in their turn told the whole truth to the Egyptian abductors, who, though perplexed at the difficulty of keeping in mind who in that complicated family was the father, sister, or brother of whom, had no reason to suppose that the strikingly beautiful woman was the tribal chief's legitimate wife. One legend has it that, just to be sure, they turned to Lot, who seemed to them to be the second in command. He, calculating coldly like the shepherds, confirmed without hesitation that the woman was the chief's sister. If we absolutely must find a partial justification for his lie too, we can imagine that in his healthy amorality, he was privately convinced that it would be a much better arrangement for Sarah to become Pharaoh's concubine than to go on being the wife of that beggarly uncle of his!

We hope to have made it plausible that Abraham's great crisis was genuine, even if it didn't end with his death. After Sarah was taken away, Abraham realized that to endure the state of spiritual and moral death was more difficult than he had imagined. We have no intention of inflicting on either our readers or ourselves a description of the tortures that Abraham had to endure in the days and weeks that followed the tragic event. We cannot rule out the possibility that, as a conclusion to his spiritual suicide, he also contemplated actual suicide. But on this point it's worth pausing to ask ourselves: wouldn't it have been an abominable act of madness, or in any case a real blunder with universal consequences, if Abraham, in that moment of despair, collecting what remained of his human dignity and merely for the purpose of satisfying our taste for dramatic gestures, had truly committed suicide? And here again we run up against the alternative, peculiar to tragic spiritual conflicts, of dying or surviving: while at first sight we tend to ascribe to cowardice a failure to destroy one's physical life after the meaning of life has collapsed, it is precisely the case of our protagonist that induces us to change our mind. Isn't it less a question of a craven fear of killing ourselves than a vague presentiment of a possible rebirth? Can it not perhaps happen that by discarding all our ideals and confronting our *nihil*, we are already unconsciously on the verge of a rising vitality that will help to lift us like the Arabian phoenix from the ashes of our failed world? There is no lack of examples of those who in their despondency think they are creating the void with a final desperate gesture, but in reality all they are doing is clearing the ground in order to build a new world on it. The moment of spiritual suicide is already frequently pregnant with the seeds from which new creative gestures and acts will grow; they may not stand comparison with the ones that have been destroyed, but sometimes, perhaps, a masterpiece will be born.

Thus Abraham, even as he sought to annihilate himself, instinctively felt that he still had things to do in this world. To his great regret, he discovered little by little that he still had a surprising amount of vital energy available, even if it was slow in coming forth. Now that it was irreparably too late, he felt that he would have been capable of defending Sarah even at the cost of his own life, since he loved her, desired her, adored her, yes, adored her more than ever, now that he'd lost her for good. The upsurge of shame and impotence made him furious, and it was all Lot could do to keep him from manhandling Pharaoh's messengers and refusing the cows and sheep they had brought as compensation from their master. The fervid prayers with which he pestered the Lord for a miracle were likewise a sign of vitality, and showed that he still believed in the full value of his discovery.

Several weeks went by, during which Abraham completely gave up the idea of becoming another man and devoted himself intensely to mourning the past. He was abruptly awakened from this torpor by an astonishing event. One fine day he watched speechless as, under military escort and led by a court functionary, a caravan formed by hundreds of *sheep, and oxen, and he asses, and menservants, and maidservants, and she asses, and camels,* loaded with gold and silver, came marching toward his camp. Abraham could hardly believe his eyes, not to mention his ears, when he heard that all this was his. And he would have liked to become deaf when he learned that all this was Pharaoh's gift as an expression of his full satisfaction with the young lady his sister.

All this made Abraham understand that he would have to relinquish his wife forever. Only secondarily did the sneaking thought cross his mind that as a result of Sarah's loss he had suddenly become rich, richer than he had ever dreamed of being. But to make him rich had been one of the Lord's first and most important promises, and if his unexpected fortune could be considered as the first stage in the fulfillment of the divine promises, it meant that the Lord hadn't abandoned him after all! The Lord, though apparently absent and hidden, had always been watching over him! If nothing else, He seemed to keep His promises. But good heavens, at what a price! Had he been able to sum things up from a single experience, Abraham would already have realized that from the Lord's viewpoint even keeping promises was not an act of pure altruism, but simply another move in carrying out His plan. But at the moment, all that mattered to him was that the Lord, though invisible, was listening nearby, and that his prayers had not been in vain. Now he wanted to make Him understand that riches alone would never satisfy him unless he could have his wife back. He went so far as to offer to the Lord to renounce these riches and the stupendous future that had been promised him if only he could have Sarah back. Goaded beyond endurance, he demanded a miracle.

The miracle took its time in coming, but it had of necessity to happen, certainly not to lift Abraham's morale, but to serve the inexorable egotism of the Lord. Having assigned a fundamental role in His plan to this married couple, He naturally had to rescue Sarah from Pharaoh's harem, and since the latter would be opposed to the idea, this could only happen through His miraculous intervention. Miraculous, yes, but not thereby hasty. Perhaps, but one can't be sure, the prolonging of their sufferings, as punishment for Abraham's pusillanimity and Sarah's pride, was one of the divine intentions. In any case, before miraculously intervening, the Lord, with wisdom and foresight, had to wait for the beginning of the rainy season in Egypt and beyond its frontiers, so that pastures in the land of Canaan would be green and provide forage for His faithful follower's increased droves.

Everyone knows the form the divine intervention took. *And the Lord plagued Pharaoh and his house with great plagues*, and the news spread rapidly throughout the country. To the people it was obvious that the gods were striking the sovereign because of some secret sin of his. The news also reached the refugee encampment, and it occurred to Abraham that in these grievous events one should see the hand of the sole true and living God. So the Lord was giving him his due! All of a sudden, he became feverishly agitated, haranguing his people and declaring that, yes, the whole truth might satisfy and deceive men, but not the Almighty, who knew the essence of truth and did not allow it to be violated. In their turn, Abraham's shepherds and servants spread their leader's theory among the other refugees, and in the end it was murmured throughout the country that the cause of the mysterious disasters was the foreign beauty in Pharaoh's harem, whom he had abducted even though she was the legitimate wife of a tribal chief who had come seeking hospitality. The murmurs ended by reaching the court of Pharaoh, who either because he was superstitious, or wanted to yield to public opinion, or else because he respected his own principles, after an explosion of just anger, restored Sarah to Abraham, and under police escort expelled them and their people and goods from his country.

Abraham departed from Egyptian soil accompanied by his Lord and his lady, and also a good deal richer, but with a wound. For he was soon to realize that Sarah would never, for all the riches in the world, forgive him her humiliation in Egypt. Her pride did not allow her to reproach him directly, or even to take revenge by recalling with ostentatious nostalgia the luxury and magnificence with which she had recently been surrounded. Nor did she try to humiliate him by saying that Pharaoh's bed had aroused in her no more horror than the matrimonial couch. In her pride, the "princess" preferred to keep silent, and with her silence she became a living statue of reproach and vengeance. If Abraham in leaving Egypt was richer than when he had arrived, Sarah departed even more beautiful than before, endowed besides with a new and disturbing allure. Her enhanced, radiant beauty was the cruelest means by which she punished her husband. Not knowing what her suddenly regained freedom held in store for her, she had prepared herself for any eventuality by bringing with her some of the splendid clothing and costly jewels that she had earned during her brief career as a concubine. When she flaunted them, as she often did, she had no ulterior motive, nor any intention whatsoever of tormenting her husband: she simply wanted to enjoy the intoxicating spectacle of herself, wanted happily to admire her own divine beauty in her mirror with its gold frame—another gift from Pharaoh. Undeniably, her beauty had met with the highest approval from the Egyptian king. And for Abraham this splendid woman was taboo.

Certainly life in the harem had been a long series of humiliations for Sarah. To accept orders to play disgraceful roles, and to be one among many other women inferior to herself in every respect, could hardly have been to the liking of a born "princess." And to have to perform, without being able to refuse, a service for which she was accustomed to being asked, was another inexhaustible source of bitterness for her pride. But, all things considered, at least her vanity was not deprived of certain satisfactions, the memories of which were softened by distance and coalesced to form for her a solid moral capital. And how! Even though Pharaoh was such and so, and had communicated the invitation to gladden his couch in the form of a command, the fact that he had preferred to address this command more frequently to her than to the other women had certainly been a sign of his high esteem for her womanly qualities; even though at the time she had received this esteem with hostility, it appeared to her retrospectively as pleasant and flattering. Even though Pharaoh was such and so, the fireworks of endearments with which he had extolled her beauty had far surpassed in poetic intensity even Abraham's hyperbole, if for no other reason than having been uttered in Egyptian, with the magical seductiveness of a foreign language, and had almost surpassed the splendor of the clothes and jewels with which Pharaoh, as a reward and a sign of gratitude, had adorned her beauty. Even though Pharaoh was such and so, he had adored her and treated her with consideration, and the undeniable result of this was the by no means negligible wealth he had chosen to bestow on Abraham. And Pharaoh, even though he was such and so, in the final analysis was still Pharaoh, the most powerful ruler in the world, who had singled her out for her charms among thousands of concubines and had treated her as the favorite.

Only hypocrisy or insensitivity could fail to understand Sarah as little by little she transformed her shameful memories into a solid moral capital. In truth, she had long considered her name as something becoming to her, but now this name, after Pharaoh's sanctifying touch, signified her true standing. To become Pharaoh's favorite may have been humiliating in itself and at first unbearable, but in her relations with the world, and first of all with her husband, it ensured her an unbridgeable social superiority. As a result, not only the indelible offense inflicted on her dignity as a woman, but also her awareness of her own lofty standing, a kind of class pride, now helped to maintain below zero the temperature of the curtain of ice that she had lowered between Abraham and herself since the first day of her liberation. Never again did she intend to consider as a husband the miserable worm who, with undeniable skill and luck, now devoted himself to multiplying the riches that had come to him *because of* her: neither riches, nor power, nor prestige would have made it possible for her to see him once again as a human being. And accordingly she treated him worse than a mangy dog.

In Abraham's shoes, any other husband would have given up hope of re-establishing relations, even if only of peaceful cohabitation, with Sarah. Actually he was obliged to resort to the most various pretexts merely to be received by her, and it cost him a superhuman effort to look in the face that reproach made flesh into which his wife seemed to have been transformed. The "princess," in her statuelike rigidity, became frightfully similar to the one who bore her name as a sobriquet, and Abraham, in the presence of this apparition, felt increasingly crushed by his own insignificance. As a born mystic, he proved completely incapable of planning the tactical moves to which any enamored husband would have had recourse in such a situation. By clinging rigorously to the unwritten rules governing the relations between adorer and adored, he adopted the only suitable attitude to follow in this phase of such relations: he did not try to deny or minimize his guilt, nor to hide his remorse; on the contrary, he seized on every opportunity to show his repentance and accepted the signs of Sarah's horror and contempt with real enthusiasm, constantly insisting on how much he deserved such treatment and almost rejoicing in it, since to expiate his cowardice required a cruel penitence. His wish for expiation and purification was so powerful that he succeeded in judging as adorable Sarah's crude manifestations of loathing and disgust, with which she was unstinting in his presence and that in other circumstances would have driven him to despair. But this was exactly the kind of treatment he expected from Sarah, and no one was better able than himself to appreciate its cathartic properties. And when Abraham's admiration and exaltation reached their height, he could not help but give vent to them. No doubt about it, he was a true mystic, and with the return of his vital energies, he came to be convinced of it himself.

Finally, with the passage of time, Sarah could not remain indifferent to such exuberant adoration, and though she did not go beyond the stage of astonishment, she gradually gave up her rigidly negative attitudes. She could not doubt the sincerity of her husband's feelings and expressions, at most she could be amazed by them, and she ended by bestowing on him a certain admiration, albeit full of reservations. If hitherto she had tortured and humiliated him with thoughtless spontaneity, she now began to torment him scientifically, driven by curiosity to test the limits of his capacity for endurance. And although she did not realize it, this was already an indulgent attitude on her part, and at the same time an enormous step forward from Abraham's point of view. Little by little, the idea began to make headway in Sarah's mind, even though it was received with some hostility, that this craven husband of hers was more complex than he appeared. Simply to call him craven was not enough to define him; indeed, there was something singular about his cravenness, and it was just this that had been the means for releasing the volcanic forces that held her spellbound. Without realizing it, Sarah remained subjugated by the impetuousness and lack of restraint of this miserable worm's adoration, compared to which Pharaoh's fervor seemed less than a lukewarm courtship. There was something moving in Abraham's perseverance, something agonizing and heartrending, enough to make you cry. Sarah almost reached the point of feeling sorry for him and of reproaching herself for being unable to forgive him.

Had anyone ever asked her, Sarah might not have admitted that with the passing of the years her hostile feelings toward her husband had noticeably softened: indeed, she was always ready to retreat to her initial positions of implacable contempt and rigid withdrawal. But Abraham's sensitive soul registered even the most microscopic concessions, it wallowed in boundless happiness, and its ecstasies conquered heights never reached before. By now Sarah sometimes even allowed him to enter her tent, which had been transformed into a kind of *sancta sanctorum*, to let herself be witnessed by this specialist in worshipful rites while she admired her own beauty, and once in a while she even decided to give a hint of a scornful smile to express her pleasure at the clothes and jewels that her husband had taken the liberty of presenting her with, frequently and with total devotion. To her surprise, Sarah even had to admit that Abraham, in overwhelming her with all these beautiful and costly things that his wealth made it possible for him to obtain, was far from making a shrewd gamble to buy her favors, but was doing it purely and simply out of devotion, driven by the wish to construct a worthy frame for her incomparable beauty. And this was another point in Abraham's favor, making Sarah feel even sorrier that she must hate him and be unable to forgive him.

Sometimes she felt so keenly sorry for him that she was even forced to seek out or create something to nourish her contempt and horror: it was to this alone that Abraham owed the favor when from time to time Sarah yielded to his supplications and allowed him into her bed. But even there Abraham brought with him his humility and contrition, and never again did it occur to him to give himself the airs of a conqueror. He always took care to declare that he was truly unworthy of such an honor, and demonstrated at every moment his profound regret that her incomparable features provoked in him certain reactions that made it impossible not to molest her. Alas, he no longer appealed to his rights as a husband, blocked once and for all in Egypt, nor to the wifely duties from which Sarah had excused herself for good. This was a matter of true mendicancy, of humble but erosive begging, and Sarah saw herself obliged from time to time to drop him a few small alms, if only to get rid of him for a while and grant herself another more or less lengthy period of untouchability.

To be tolerated by Sarah, and at times be able to embrace her, was for Abraham the height of bliss, the intensity of which was strengthened rather than diminished by all the difficulties, humiliations, and rejections that often preceded it. Nevertheless, Abraham could imagine bliss even more perfect than this, which in itself was almost unsurpassed, a bliss that he was not ready to renounce and intrepidly sought: that of being not merely tolerated, but loved and respected, or at least rehabilitated, if not forgiven for the shame of Egypt. And a marvelous opportunity for this rehabilitation seemed to present itself when Lot fell prisoner to Chedorlaomer, king of the Elamites.

Unless we bear in mind the bond between Sarah and Lot, which in all probability was that of brother and sister, but in any case was cemented less by blood than by nostalgia for the world and gods of their youth, as well as by a kind of alliance or rather complicity against Abraham, we would find it unbelievable that our hero, hotheaded and impulsive to be sure, but basically a coward, had on hearing the news of his nephew's capture unsheathed his weapons in a twinkling and hurled himself against the combined forces of four enemy kings. He had brought Lot with him from Chaldea out of a pure sense of moral duty (perhaps because he did not have a completely clear conscience over the premature death of Lot's father), but actually he had always disliked his nephew, if for no other reason than his great resemblance to Sarah. Except that all the features that in his wife were elevated to the realm of the divine had in young Lot been stabilized at a very low level, taking the appearance of unforgiveable faults and repugnant vices, from impudent egotism to vanity and lechery, which led Abraham always to consider him the perfect personification of idolatry. Undoubtedly it had been more than providential that in Egypt Lot had given him a hand by attesting before Pharaoh's men that the beautiful woman was his uncle's sister, and by no stretch of the imagination his wife, but Abraham never doubted for a moment that Lot had acted not out of a sense of solidarity, or even understandable fear, as had he himself, but out of repugnant selfishness and ignimonious greed for material gain: motives that were all the worse since even with the most unbridled optimism Lot could not have hoped for more than a few cows and sheep in exchange for Sarah, in all probability his sister, but in any case his beloved ally and accomplice. And it had been especially repugnant and ignominious that Lot, citing his own contribution, had had the effrontery to demand his share of Pharaoh's remarkable gift, and had thus ended by filling his pockets while having risked nothing, getting fat on the shame of his relatives. But what to the unhappy Abraham was the unkindest cut of all, shocking him more than anything else and making him hate his nephew irrevocably, was the fact that Sarah, though determined never to forgive her husband, immediately renewed her ties with Lot, and joined him in cursing Abraham or mocking him, depending on their mood.

The *strife between the herdsmen* of their respective droves was an excellent pretext for their separation. Abraham heaved a sigh of relief, but Lot himself was no less pleased. When Abraham offered to let him choose which part of the promised land he wanted to go to, Lot, who had always dreamed of the comfort and pleasures of civilized life, chose without hesitation the plain of the Jordan, with the idea in mind of settling eventually in the city of Sodom. Presented by the Bible as a sink of iniquity, this was above all a rich and cultivated city, where among other things the luxury and refinements of life required a good deal of money, but where money, in skillful hands, could also multiply and accumulate. In view of these possibilities, Lot sold his herds and found himself a highly profitable burgher's profession. The legend tells us that he enjoyed lending money, especially at high interest rates, to the gilded youth of the city—that he was, to put it bluntly, a usurer. And since he was not the type to let himself be taken in, his business thrived. He lived well, got married, and produced numerous offspring.

It was one more thorn in Abraham's side that Lot easily succeeded where he didn't, that his nephew was already several times a father, while he was still condemned to go on begging to be admitted from time to time to his wife's bed. The news of Lot's capture filled him at first with a diabolical joy, but even when he felt ashamed of his feelings, he was unable to go beyond that formal compassion that throws a handful of dust in the world's eyes. But anything could be attained by Sarah's despair, spasmodic weeping, and hysterical cries of pain! It was almost as though with that scoundrel Lot she had lost her dearest treasure! Abraham was dismayed to see that even this event was being used by his wife to humiliate him. "And you," she screamed, beside herself, "how can you sit here with your hands folded when your own flesh and blood has been dragged away into everlasting slavery? You don't mind seeing part of the wealth that came to you at the price of my body going to ruin? You do nothing but boast about your strength, your prestige, your powerful friends! What would it cost you to take a few armed men, go after the enemy, and free Lot with his family and property?" So little do wives sometimes know their husbands! Abraham, however, did not dare tell her what all this would cost him. To take to the battlefield, fight the enemy, and risk his hide were surely the most absurd ideas ever to emerge from anyone's head! On the other hand, Abraham feared nothing so much as Sarah's wrath, and although later, and for the same reason, he was to commit the other two most dastardly acts of his life at the expense of Hagar and Ishmael, at this moment, again for the same reason, he found himself forced to perform a heroic deed. Death is preferable to Sarah's anger, he decided despairingly; but at the same time an idea flashed through his mind and lifted his morale: if with the help of the Lord and his own powerful friends, everything were to go smoothly, he would be able to reappear before Sarah surrounded by the halo of a victorious general, worthy of her love! And so Abraham did for the hated Lot what he had not done for his adored Sarah: he risked his life.

As we know, the general *malgré lui* achieved a great triumph, which consolidated his prestige in the land of Canaan and in the eyes of his royal friends, but made no impression on Sarah's imagination. The conqueror of kings found his wife's bed no more accessible than had that coward for whom he had previously been taken. Thus do men delude themselves that their virtues count for something in the love of women! Everything went back to the way it was before.

Such, then, were the relations between Abraham and Sarah around the tenth year of their sojourn in the land of Canaan, unsatisfactory relations by any standard, but at the same time not unbearable, since in the final analysis—granted it would take a miracle—they might even improve. But although the possibility of improvement was not to be ruled out, it unfortunately assumed different aspects for each of them, so different as to be in conflict. In short, Sarah, having become accustomed to and almost fond of Abraham's adoring attitude, hoped that it would end with his being content to go on admiring and adoring her, while giving up the coarse desires that had gained him so many unspeakable humiliations. Abraham, on the other hand, hoped that Sarah, by now intuitively aware of the incomparable force and singular spell of the religious and erotic worship he bestowed on her, would end by returning his love and—if not in the drunken ecstasy of the senses, at least in the placid warmth of forgiveness and affection—stop rejecting him.

For both of them, the miracle, from which they hoped to obtain diametrically opposed results in order to improve their marital relations, would have been Sarah's maternity. Beyond the fulfillment of one of the Lord's promises and commands, and the satisfaction of an ardent desire of his own, Abraham also expected this event to soften his wife's frigidity. It's curious that in the first years of their marriage Abraham had even been content to delay this event, expected from the first moment, for fear that maternity might spoil Sarah's beauty. To cause her lovely virginal shape to change seemed to him not only a risk but a sacrilege. But, in truth, neither of them ever took precautionary measures against this eventuality. For Sarah, becoming a mother was in the order of things, and even when she tried every means to limit, or even block, her spouse's conjugal zeal, she never protested against the idea of an eventual maternity, only against sexual intimacy with a man who in this connection was hopelessly odious to her. And, in reality, this man sometimes succeeded in making even the idea of having a baby odious as well. This happened whenever her husband, having met with his mysterious Lord, accelerated the pace of his efforts to beget an heir. There was no need for him to evoke her duties as a wife to offend and humiliate Sarah, who seemed only now to understand her husband's true intentions. "It's clear to me now that your declarations of love and gestures of adoration were nothing but vulgar lies. It's not true that you love me, you don't desire me, you just want to get me pregnant so as to please your imaginary Lord, whom I don't believe in, and if I did, I'd hate and despise! I have no intention of lowering myself just so you can use me a means to please others!" After such scenes, the dejected Abraham was hard put to dispel his wife's bad mood and make her understand the purity and disinterestedness of his love. When things were back on track, Abraham yielded once again to his mystical happiness in the brighter atmosphere of family peace. Still, he did his utmost to make Sarah pregnant, and she, in her turn, did nothing to prevent it. Indeed, had he known another way to promote the possibility of a pregnancy other than the customary one, he would not have hesitated to use it. She too saw no other solution to improve her marital situation but maternity: with the birth of an heir, Abraham would have one less excuse to pester her.

And yet it seemed to her that it would take a miracle for her now to become a mother. Too many years of marriage had gone by (almost ten spent wandering through the land of Canaan, and perhaps many more before: our sources say nothing, or contradict each other, about the date of our two protagonists' nuptials) to encourage any hope of success in this matter, and Sarah wisely began resigning herself to the idea of her own sterility. It's always a sad thing to call a spade a spade, and it was very painful for Sarah to admit the crude reality and feel herself, the most beautiful of all women, somehow impaired in her splendid femininity. As the one slim consolation for her sad condition, the hope dawned on her that Abraham would finally realize that it was hopeless to expect a child from her and desist from his stubbornly amorous siege. He, however, took nothing for granted; for him this hypothetical sterility remained unproved, and was at most another excuse to give vent to his imperturbable, inexhaustible love. "I adore you," he announced with passion, "quite apart from the fact that you may or may not give me any children." And one fine day he came up with a surprising idea. "My princess," he burst out, all red in the face, "I've been thinking a lot about your supposed sterility. But how can we be sure that I'm not the sterile one?"

But just look how Abraham's ideas were more fecundating than his loins and Sarah's cerebral cortex more receptive than her womb! From that moment on, the beautiful wife began urging her husband to put himself to the test with a servant woman. For Sarah it was an upsetting experience to find out how painful it was for her, in the final analysis, to give this advice. It deeply humiliated her and made her almost furious to admit that much as this man repelled her, she was still unwilling to yield him to another woman. To admit all this meant also to recognize that in one way or another she had need of her man, if for nothing else than the mystical adoration he bestowed on her; and the pain she felt was a disturbing sign of the fear that struck her at the mere thought that by giving him up physically, she would also be giving up to another woman part of his heart and soul. A flush of indignation spread over her lovely face at the very idea that Abraham's love might lose its intensity and exclusivity were he to have something else to do besides adoring and pestering her. On the other hand, not to insist on this proposal would mean perpetuating their troubling relations, with no way out. But Abraham relieved her—as, in truth, she was hoping and expecting—of all these worries by rejecting her idea, which he judged humiliating to himself. "The Lord," he said, "has promised to make me the forefather of a great people, but that's His worry. I'd rather die without children than, having loved you, lower myself to a servant woman!" These words were sweet music to Sarah's ears, but meanwhile her annoyance was multiplied by Abraham's increased conjugal enthusiasm, and at times she found herself obliged to be nasty and cruel in order to free herself from it.

Due to this state of affairs, Abraham was downcast and in a foul mood when the Lord made him the ingenuous and explicit promise of a son from his bowels. On this occasion, it already seemed to him an impossible task to inform his wife of the news, for she was tolerating him even less than before and lost even a glimmer of reason at the mere mention of the Lord. On the other hand, how was he to keep the divine announcement hidden from her, since it concerned her directly and required her active collaboration for its realization? As he did in every delicate circumstance, once again he left it to his wife's discretion, and trembling with remorse and a sense of guilt, made a full confession of the recent divine appearance. Thanks to his unconditional surrender, Sarah did not fly off the handle; on the contrary, buoyed by a sudden idea, she treated him gently, almost maternally. She explained to him with shrewd, tender, but clear words that she was neither suited nor disposed to submit to procreative experiments, and besides, this whole business had nothing to do with her. The Lord hadn't said a word about the promised son coming from her bowels, all He had said was that he would come from Abraham's. "Get it through your head, my friend, that your Lord (who for me is just your fixation, and in whom I don't believe) has closed up my womb for good. So once again I give you the same advice: look elsewhere for the proof of your powers of procreation. Just to show that I understand you and respect your concern, I'm ready to make the greatest sacrifice that it lies in my power to make. Look, I'm not urging you to try your experiment on any little servant girl. I'm offering you my personal handmaid, Hagar. It's a considerable sacrifice on my part, since it's her job to look after me personally, attend me when I bathe, comb my hair, perfume my body with precious unguents, and in short assist me in my toilette. But, all the same, Hagar is a decent girl, young, attractive, appetizing, well groomed and also well trained—you can easily see she was one of Pharaoh's gifts. You certainly can't say I'm sentencing you to horrible forced labor . . . And anyway there's another point to be considered. You know as well as I do that if Hagar gives birth, from the practical and legal standpoint it would be as though I'd given birth myself. *I may obtain children by her.*"

It was a shrewd, affectionate, almost maternal speech, but Sarah still found herself faced with Abraham's dogged resistance. She was now determined, however, not to give in either to him or to her own misgivings. She guessed that this ingenious idea of hers would take the place of a miracle and bring about the desired solution to their marital problem. With soothing violence she thus persuaded Abraham to make use of the Egyptian slave, and finally, weeping, overcome with remorse, and with protestations of love for his adored wife on his lips, he decided on the fatal step and approached the girl's sleeping mat, no less distressed than if he were on his way to a torture chamber. But he wept more copiously, and was even more cruelly tormented by remorse, when he emerged, since, alas, not only had he survived the ordeal, but it hadn't been all that bad! He was then left truly aghast when, a few nights later, he found that in going to Hagar he no longer had to overcome any personal resistance; on the contrary, it was all he could do to restrain his impatience until the hour agreed upon. It was a terrifying discovery. And if in the first days he tried to avoid his wife so as not to have to look her in the face, now, driven by remorse and the need for penitence, he visited her to demonstrate his loyalty and to find in her company the only happiness of which he was worthy. With the force of desperation he begged her, pleaded with her, to allow him to suspend the extramarital practices that were not to his liking, and to come back to her. But Sarah would not be swayed. She explained that Hagar lay next to him in her name and as her representative, and admonished him to concentrate all his attentions on the girl and not even dream of interrupting his experiments until he had impregnated her.

Abraham, dismayed, foresaw storms in the near future. "And what if it takes weeks, or months, for her to get pregnant? What if she never gets pregnant?" he cried despairingly. "Not only do you force me to go to bed with a woman I don't love, but what's worse, I have to live without you!" But when he mentioned the possibility that Sarah, at least once in a while, might readmit him to his mystical paradise, she made it plain, in words as gentle as they were adamant, that she would consider any attempt on his part to return to conjugal intimacy as an offense and outrage, so long as his relations with the servant continued. Thus Abraham came to realize with actual terror that his wife had assigned him Hagar less as her representative than as her replacement, in other words as a surrogate for herself. He began to hate the Egyptian woman, with whom he nevertheless found himself more and more at ease, and as soon as Hagar became pregnant, he felt truly relieved. Reassured now about his virility, he intended to devote all his energies to Sarah, lavishing on her the flood of adoration that had accumulated in his heart during the long period of abstention. He was in for an even graver and more bitter disappointment.

Sarah repulsed him with unconcealed rage. Abraham had never seen her so furious, nor could he even have imagined it. The "princess," always so composed and impassive, had become irritable beyond measure, losing her temper for the most trivial reasons. It took Abraham a while to realize that Sarah was even able occasionally to forget the outrage she had suffered in Egypt, but that never in her life would she be able to forgive the fact that he had had his way in another woman's bed. And not even Abraham could forgive himself this time. When he thought it over, his extramarital exercises now seemed to him a trap laid for him by Sarah, with cunning but also with jealous love and the anguished hope that he wouldn't fall into it. Now it was clear to him that Sarah only wanted to put him and his fidelity to the test, to see if he was capable of sacrificing the purity of his mystical adoration for vulgar sensuality, albeit skillfully disguised as the desire to reproduce. And look how he, deceived by this desire no less than by his wife and the Lord, had fallen into the trap!

Everything threatened to collapse. Sarah not only rejected him with indignation and in no uncertain terms, but what was still more painful, she made fun of his acts of submission, of his wish for atonement, and of the fervid words with which he reaffirmed his unalterable love. But what wounded him even more was that Sarah, with hellish sarcasm, exhorted him to go back to Hagar's bed, something he wouldn't have done if his life depended on it. By now he wholeheartedly hated the unhappy girl, the cause of all his troubles, and stood by, albeit reluctantly, when Sarah discharged her unworthy anger (perhaps worthy only of a goddess) on her innocent handmaid. Frightened and mortified, Abraham thought it right that from now on everything in their lives, and even in the whole world, should go according to Sarah's will. This is why he stood by, likewise reluctantly, when Sarah drove out the woman who carried his heir in her womb, the son wanted by God . . . or rather who had seemed to him wanted by God. Such was the high price Abraham had to pay for the misunderstanding of having begot Ishmael instead of Isaac!

In any case, the expulsion of Hagar was a kind of storm followed by relative calm in Abraham's domestic life. Once the act, which seemed irrevocable, had been committed, everyone had second thoughts. Sarah, once more composed and impassive, regretted her cruelty, and Abraham, tormented by remorse, was ashamed of his pusillanimity and feared the anger of the Lord. In the sobering desolation of the desert, Hagar too may have realized that she had behaved insolently toward her mistress and that she ought to heed the Lord and return home, where by now the ground was prepared for a warm welcome. It was a relief for them all to shed the burden of guilt and make peace with each other under the auspices of an impending birth. One by one they came to understand that a fundamental problem had found its solution. It seemed that all of them had done their duty, Hagar by her mistress, Sarah by her husband, Abraham by his Lord, and even the Lord by His elect.

IV. Love's magic

THE BIBLE PASSES IN SILENCE OVER THE LONG PERIOD OF FOUR-
teen years between Ishmael's birth and the announcement of
Isaac's, obviously because nothing of importance happened for the
further development of the story. During that period Abraham did
not change his residence, had no more children, did not sell his
wife again, and didn't die. These, of course, would have been
events worth recording, in addition to any meetings with the Lord.
But no such meetings took place: in those fourteen years the Lord
never appeared to the man who was His discoverer and sole follower.

We, however, who are less interested in recording events than in
understanding them, finding the psychological connections between them, and probing their development, are not similarly
disposed to skip over that long period of time. And just as the
sacred text is silent on the events of that period, since even though

they happened, they have no importance for the story as such, so we, for the requirements of our narrative method, have to turn the spotlight on some of them. Far from inventing new events, we draw our readers' attention to some that surely took place, almost banal ones, implied even in the biblical story, but which should be taken into account.

First of all, we ought to point out that we now find a profound change in our protagonists and the atmosphere of their home life. To begin with, we must reckon with the presence of a character who fourteen years before had only just been born, but is now almost a youth—Ishmael, the patriarch's first and only son, presumed heir to his name and worldly goods, his prestige and power, the repository of so many promises and hopes, and the apple of his father's eye. It must not be forgotten that Ishmael was the center of attention for his three parents and the whole tribe, and that Abraham's family life pivoted around him.

Sticking strictly to the facts, we should note that fourteen years ago we left an Abraham who by his pusillanimity had set himself against the divine will, driving into the desert the Egyptian slave woman with his own son in her womb, while now we find an Abraham ready to perform the cruel operation of circumcision in order to comply with the will of God. This means, at the very least, that the patriarch's faith had grown stronger in this long period of time in which he'd had no opportunity to consult the Lord. And we might simply add that this had happened precisely because he hadn't seen the Lord again. For, thanks to the fact of not seeing Him in person, the terrible aspects of the desert god had paled in Abraham's memory, giving way to a luminous image more in keeping with the idea he had originally formed of Him in the great intuition of his discovery: the image of God as pure and absolute spirit, whose one concern was to help and promote His discoverer and sole follower. In that long period of fourteen years the Lord, while withdrawing into inaccessibility, had not been stingy in His gifts, leaving Abraham increasingly convinced of His infinite goodness. It was in these years that the patriarch forged the fatal thesis that has lasted for thousands of years and remains stamped on human consciousness: that whatever the Lord wants is good, and that things go well when the Lord wants them to. The pact concluded between God and man functioned to perfection on both sides.

All this needs to be pointed out lest we think that in the ease and relative calm of his family life Abraham's personality had been completely absorbed by his duties as a happy father and administrator of his worldly goods. Just as during the time of the Egyptian sojourn, the harsh blows he suffered could in no way change him, so not even his growing prosperity and the knowledge of work well done could stifle in him his true vocation. In those long fourteen years, vast new horizons opened up to his religious genius, lifting him to heights never before reached as he succeeded in spiritualizing God and making Him a suitable object for adoration.

But the true path of mystical elevation still remained his love for his wife. Having left our protagonists fourteen years ago in a climate of bitter calm, when Abraham was denied the opportunity to exercise his rights as a husband and Sarah abdicated her duties as a wife, we might think that the vivifying source of mystical love had also gradually dried up, especially now that the youthful ardors of the body no longer fed the desires of the spirit so readily. For we must also keep in mind an important physiological factor, closely related to the passage of time and on which the Bible itself lays great stress: in fourteen years our protagonists had considerably aged, to the point where Abraham could laugh in the Lord's face when He spoke of a son to be born to him from Sarah. But, as we know from the rest of the story, their old age was quite exceptional. Indeed, as we've already mentioned, much as Abraham thought of himself as old and decrepit—and in his outer appearance he did look worn out—he succeeded beyond the age of 137 in begetting half a dozen sons, while Sarah, though old clinically speaking, since it was years since she had stopped menstruating, remained a splendid woman, attractive enough to arouse the desires of King Abimelech. But while all this is marvelous, there is no need to see in it any supernatural intervention: this different way of aging and nevertheless staying young was the direct result of the relations between our extraordinary hero and heroine.

One other thing needs to be emphasized: while the birth of Ishmael resolved the most pressing issue in Abraham's family, it could not be, as had been hoped, the panacea for all ills. It would be gratuitous to believe that as a result of the appearance of an heir, Abraham had ceased to love Sarah, just as it would likewise be unreasonable to suppose that by the mere fact of being shielded from her husband's amorous harassment, Sarah had achieved the peak of happiness. If before she had lightheartedly done without it, now she would have been humiliated and desperate if she had had to give it up for good. Had Abraham come to his senses in this respect, it would have been a deadly blow for her susceptibility, all too strained, and which she scarcely managed to conceal under an appearance of serene apathy; in truth, the feeling of her own uselessness cast a faint shadow on the depths of her soul, and she was terrified by the idea that the meaning of her existence as a woman was about to be lost, without ever having come to fruition. For the first time in her life she was seized by the bitter presentiment that youth and beauty, the inexhaustible sources of her pride, were not necessarily eternal, and that they would never give her the satisfaction that had been expected. The nightmare of an embittered old age appeared on the horizon of her thoughts.

Alarm bells went off in Abraham's sensitive soul. When Sarah at first told him of her fears, he judged them premature, and thought his wife's talk about her incipient old age was only meant to discourage his overtures. Ever since Hagar's pregnancy, Sarah had always rejected his love, first with scorn and hostility, then with polite coldness, but always with unshakable firmness, and it was with an air of serene melancholy that she gently but stubbornly defended her chastity. "I'm getting too old for certain things, my poor friend," she would say, and when Abraham for the first time heard a note of bitter sincerity in the tremor of her voice, he was thunderstruck. New problems, hitherto inconceivable, appeared before him, deeply threatening the meaning and the very essence of his existence.

The possibility that even Sarah's youth was subject to the laws of time was something he would never have foreseen: an aged Sarah, deprived of her loveliness, would be an unexpected element, not only in his life, but in the entire cosmos, and would make it necessary to re-examine and redefine the order of the universe. But this was easier said than done. How could one go on living in a world in which it was no longer possible to venerate Sarah's divine beauty, and to adore and desire her? How could Abraham go on living in such a world if he could no longer look forward to the day when Sarah, young and beautiful, would return his love and give herself to him wholeheartedly? Such a world would be a horror, senseless and intolerable, a world in which there would be no place for Abraham . . .

For the moment, however, the danger was more imaginary than real. Sarah was still strikingly beautiful in both face and figure, and her youth, for the moment, showed no signs of decay. That this was not simply the illusion of a starry-eyed lover, Abraham could note every time he exchanged visits with neighboring dignitaries or itinerant tribal chiefs: men's eyes, ablaze with desire, almost popped out of their sockets at the sight of Sarah, while the faces of the women turned yellow with envy. The only worrisome thing was the adverbial locution *for the moment*, which came to him spontaneously every time he thought of his wife's youth and beauty, almost as though to demonstrate that the danger was remote. On the other hand, unfortunately, this locution was also at the same time a sad *memento*, constantly reminding him of the relentless approach of this future danger.

The tutelary religious spirit within him would help him overcome the problem, and he ended by imagining that he could adore and desire an even less young and beautiful Sarah, especially now when her slight melancholy, which seemed to shroud her splendor like a veil of burnished gold, aroused in him a secret emotion never felt before and enriched his love for her with new and tender nuances. But it was precisely Sarah's hidden sadness that worried Abraham. By developing the infinite resources of his own mysticism, he would be able to attain untold heights of ecstasy, but how would this solve Sarah's problem? For the first time in his life, he was able to put aside the selfishness of his adoration and concern himself with the woman who was its object. Obviously, Sarah would not allow herself to be deceived for very long by his effusions, and her wounded pride would rebel against what would seem to her a humiliating farce. Abraham came to the realization that there was only one solution that would satisfy them both: Sarah must remain young and beautiful until the end of time.

Thus began a new period in Abraham's life, an intense and emotional one, which we might call "magical," since even if it did not have all the characteristics of magic, in substance it belonged to that sphere. Abraham determined to arrest fleeting time, well aware that he was thereby violating nature's—and therefore God's—laws. Convinced that he could not invoke His help in an undertaking directed against the order that He Himself had established, he set against this natural order, as a compelling supernatural force, the overwhelming strength of his will and love. Drawing an imaginary magic circle around Sarah's tent, he built inside it his world, resistant to the corruption of time, creating and re-creating it day by day, in the holy furor to preserve intact and unchanged the object of his adoration, without which his existence would collapse.

We are convinced that Abraham could have saved himself a lot of trouble if, instead of indulging in magical practices, he had begun praying ardently to the Lord: he might thus have been able to call His attention to the situation of the woman who would become Isaac's mother, and we cannot rule out the possibility that the Lord, as though awakening with a start, would have given him the true heir in advance, or anyway would have taken the initiative in tenderly preserving Sarah's precious youth, which was indispensable to His by no means distant ends. In shouldering this task, which was beyond human power, Abraham could never have imagined that just when he thought he was acting against the order established by the Lord, he was walking with Him more than ever on His path!

So Abraham, instead of reminding the Lord that Sarah's youth was one of the pillars of His eternal plan, committed himself to a heroic struggle against the implacable law of nature. Sarah was amazed to discover new and unsuspected strengths in her husband, who, in response to her melancholy observations on the infallible signs left on her body by time, flew into a rage; shouting and screaming as though he were quarreling with someone, he never stopped pointing out to her that her beauty had suffered no change in the course of their long marriage. In his magical fury, he went so far as to repudiate completely everything he had stated daily during the decades of his amorous ecstasies—that Sarah was becoming more beautiful each day—and modified his previous thesis by declaring that she was *exactly* as beautiful as on the day of their wedding, making her beauty appear as a constant element in the cosmos, a non-perfectible perfection, and therefore incorruptible. In his outbursts of rage, he was impressive and frightening, intolerant of any objection, and Sarah, ever more astonished, ended by refusing to discuss the matter. When, as sad proof of the reality, she discovered in her splendid tresses the first strangely lifeless and stiff white hair, she showed it to Abraham with a smile of bitter triumph; but after he had rebuked her, derided her, and proved to her with irresistible eloquence that nature allowed herself jokes in bad taste even at the expense of sixteen-year-old girls, she pulled out the second white hair without saying a word. Aware by now of her husband's furious reactions, Sarah complained of the slow deterioration of her beauty only to the small extent that sufficed to persuade her of the contrary; of the rest she no longer spoke, and wisely took care to cover up all those things that now seemed to her merely tiresome phenomena that disturbed the harmony of her physical perfection, rather than fatal and infallible signs of decay. And in those curious, and increasingly frequent, erotico-religious orgies that they staged together before the Egyptian mirror, and which always took on the appearance of a magical rite, Sarah succeeded in dispelling her bitter worries. Actually it would have been madness to doubt her youthful beauty and start dreading old age, true old age, in which her person would arouse horror instead of desire!

The most effective element in Abraham's magical treatment was the fact that it didn't at all seem like a treatment. Even though at first the suspicion crossed Sarah's mind that the good man was merely trying to rouse her out of the melancholy that had ensnared her, she must have realized quite soon that this was not the purpose of Abraham's magical practices, but rather a very beneficial by-product. Already uncertain whether it was right to consider this paroxysm of adoration as a series of conjuring tricks, Sarah gradually realized that Abraham did not intend to deceive her, but at most himself. And while this discovery deeply touched her heart, it simultaneously aroused in her the desire—a desire that almost bordered on a sense of duty—to match the illusion of that engaging madman her husband. This truly cost her no effort. Her extraordinary beauty, which even by itself would long keep resisting the destruction of time, now attended and shrewdly framed, livened by the spell of the new goal, and exalted by the furious, almost threatening will of the holy madman, ended by becoming incandescent and throwing off astounding and dazzling sparks. To Sarah's surprise, she suddenly began to believe in her husband's magical strength, while for his part, he had to admit that never in the past had his wife been so intoxicatingly beautiful as now.

If at the beginning of this chapter we were inclined to think that Abraham's worship of Sarah had an empirical importance for himself, we can now, as our story proceeds, state unequivocally that with the passage of the years the erotico-religious mysticism of the man constituted an inexhaustible source of energy for the woman as well. She, who in the course of a long conjugal life had been more irritated than flattered by this immense, volcanic adoration, having reached the critical period in her life as a woman, made it a solid base for the present and future. The sense of the emptiness and uselessness of her own existence, which had fallen on her since Hagar's pregnancy and the birth of Ishmael, was dissipated by the love spell whereby Abraham restored her faith in herself and her will to live, regenerated her youth, and redoubled her beauty. To her great surprise, she began to look at her husband differently, almost as though her eyes had been reopened by the enchantment.

Of course, Sarah's change of heart still did not mean that the gates of Paradise had been flung open for Abraham, and that he could now bask voluptuously in the languid rays of the setting sun. But still she began to admire him and to realize that he stood above the category of evils that one had necessarily to put up with. For the first time in her life, she felt spontaneous gratitude toward her husband; a sort of sense of duty seemed to rise from the bottom of her heart, actually inducing her to be grateful to him; and after their ecstatic erotico-religious orgies she no longer felt that singular disgust in yielding to the turgid desires of the holy madman, and submitted patiently, with mild resignation and no resistance, like any ordinary wife. Since, however, she never succeeded in feeling any sexual rapture for her admirable spouse, so indispensable to her existence, but if anything the opposite, her capitulations inspired by gratitude were followed by long periods of rigorous abstinence. Actually there was no other way of dampening Abraham's conjugal optimism that to resort once again to extreme aloofness, first of all by suspending the tempting orgiastic sessions before the mirror. But, unfortunately, in these periods of fasting, Abraham immediately fell to the mystic's lowest point, considered himself beaten and a failure, sulked, and in his discouragement lost all initiative. And then there appeared in Sarah's heart the terror of the end, the end of everything, the moment when she would cease to be attractive even to her great worshipper. When they reached this point, Abraham, with his peculiar sensitivity, was alerted by the shadows of melancholy that darkened his wife's brow, his unsatisfied erotico-nystical alacrity was aroused, and the practices of love's magic were resumed . . .

This, then, was the golden period in Abraham's married life. From the standpoint of his mysticism, things were not going badly: the being he adored did not constantly hide from him, at the very least she was not rigidly and rudely reluctant or unsociable, and from time to time she allowed him to approach her, without later taking measures of reprisal. But Abraham was also wallowing in a sea of happiness in his position as an ordinary husband; Sarah, even without admitting it, admired him and was grateful to him. Were not these two sentiments perhaps separated from love by only a hair's breadth?

Leaving Abraham to his illusion, which mistook an abyss for a hair's breadth, we might note that his happiness might theoretically have lasted forever if an insignificant trifle had not abruptly, not to say prematurely, destroyed it. For since no provision had been made for it in advance, the moment when "it ceased to be with Sarah after the manner of women" had all the appearance of a snag in the dawning of their love.

Oddly enough, they had never reckoned on the possibility that this could happen even to Sarah. Despite the passage of calendar time, the woman still seemed so young, her beauty was so appealing, and Abraham saw himself so much at the beginning of love and a happy married life, that the bureaucratic precision of nature unleashed a storm of desperation and revolt in their souls.

Menopause is a melancholy moment in a woman's life, but it seldom has a tragic effect on married life. When this moment arrives, the two spouses have either been out of the habit of each other for some time, or have become so accustomed to each other that no real obstacle can arise in the normal course of their lives. At that age, a wife has in most cases already performed her strictly female tasks. She has given birth to her children and raised them, and has come through the disturbance of the spirit and senses that follows the menopausal crisis. In short, she is psychically and morally prepared for the inevitable. Not even in the marriage bed does she have greater or lesser duties than before: everything depends on her husband's zeal. In the final analysis, a woman is still a woman so long as the man lying beside her feels like a man in relation to her. What makes a woman's life melancholy after menopause is something psychological in nature, namely, the sad certainty that sooner or later the external symptoms of old age will stand forth, no longer capable of being suppressed or hidden, that those already evident will be accentuated, and there will be no panacea to prevent the beautiful woman in her final bloom from becoming old. All this is a question of time, but unfortunately a very brief period of time, whose pace keeps accelerating.

This event, which fell, if not prematurely, at least unexpectedly on the married life of Abraham and Sarah, overturned their twilight idyll insofar as their relations had never been the result of a natural development over many decades, but of a compromise that both ceaselessly sought to go beyond in diametrically opposite directions. Sarah immediately used the melancholy moment to declare herself old and to reject her husband for good. Her crisis was terrible, and she would have found it unbearable had she not found a scapegoat in the person of Abraham. Now that the terror of old age loomed before her, she realized better than before that her youth and beauty had passed without having borne much fruit, that her life as a woman had not given her any satisfactions, that her womb remained barren, and that she did not even know the voluptuousness of sex. It was convenient, and at the same time comforting, to throw the blame for all this on Abraham. But she also blamed him for the devious attack by nature, since nobody would have been able to dispel her notion that her menopause had been hastened by Abraham's sexual appetite. Her reasoning was not entirely devoid of logic: so long as she had lived as though enclosed in her almost virginal abstinence, her beauty had always thrived and her organism had functioned with regularity. But no sooner had she let herself be tempted by her husband's abstruse theory that a more intense conjugal life would help to maintain her youth and beauty than her disturbances had begun, and all of a sudden she had stopped menstruating! No one would have been able to dissuade Sarah from evicting her husband from the marriage bed for good, determined as she was to save whatever could be saved.

Sarah's singular theory and her anger were now just one more element in Abraham's drama: he collapsed on his own, more defeated than Sarah herself, since he found no one to accuse. Sarah's menopause simply deprived his life of its twofold meaning. He had to bury forever his fond dream of the adored woman who, languid and enamored, was to yield herself in his arms. But there was something more serious: he realized that not even his adoration would last forever. The mystic and the husband failed in him simultaneously.

But after a dark period of despondency and fits of despair, both were able to look the objective reality in the face, and it turned out to be less harsh than the imaginary one. They realized with surprise and relief that despite the fact that months had passed since the melancholy moment, Sarah showed no tendency to age—if anything, she was more beautiful than before. Sarah, noting this fact, became almost arrogant: now she was the one who refused to succumb and was prepared to resist nature's devious attack to the last breath. With even greater diligence and care, she examined herself in the mirror that Pharaoh had given her, and a thousand times a day she noted with proud satisfaction that not a single wrinkle threatened the harmonious beauty of her face nor had even an ounce of fat been added to her hips. Thanks to her original and exceptional beauty, destined to last longer than normal, she really did not have to resort to extraordinary methods to combat the advancing forces of old age. With a throbbing heart, she could not help thinking that Ningal was protecting her, and that she herself, a princess in name and rank, was somehow like the goddess immune to the laws of time. Now that she was reassured about her unfading beauty and the tenacity of her youth, her anger toward her husband abated, and with the tension in the domestic atmosphere once more relaxed, Sarah ended by re-admitting Abraham to the worship of herself. But she told him, in no uncertain terms, that from now on their relations could not go beyond the limits of a brother-and-sister friendship and that she considered the physical aspects of their marriage to be over. All this, she explained, because it was her intention to grow old with dignity.

An old dream was shattered, but Abraham realized that their good relations would never be re-established without his renunciation. He would not, however, have been Abraham if he had not made a virtue out of necessity. A simple, resigned, humble renunciation would not have suited our hero; his was an active and dynamic renunciation, relived and suffered daily. He understood very well that renouncing an object—namely, the youth and beauty of his wife—no less presupposed its desirability than conquering it. He realized that now there were no other assets left to him to be turned to account in his life except this renunciation, and that he would have to renounce even this renunciation if Sarah became old and ugly. And what profit, what fascination would there be in renouncing a woman who was neither desired nor desirable? In order for his renunciation to remain an operative virtue and procure him the delights and torments of erotico-mystical rapture, Sarah had more than ever to keep herself beautiful and alluring. The orgiastic sessions before Pharaoh's mirror were resumed, and Abraham, with the magical power of love, created and re-created day by day, hour by hour, the youth and beauty of his wife. And if previously he had lavished on the adored woman magnificent and costly clothes, precious jewels, perfumes, cosmetics, and rare spices supplied to him by the caravans arriving from remote civilized lands, now, as a sign and outlet for his overflowing adoration, all this fabulous merchandise became magical means in the service of the operative virtue of renunciation. Never could Sarah have dreamed of a more tender, more generous, and at the same time less demanding adorer.

It is not absolutely true that giving up a fixation wherein we have identified the meaning of our existence necessarily involves the impoverishment of our lives; on the contrary, when we get rid of a crushing burden and our mind and nerves relax, our eyes open wide to the pleasures and other good things that hitherto went unobserved, even though they were within arm's reach. In ourselves as well, and in those who live around us, we detect new resources and qualities previously neglected, the discovery and enjoyment of which, even if they don't make us happy, yet amaze and console us. Abraham was almost tempted to persuade himself that he had done an excellent thing by letting go of what had hitherto seemed to him the meaning of his life. Sarah, for example, feeling spared from amorous vexations and excused from the odious role of paramour, was almost reborn. She became a new person, rich in kindness, affection, and disinterested concern for her family. Once again she was able to appreciate her husband's extraordinary personality, and did not conceal from him her gratitude and sympathy: she treated him not only with humanity, but tenderly like a friend or sister, or else a mother. She even went so far as to be concerned with his personal welfare, and also began, from one day to the next, to take an interest in the household, making more frequent appearances in the kitchen, where with her own hands she prepared a certain kind of pancake on which Abraham doted. The patriarch sometimes felt he was in seventh heaven, and his peaceful existence was also brightened by the fact that Sarah had overcome her aversion for little Ishmael and had ended by becoming almost fond of the heir to her husband's name and worldly goods.

Sarah, however, was far from becoming a housewife. Beyond the affectionately human features of her behavior as friend, sister, and mother, Abraham continued to experience the spell of that *je ne sais quoi* of the "divine" that made her superior to any other woman. Often there came to his mind those magnificent figures of Eastern goddesses who with cold coquetry promised love and death to their mortal lovers for the coming spring. For Sarah, although she had rejected his love, never stopped being attractive to him, and to everyone. She had remained young and beautiful in the manner that for some exceptional women is the same as growing old: she was like a rare exotic flower that wilts in a precious crystal vase, while preserving intact the exuberant magnificence of its petals and continuing to emit its soft intoxicating aroma. In plain words, this meant that Sarah, despite the appalling number of her years as recorded in the Bible, was still a woman not only beautiful in appearance, but even alluring and desirable, who when she cared to or had some reason—for instance, when entertaining guests—knew how to look splendid and exercise an irresistible charm. Men, especially young men, still looked at her with eyes burning with desire, and women, not only old women but young ones as well, could feel themselves turning pale with envy. On these occasions Sarah's heart beat feverishly and her secret happiness rendered her beauty youthful and her refined elegance regal. The difference with respect to real youth consisted in an unpleasant drawback: the emotions of her success exhausted her and next day she looked tired and worn out. She seemed—let us go ahead and say the bitter truth—aged. But Abraham, gallant suitor and mystical egotist, insisted pedantically on the meaning of the verb "to seem." On her bad days, she only "seemed" aged, but wasn't. And the unwelcome appearance vanished under the effect of love's magic, a prolonged rest, and the timely application of cosmetics.

Thus when Abraham and Sarah had reached respectively the biblical ages of ninety-nine and eighty-nine, peace, serenity, and harmony reigned in the encampment at the terebinth grove of Mamre. It was happiness of a sort, in a minor key, but built on unacknowledged failures, repressed desires, terrifying anguish, and binding prohibitions. This shaky equilibrium, which threatened to collapse at the touch of a finger, was the most notable result of that period of fourteen years that the holy book passes over in silence.

We have tried to bring to light a few facts and events implied by the biblical account. But it would be deplorable negligence on our part not to stress the most important event that marked the end of this period and gave a decisive turn to the story of our protagonists and that of the world. No words of ours can sufficiently emphasize the importance of this event, namely, when the

Lord all of a sudden woke up to the fact that His naïve chosen
follower, so full of good intentions, had begot a certain Ishmael
instead of that Isaac who figured in His predictions, which were
supported by infallible prescience! There was just barely time to do
something about it . . .

It was hardly the touch of a finger: for Abraham's precarious
equilibrium, the divine decree was the explosion of a bomb! The
poor man remained paralyzed, and it was precisely his terror and
feeling of impotence that suggested to him the only decision possible: to do nothing, not to open his mouth to anyone, not to move
a muscle to assist the divine plans. It was up to the Lord to do what
He wanted and what He could . . .

When later he recovered from the initial blow, he discovered a
comforting point in the divine declaration. What had seemed to
him at first the most terrifying detail—that the child would be
born a year hence—now appeared as a reason to be immensely
relieved. If one could trust in the words of the Lord, he, Abraham,
still had three months to think about it and—to act!

V. *A little apologetics*

HAD HE BEEN ALLOWED TO, ABRAHAM WOULD HAVE EXPLAINED
to the Lord most energetically that the birth of another son would
serve no useful purpose and be replete instead with serious dangers
for the equilibrium of his private life. But having been reduced to
the situation of having to keep his opinions to himself, all he could
do, in his impotent desperation, was to upgrade his knowledge
about the Almighty by adding this new observation that the Being
he had discovered was not only completely arbitrary and stubborn,
but maddeningly deaf and blind to the personal outlook of His first
and only follower.

It seems to us that after our attempt to familiarize them with the
figures of Abraham and Sarah, our kind readers would remain
justifiably dissatisfied if for the rest of our story we were to be
content to convey only the subjective impressions of our two protagonists in relation to the Lord, who no less than they deserves the

title of protagonist in the biblical episode we are treating, not to mention all of sacred history. We now consider it our duty to take a closer look at this elusive character.

Having arrived at this point, the author would like to put in a personal word. A previous text we wrote (as a literary genre, a twin of this one, but since we'd be unable to say what sort of literary genre this one belongs to, let us call it, noncommittally, a "text") was accused from many sides, more or less jokingly, more or less seriously, of "mistreating" the sole true and living God, or of not paying Him proper respect. We rejected these reproaches each time with a kind of astonished regret. First of all, our upbringing and inborn politeness have always excluded the wish to offend anyone, even those who presumably would not take serious and immediate reprisals (or who in all probability would never take any). The accusation may derive from the misunderstanding that attributes the opinions, impressions, and experiences of our biblical characters to the author himself. The truth is that he has limited himself to drawing them forth from the abysses of primordial time and bringing them to the surface with a writer's particular methods and meticulousness. It is our conviction that never has the figure of God, in the plurimillenial literature in which it appears, ever been so "well treated" (except for Voltaire, who was even prepared to invent it in case it didn't exist . . .) as by ourselves, who are being unjustly accused. Indeed, the most important of the modest results that our unorthodox researches may yield is to dispel the erroneous and superficial ideas that honest and blameless believers have formed in the course of thousands of years about the Lord and—to put it bluntly—to His detriment. In view of some of His deeds, which baffle the ordinary mortal and give him gooseflesh, we refrain from proclaiming at every turn that our God is boundlessly good, wise, and just, nor are we in a hurry to find an "excuse" for Him in the incomprehensibility of the divine plan or the insufficiency of the human intellect, to which believers and those who guide them like to refer. To us, the Lord, for whom we are accused of lacking in respect, is not a being capable of "punishing" Adam and Eve (and with them all subsequent generations for all eternity) for an act of "filial disobedience"; He is not a being capable of annihilating humanity with the flood because it was "wicked," nor one who "accepts" *sic et simpliciter* the sacrifice of His only begotten son in order to redeem the human race—things that instead seem logical and unquestionable to those who, out of blind love and respect for Him, silence their own doubts. Actually we consider our "excuses," or the reasons by which we seek to "exculpate" Him and explain His actions to ourselves, to be much more worthy both of men and of God. And we cling to these more "worthy" excuses because—even if most of our readers have not realized it—we also pride ourselves on having a taste for apologetics, if for no other reason than that we find it extremely humiliating for humanity to have had to deal for thousands of years with a humiliated God.

We would never, for instance, fall into the sacrilegious error into which Abraham himself fell—though he, no less than Noah and the heroic Daniel, walked with the Lord—namely, that of calling some divine measure absolutely pointless. It required a considerable dose of naïveté on Abraham's part to form and sustain such an opinion, when instead he could easily have seen that the Lord had firmly desired—repeating it three times so as to avoid any misunderstanding—the very thing he judged pointless and harmful. Of course, Abraham has the undeniable excuse of being barely a beginner in knowing the Lord. Even had he fully submitted, he would have been unable to grasp the divine insistence on this point: for that he would have needed nothing less than a historical perspective. We, on the other hand, know that from Isaac came Jacob, from Jacob came the Jews, and from the Jews came Jesus Christ, to whose credit it is that today the Lord has as many followers as there are grains of dust on the earth and stars in the sky, just as He Himself had predicted to Abraham. Had he been in possession of this knowledge, our hero would certainly not have said that the birth of Isaac would be an event of no importance, at least from the Lord's standpoint.

But, in Abraham's view, Ishmael would probably have sufficed for all this, and we suspect that he died without ever changing his mind. Far be it from us to reproach him, and we would drop the subject if still today we didn't see masses of honest and blameless believers playing with equal irresponsibility at interpreting the Lord's will. Indeed, the more honest and blameless the believer feels himself to be, the more he thinks it his duty to believe that "everything is the will of God," that "everything is good the way God wanted it," that "if God had wanted things to be different, He would have made them different," and so on and so forth. And all these convictions, which manifest an absolute faith but nevertheless contradict each other, give rise—obviously by the will of the Lord—in brains untrained in philosophy, to confusions and doubts that no one succeeds in dispelling (perhaps likewise by the will of the Lord). For a true and self-respecting believer, nothing is more natural than to side with Abraham and insist along with him that—had God been willing—the whole series of aforementioned events and the present situation of the world could just as well have begun with Ishmael. For *is any thing too hard for the Lord?*

These are very old and familiar problems, and for thousands of years a copious literature has been devoted to them. Numerous heresies and still existing creeds have been built over the course of the centuries on the various proposed solutions to the question of divine will. One gets the impression that divine will is more a question of faith or opinion than an objectively existing attribute pertaining to the divine nature of the Lord. The fact is that everything that theology and philosophy have been able to adduce in support of this or that thesis has already been said, and to try to make headway in this field would be an undertaking marked by such audacity or immodesty as to border on stupidity. If nevertheless we do not go out of our way to avoid the problem, this should be attributed both to our unbridled passion for apologetics and to the temptation to try out our method of research, which consists in remaining slavishly attached to our sacred texts.

In truth, the idea of God "wanting" something would be the

fruit of human imagination if the Holy Bible, which we take to be our only authentic source, did not testify to various manifestations of divine will. Indeed, whenever something happens in universal history or the life of the individual that suggests a direct manifestation of the Lord's will, one has every right to be suspicious. This is not the case with the Bible, and particularly Genesis, whose compilers had their hands tied by tradition, the storehouse of ancient knowledge. From this source, the only reliable one we have, it emerges with certainty that on numerous occasions God has intervened directly and insistently in the destiny of the universe, and the same texts seem likewise to show that, in the divine nature as well, an intentional action is preceded by an act of will. The Holy Scriptures leave no doubt about the fact that God *is able* to want and that *sometimes* He decidedly does want. They do not, however, show that His will is exercised permanently and extends over all moments and all acts in the flow of history: indeed, they show just the opposite, since He usually starts wanting when something in the world goes against His intentions, that is, in a way He would *not* have wanted.

The Holy Scriptures, and primarily the Book of Genesis, offer no arguments in favor of the thesis of predestination, at least not in the absolute sense, and to suppose or accept as a fact that the Lord has a plan for the world and the human race, a plan moreover pre-established by the dual act of wanting and foreknowing, does not necessarily confirm the above thesis. In our human world at least, a farseeing plan, however conscious of its own end and calculated in all its possible details, is still subject to mishaps and thus also to changes and modifications: its perfection and workings can be weighed precisely on the basis of the degree to which it remains unchanged and achieves its purpose despite the unforeseen reactions of reality. A superficial faith may believe that it moves closer to the idea of the Lord's greatness by attributing to Him a mechanically perfect plan that runs like clockwork or a precision instrument, a hypothesis that cannot, of course, be excluded *a priori*: it is on this very hypothesis, the idea of a "pedantic" God, that the tiresome doctrine of predestination has been erected. But by the same token, we can imagine a magnificent and self-assured God, who, although He knows what He wants and wants what He knows—meaning that He has His plan and knows its purpose and outcome—makes every allowance for unforeseen mishaps, and therefore defines only the broad outlines of His plan. This is the image of the Lord suggested by the Bible, without thereby diminishing His greatness.

For we must not lose sight of the fact that, for man, the direct consequence of original sin was free will, the freedom to choose between good and evil, between acts either in accord or in conflict with the divine plan and the Lord's directives. Unless we want to lower the relations between God and men to the level of a horrible joke in which the Lord, by the very fact of knowing the future in advance, binds our freedom of choice and thereby forces us to want something or other "freely," we must state that man is capable of wanting and doing the opposite of what God *would like* him to, and from this it follows that things really happen in the world that God would like *not* to happen. Thus the believer who thinks to please the Lord by proclaiming that not even a leaf can fall from the tree without His will may not be doing Him a service. The truth seems to be just the opposite. The Lord gives a free hand to the laws of nature, and likewise to man's will, just so long as He doesn't see His plan and its outlines seriously compromised. Therefore many leaves fall from the trees and many men live, suffer, sin, feel pleasure, and die without the Lord taking the slightest interest. All we can say is this: *if* and *when* the Lord wants the leaf to fall, it falls; *if* and *when* He wants it *not* to fall, it doesn't fall; but if and when He is not in the mood to want, the leaves must reckon with the contingencies of existence.

Just as all this does not conflict with His incommensurable greatness, so it does not necessarily even conflict with His infinite goodness and infinite wisdom, since sacrifice and prayer may well recall His attention to human needs and desires and suggest to Him an act of will. And even if He stubbornly refuses to answer our prayers, there is no reason to accuse Him of deafness, indifference, or harshness, which might instead be the sign of His wisdom. For we can never know if some irresponsible or foolish prayer of ours may not itself threaten to compromise the divine plan. It is always well to keep in mind that infinite divine wisdom may look to us like indolence, and that His infinite goodness may appear capricious only because these divine qualities are consistent with themselves and not with our imaginings.

Presumably all these apparent contradictions, along with the aforesaid one between will and prescience, are peacefully reconciled in the divine nature, and this is no one's business but the Lord's, and to some extent the theologians'. Meanwhile, emboldened by our previous statements, we are automatically freed from any need to bother with a large number of naïve questions, now that we are preparing to confront certain moments at the beginning of human history, moments that *seem* to have caught the Lord by surprise and aroused His fury, in that—it *seems*—they happened against His will. These are the great circumstances in which the Lord, with absolute resolution and total commitment, in a series of sudden, sometimes catastrophic, sometimes shocking interventions, took a personal role in the fortunes of the human race, giving them a radically new twist in the direction of the goals foreseen by His mysterious plan. Faced with these facts, our question has nothing to do with whether or not such interventions are compatible with divine qualities, but rather with the motives that provoked the Lord to act willfully and rationally in conceiving and carrying out His blatant interventions. The Bible leaves us in no doubt about the motives: the reason for the expulsion from Eden was the fall of man, and the reason for the flood the disproportionate development of human wickedness—phenomena that the Lord could hardly have desired even had He foreseen them.

Since we're now beginning to realize that being God is a much harder task than a good church-going housewife might imagine, we can hazard a guess that the Lord from the start was not prepared to arrange things in advance so as to exclude the need for His occasional personal interventions. But to suppose this is the same as supposing a limit to His omnipotence! To halt *in statu nascendi* the tremendous storm of indignation with which blameless and upright believers threaten to overwhelm us, let us immediately add that we're thinking of spontaneously accepted limitations, perhaps suggested to Him by His infinite goodness, even to the detriment of His infinite wisdom: the Lord may not have cared to know what He knew beforehand, and may have known that He was making a mistake. It would truly have been a fine thing if man, first in a state of innocence, and later thanks to free will, had loved, respected, and worshipped his Creator . . .

We are fully aware that we are childishly playing with tremendous problems, but since it is known that in addition to need it is precisely "play" that leads to progress in all fields, we allow ourselves this decidedly methodological game. We have no right to suggest that the prescient God had not foreseen from the beginning the fall of the first man and the degeneration of humanity in the times of Noah. But if that's how it is, we must also resign ourselves to the idea that He had likewise foreseen both the expulsion from Eden and the havoc of the flood. Except that such a result, fraught with frightening implications, prompts us in our melancholy game to insist on raising methodically naïve questions about serious problems that promise no comforting solutions. The first question, which arises spontaneously, is this: Assuming He knew everything beforehand, what was the Lord hoping for? And the next: Since He knew everything beforehand, why was He so cruel as to spare man's life?

Of course, the game broadens our horizons, but at the same time it reveals the inconsistency of our questions, which are more human than childish, all too human, *allzu menschliches!* On the other hand, if a game leads to such revelations, that alone makes it worth playing. Indeed, it's most helpful to realize that our terms, typical products of our mental categories, cannot be applied to the things of God, and it is well to get it through our heads at once that the Lord, who knows everything, does not have, for example, any reason to hope or even the possibility of doing so. And one might do well to consider the probability that divine cruelty and goodness had nothing to do with the problem of whether to leave humanity alive or not. At most, we are entitled to put the question in this form: Why did the Lord, who knew man's corruptibility beforehand, not extirpate him completely? Since He did not extirpate him, it seems to us a reasonable suspicion that the answer lies hidden in the divine plan, which is still in the process of development, and in which man's knowledge of good and evil was calculated from the beginning. Obviously, the Lord knows how His plan will end. We are the ones who don't know what He knows. We, for instance, don't even dare to think that God has any doubts about the success of His plan. Why couldn't this be the case? Because the idea we've formed of His omnipotence excludes the possibility that the Lord should not always be victorious . . . Because we do not keep the fact sufficiently in mind that omnipotent God, having accepted the unknown quantity of man endowed with free will, must continue to operate with it . . .

It is a singular fact, for example, and more compatible with our ideas about divine omnipotence and omniscience, that original sin caught the Lord by surprise and in some way embittered Him. The incontrovertible proof would be His fury and His violent reaction. Without wasting too many words to remark that even a feared or foreseen affront can arouse anger, pain, and exasperation, or that external manifestations of these emotions can be a simulation for pedagogical purposes on the one hand, and a mere impression on the other, we feel it more essential to point out that such superficial reasoning risks denying the Lord the quality of prescience precisely when He would have needed it most—in the course of creation. Moreover, it is both the basis and supreme pleasure of any creation, human as well. Wouldn't it be more prudent and reasonable on our part to get rid of this fixation and stop considering man's first sin as a "defect" in creation? For we could call it a defect only if God had not foreseen it from the beginning. But why shouldn't He have foreseen it?

Keeping to the order of ideas in our methodological game, we might go on to ask: Why did the Lord, if He is "all that" omnipotent, not create man perfect? Or, if man had been perfect at the moment of creation, why did He make him corruptible? Or else—and this is as far as such questions can go—if this man had given Him so many headaches and so little pleasure, why didn't He throw him back in the mud and dust from which He had taken him and mold a new, perfect, and incorruptible one who would have been more to His liking? But the Bible, almost as though foreseeing the most unheard-of questions, has the answer ready: *"And God saw every thing that he had made, and, behold, it was very good"*—perfect, we would say, including the imperfect man, whose imperfection He had foreseen. We therefore have no right to suppose that the Lord, even had He decided to wipe out His whole creation and create a new world, would not have created it the same, and if not exactly the same, still nevertheless with the imperfect man, or else another similar being, who being endowed with soul and spirit, would still end by acquiring the knowledge of good and evil. If God did not create something better, it means that He didn't want to or couldn't, at least as far as man is concerned.

But then, you might ask with mounting exasperation, why did He create man, this blot on the beauty of the universe and cause of all evils? Perhaps the only answer is to recall that for the Lord everything "was very good" after the creation of man. But it takes no particular courage to add, however foolhardy it sounds: Man, beyond all doubt, is the height of Creation! This was what the Lord, who set him above all creatures, wanted when He formed him *"in our image, after our likeness."* Man was the masterpiece of creation, its most complex structure, a purpose worthy of a nevertheless incommensurable creator. *He was made a living soul*, and superior to other living beings, absolutely distinct, from the beginning, from plants and animals in what made him similar to the Lord: his intellect, of which they were devoid or incomparably less endowed. It is impossible to grasp what this meant, or what this human intellect was capable of at the moment of its creation or in the first phase of its existence, but the Lord intended the intellect to be the means whereby man would form for himself an idea of his own Creator, admire and enjoy Creation, rejoice in the good and the beautiful, praise the Lord, and be grateful to Him. To get a vague idea of that primordial state, imagine a happy child who is allowed to do everything and somehow realizes that he owes his happiness to his parents, who rejoice along with him.

Here is man's singular task, perhaps his only vocation, for which he was drawn out of the mud: to admire Creation, praise the Creator, and be grateful to Him. Doubtless the universe would be a marvel of perfection even without man, but who would be aware of it if man didn't exist with his intellect, already similar to God's when he is still only a little child? From the Lord's point of view all of Creation would be worth nothing without the applause of an intelligent and grateful public. God in his capacity as creator has need of men.

What is there to say? We've reached the threshold of creation with giant steps and a rapidity that may seem insolent compared with the overwhelming monumentality of the subject. On the other hand, we are somewhat bolstered by the hope, not really worthy of a writer's ambitions, that basically we have not said anything new and that our account could be endorsed without hesitation by even the most pedantic theologians. The most they will do is to observe that it was less the need for spiritual order than His own infinite goodness that induced the Lord to allow a being endowed with intellect to share in the magnificence of the Creation. But whether He created man out of goodness or necessity, both the most blameless and upright believers and we ourselves, mired in our game of methodological naïveté, have a trick question up our sleeves. Why, in fact, did the Lord, if He was so satisfied with man's state of innocence, not let him stay there, instead of exposing him to a strong temptation, knowing beforehand that he wouldn't be able to resist it? Believers, especially the more naïve ones, for whom divine goodness is unlimited, are obliged to think that the Lord could have spared man his disobedience, with all its cursed results, and given a much more eloquent proof of His paternal love if, instead of kicking him out and inflicting on him atrocious sufferings, He had given him a good scolding and made him stand in the corner as punishment. Man, after all, when he committed the first sin, still lacked the faculty of choosing between good and evil, and thus his sin was merely a childish prank.

Now comes the moment when our passion for apologetics reveals its secret goal: our most ardent wish has always been to produce a decisive proof of the Lord's "innocence," one that with a stroke of the pen would clear Him once and for all of the endless, bitter accusations of being deaf, cruel, and capricious (and also at the same time protect Him from the endless, unctuous, and unfounded "excuses" by which believers have tried to justify His actions for thousands of years). And we believe we can already absolve him in a pretrial hearing, by stressing a fact that has generally been ignored or not taken sufficiently into consideration. We will certainly not be saying anything entirely new, even if it may come as a surprise to some of our readers, when we point out that the Lord forbade the first man to eat the fruit of that famous tree, not to test His favorite creature's filial obedience, but because He really "would have wanted" and "would have liked" the latter not to eat it, or to put off eating it as long as possible—and we are unable to find better words to say it, since the Lord from the beginning had foreseen the inevitability of the tragic event. Yes, the Lord "would have preferred" that man remain in a state of innocence, since in this condition the supreme creature would have satisfied to perfection all the requirements that the Lord had hoped to satisfy by creating him. But from the beginning He knew very well that man, sooner or later, would eat the fruit of that fatal tree, and that from that moment on a struggle would begin, with no holds barred, between Him and man: a struggle that would take place in Time, subdivided by the calendar, and be called by the name of History. In a certain sense, it hardly matters whether the outcome of this struggle was known beforehand or not: more im-

portant was the fact that the great Sunday, in which divine existence was so beautiful, so happy, so harmonious would come to an
end with man's sin. How to make Edenic conditions last? How to
prolong the Edenic moment of His own existence? The expedients
at His disposal were, by their nature, precarious: the Lord had
either to leave it to chance whether man would eat or not, or forbid
him to eat under the threat of drastic punishment. As we know,
the Lord chose the second path.

Now, if we put our minds to the fact that the tree, as attested
by the Bible itself, was the tree of the knowledge of good and evil,
and that man's tasting of the fruit involved huge and manifold
dangers for the Lord, we can easily see how He couldn't rely on
chance, much less listen to the voices of His infinite goodness. On
the contrary, He had to be prepared to thwart and stave off the
advent of that moment that had nevertheless been foreseen, and to
take His drastic measures for the future. For the Lord knew very
well beforehand that human reason, stimulated and fortified by a
single morsel of omniscience, and at that moment becoming the
human Intellect, would soon allow man to do without Him by
making himself God. The Lord was likewise well aware that at that
moment human consciousness would emerge; the Serpent's seductive words leave no doubt about the great consequences of that
decisive gesture, the first human gesture worthy of the name: *"For
God doth know that in the day ye eat thereof, then your eyes shall be
opened, and ye shall be as gods, knowing good and evil."* And to know
good and evil, and at the same time have one's eyes opened, could
lead to a being more powerful than God Himself, an electronic
brain endowed with consciousness and thus always awake, unlike
the Lord who from time to time allows Himself to doze off. Therefore the Lord had no choice but to forestall an overdose of omniscience by immediately driving man away from the vicinity of the
fatal tree, since now his eyes could never again be closed . . .

Someone might still ask why the Lord should have tolerated that
baleful tree in the middle of Eden, predestined to blow sky-high
the soft Sunday languor of Creation. We hasten to assure anyone

who may raise this question that of all questions relating to the beginning of the beginning, he has come up with the most essential one. Indeed, it is hard to understand why the importance of the tree, although it is the key to the tragic clash between God and man, has almost entirely escaped general attention. That the fatal tree stood right in the middle of Eden is seen by most people as a given fact requiring no further investigation.

Actually it was a given fact for the Lord as well: its importance—about which the comparative history of religions and mythologies leaves no doubt—is also shown by the indirect proof furnished by the Lord Himself, for though aware from the beginning that the tree would be the source of all woe, He had not uprooted it but had let it stand. And this means, in plain words, that the tree had an essential role, or rather was a constituent and structural element of creation. We might infer that without the tree God would not have been able to create, or that the universe would have disintegrated: the tree seems to constitute its axis or armature. The roots of the tree—just like the roots of any tree in humus—carried on a continuous process of disintegration in the structure of the universe, and were also at the same time its force of cohesion; while the fruit, which provoked the crisis in the human world, shared with the Lord the arcane knowledge of chaos and guaranteed a harmonious of existence to living, but not reasoning, beings. This was the crucial point where the Lord had to reach a compromise with His own omnipotence: in wanting to create, He had to accept in full the laws intrinsic to the material of creation, otherwise He would have been obliged to renounce creation itself (and this would likewise have been a harsh blow for His omnipotence). By the very fact of having decided to create, He had to commit Himself to respect the restrictive conditions of any sort of creation: the physical and chemical peculiarites of matter and the necessity of choosing a form. It was, of course, a question of restrictions spontaneously accepted, of willingly sacrificing only a minuscule fraction of His omnipotence. But this renunciation constituted at the same time a basic restriction of incalculable importance: the Lord had once and for all tied His own hands.

The fatal tree, which turns up in the most diverse religions and mythologies, is rooted in chaos and nourished by chaos: around its slender trunk the Creator has molded the cosmos from chaos, and its fruits contain omniscience, the knowledge of good and evil, and the arcane wisdom of chaos, which they transmit to those who taste them. The tree of Eden was identical with this cosmic tree, an identity attested beyond doubt both by the prodigious power of its fruit, and the fact that the Lord had forbidden man to eat of it, as well as the even more significant fact that He never uprooted the tree, not even in His darkest hour, marked by the fall of man, but had set the cherubim to guard it. In the presence of the tree, the Lord had been reduced to impotence . . .

But it's time to stop rummaging among the Lord's secrets. We have neither the courage nor the strength to go on with it. And, to tell the truth, we have no need to. It's enough to have reached this point for all the naïve questions that believers and nonbelievers are in the habit of raising about the divine will—and which we ourselves have raised, albeit for methodological purposes—to fall of their own accord. A ray of new light now illuminates the relations between God and man, caught at their embryonic stage, and this new perspective will help us to see and examine them more profitably in their further developments as well.

The cosmos is ordered chaos: the principles forming and informing it are only a few of that infinite number of principles that formless chaos contains unrealized in itself. God, as Creator, chose some of these principles for His creation, when He determined its ends, means, laws, and form: these were the restrictions that He freely and spontaneously accepted. But among all the principles that operated in His creation, some were not even "chosen" by God: they imposed themselves, so to speak, automatically, with no possibility of an alternative. God was never in a position to have preferences in choosing the material of creation: it was given, it was chaos, and God had to create from chaos. The cosmos in its final form, that is, the universe with its principles and laws, eliminated the confused formlessness of chaos, in the same way, for example, that a sculpture, precisely because it is sculpture, is no longer an amorphous mass of clay. And yet . . . there is no sort of omnipotence that can guarantee that the material of a clay statue is not clay, and does not absolutely imply those intrinsic principles that make clay clay, while at the same time containing the gravest risks for the statue. For it is precisely the singular qualities that make clay suitable for creating a statue that constitute a constant threat to the integrity and durability of the statue itself. In the same way, chaos, as the material of the universe, has preserved its properties and by its intrinsic laws threatens the existence of the cosmos from the start. The tree—if it is proper to reduce the infinite riches of myth to a rationalistic concept—represents the principle of matter in the universe. Thus whether to tolerate it or not was a question that never even came up.

Let no one suppose that when we speak of the "materiality" of chaos, we are using a concept of matter in vogue in the middle of the last century. For us chaos means something more: chaos is the sum total of all those infinite possibilities that as principles, laws, ends, means, and forms were left unrealized, discarded, and condemned to atrophy by the Lord's creative act. To use a biblical term once again, we might say that if the Lord is "He who is," chaos is "that which is not"; but we might complete the sentence by adding: yes, it is that which is not, but which could have been, and indeed could be. All those who tasted the fruit of the tree gained knowledge of this secret, and in the earthly Paradise all living beings, except man, were familiar with it. Indeed, animals are still "omniscient" today, because somehow or other they "feel" chaos, they "know" when it is getting ready to burst into the order of nature and are in time to take countermeasures. The limit of their omniscience is determined by the deficiency of their reason, in no way similar to the divine. But how could everything have remained within such safe limits when man, endowed with an intellect similar to God's, was the one to taste the fruit?

Bible readers are generally left perplexed by the fact that the forbidden tree was sometimes called the tree of omniscience and sometimes the tree of the knowledge of good and evil, and are inclined to prefer the latter designation, it being apparently easier to distinguish good from evil than to know everything. So it will not be entirely pointless to take a closer look at what is meant by this "everything" that man comes to know after tasting the forbidden fruit. The truth is that the individual man's knowledge is shamefully meager compared to the sum total of knowledge, but even the frightful amount of knowledge acquired by the human race in the course of its history is a miserable thing in the face of "everything" as this concept is generally conceived. If this is the situation today, just imagine what it may have been at the tragic moment of Eden! A naïve Bible reader will never be able to understand what it was that so alarmed the Lord when man knew as little as it was possible for him to know. But was what he knew really so little? Even if it was not much quantitatively, it would have been significant enough instantly to disrupt the Sunday languor that had hitherto enveloped the relations between God and man.

The Bible itself catches the significance of the tragic moment in Eden when human consciousness was born. If the divine way of knowing is omniscience, that is to say, knowing "everything" dimly, once and for all, and as a natural gift, man's omniscience consists in knowing little, but consciously and with the unlimited possibility of knowing "everything." We hardly think if necessary to analyze the concept of "conscious being," but only to point out the essential features that fatally compromised man's position in the presence of the Lord. Adam and Eve, the moment they tasted the forbidden fruit, discovered the cosmos but also chaos. By eating the forbidden fruit, they realized for the first time in their existence a possibility that until that moment had been—perhaps because of the prohibition—beyond their horizon as reasoning beings; afterward, thanks to that morsel of omniscience, they discovered the infinite realm of possibilities behind the facade of immense reality. And a moment later, dumbfounded, they realized that everything could be *different*. And after another moment, trembling, they thought that everything could also be *better*. And after still another moment, terrified out of their minds but drunk with disquieting and hitherto unknown desires, they understood that they themselves would be able to change everything to make the world *more agreeable to man*. At the magic touch of the arcane wisdom of chaos, man experienced the revelation that the world of Eden had become dull through the very "omniscience" he had just acquired, and that a much better world could be created in its place. The Lord, who so far had been loved and admired with childish lightheartedness, all at once became an object of criticism, and also of terror. And not without reason. Punishment had been instantaneous and inexorable: man suddenly found himself exiled from the land of his childish happiness into an unknown, harsh, pitiless world. If he was to survive, it was no longer a matter of rearranging a paradisiacal garden to make it more amenable to his new needs, as had been his intention, but of confronting and overcoming difficulties and dangers beyond his strength; by gaining the possibility of creating a new world, he also found himself faced with the *necessity*, inflicted on him by God, of creating another one. Another world, predestined never to become a land of happiness, but to be just barely tolerable, and which moreover had to conform and submit to the divine will to avoid being destroyed.

We already know that the Lord could never destroy man unless He cared to destroy Himself as well, that is to say, lose the purpose of creation and come into contradiction with His own essence. The facts discovered in Genesis and our own Judeo-Christian idea of the Almighty suffice to lead us to this conclusion, and they absolve us from having to deal with other possible aspects of the relations between God and man that occupy a place of prime importance in other religions and can be traced even in the Bible. Thus we do not take up the fascinating hypothesis according to which man, by becoming a kind of titan at a certain period of his existence, may have constituted a real threat to God's position and very existence;

nor even the attractive and witty theory that "the gods are hungry" and are only able to survive because of the sacrifices offered to them by man. For our Judeo-Christian God, in whom existence and essence coincide, to be forgotten or be deprived of man's veneration, admiration, and adoration, or the mere fact of not seeing His handiwork appreciated by the human intellect, was equivalent to such tragedies as dethroning, killing, or death by inanition that befell other gods in other civilizations. Finding Himself deprived of human worship meant for the Lord to fall back into the state that had preceded the creation, to fall back, that is, into a form of existence that did not express His essence, and such a state, for the Lord, would have been a form of death from which He had to protect Himself.

It would be quite foolish to suppose that the Lord had not foreseen and known beforehand all the consequences of creation from the very birth of His idea. But the Lord "had to" create, and He was determined from the start to confront all the dangers and difficulties inherent in this creative act. And certainly He never underestimated the difficulties He would encounter. Knowing everything in advance, He never let Himself be taken by surprise, and by no means did He become that furious and desperate being that would seem to be indicated by certain biblical episodes. He was and always remained a logical being, a calculator aware of His own ends as well as His own, by now quite limited, means. The tree's presence in the universe, and the birth of the human intellect after sin, made Him almost powerless with respect to what was happening or about to happen on earth. Indeed, in the face of man's free will, God's infinite power was reduced almost to the point of being able, of course, to destroy everything, but of no longer being capable of forcing man to live the way He wanted him to. Since He knew everything in advance and nevertheless undertook the harsh struggle, the Lord obviously did not consider Himself beaten, and presumably expected to win. But what did winning mean? In our opinion, there can be only one answer: to ensure, even with His limited means, that man freely chose good instead of evil and accepted the divine order of the cosmos and of life as the best possible order. The Lord's plan is thus a pedagogic one, a program of re-education whose purpose is to lead fallen, sinful man to a state of enlightened intelligence, in which he once more becomes capable of consciously appreciating the perfection of the universe and of loving and worshipping the Creator, just as he did in his state of innocence in the delightful garden of Eden. From the Lord's point of view, it would be difficult for the purpose of History to be anything else.

This plan for re-educating humanity is a monumental and very complex one, but it is too divine to allow us to trace its general outlines, the pedagogic principles that inspire it, and the ways in which its various phases are carried out. It seems to embrace all principles and methods, from the most vulgar to the most refined: systems for subjugation based on punishment, terror, and often torture not seldom prevail. To further His plan, the Lord has not hesitated from time to time to extirpate almost the entire human race or a good portion of it, while imposing a squalid existence full of hardship on the survivors. In other periods, divine pedagogy seems to be inspired by extreme indulgence and cordiality, almost as though to lure the human race into life. We can be quite certain that the Lord, even in this respect, does not let Himself be guided by gratuitous impulses or caprices, but by an infallible sense of diplomacy on which any self-respecting pedagogy must be based.

An omnipotent God in the true sense, or in the human sense of the word, would not have been obliged to resort to such stratagems and precautions. But the Lord, who had tied His own hands, was subject to the rules of the game of History, which, in its turn, is subject to Time. Let no one think that the Lord is capable, by an imperceptible movement of His eyebrows or a loud personal in-tervention, of making the world of man, endowed with free will, appear any way He likes: the Lord, no less than His creatures, must exercise patience, await the favorable moment, and, in short, give time enough time, if He is to bring any of His actions to fruition in a useful and effective way. He could not, for example, allow

Himself the luxury of wiping a corrupt and dangerous humanity off the face of the earth at any moment He chose: in order to do so with a particular result, He had to wait for Noah, who would give reborn humanity a direction more appropriate to His plan. In the same way, in order to be revealed once more and enter again into the consciousness of the human race after having been long forgotten, He had to wait patiently for Abraham. Until the advent of His emissary, whom He could no longer *create*, but at most ensure that he *came into the world* at the right moment, the Lord remained subject to the tyranny of Time and the caprices of men, their shilly-shallying between good and evil. Clamorous interventions would have made no sense: what counted more were small skillful moves, which to our human minds usually look like extraordinary cases, unique occasions, or alluring snares, and which were better suited to smooth the path of History for the advent of those who by "walking with the Lord" were destined to give a new twist to the relations between God and man.

In His struggle to overcome humanity, the Lord was able, particularly in the most precarious situations, to make do with a few chosen individuals, for whom His incommensurable greatness and the perfection of the order He had created were obvious and unquestionable truths. At crucial moments of History He relied on these few "just and upright" men, the Seths, the Noahs, the Abrahams . . .

His singular omnipotence would have allowed Him to destroy all or almost all of humanity, and even to reduce the whole universe to nothing and perhaps create a new one. Instead He used it only to a limited extent to accelerate time. Smoothing at most the path for their advent, the Lord had to wait for His men with patience. Only with their arrival did the hour for divine action strike. Whatever happened in the meantime, painful as it might be, was of little concern to the Lord.

With these final touches to our *excursus* into apologetics we hope to have cleansed the Lord completely of the filth of obtuseness, cruelty, and inconsistency with which believers and unbelievers have smeared Him for thousands of years. He wills and acts always according to the logic and finality of Creation, ever at the proper moment and always infallibly, keeping in mind His plan, wherein man's position is established for the best. Despite the fact that man does not always succeed in understanding this. Despite the fact that, in general, man never succeeds in understanding this. Despite the fact that man even rebels against His plan . . .

For (to put it simply, if imprecisely), the crux of the matter is this: Man, from the moment of original sin—that is to say, ever since his relations with the Lord have no longer been called "walking together" but "standing before"—has had the firm conviction that the universe, grandiose and astonishing as it is, is not from his purely human point of view that cosmos of perfection that it had seemed to be in his state of innocence, and that he, by his ingenuity and wholly in accordance with human criteria, should be able to improve it, and make it even better, more beautiful, and more pleasant than the earthly Paradise had seemed to him when he was in that innocent state. But at the same time he cannot silence a kind of inner voice that tells him that all these ideas and ambitions are somehow sinful because they are contrary to the intentions of the Lord, who with His laws, His arrangements, and His interventions does whatever He can to thwart the dreams and efforts of human hubris. According to the Bible's testimony, humanity has only felt completely at ease three times, in the three great periods of its march, specifically those when the Lord was not constantly looking after it. But no sooner did the Lord start meddling in man's affairs than the human world, until that point prosperous and thriving, all of a sudden collapsed. This is how it was in the preconscious, animal-child period of Eden, up to the moment of the prohibition. This is how it was in the period of nine generations from Adam to Noah, in which man emerged from prehistory. And this is how it was in the period of nine generations extending from Noah to Abraham, in which the first high civilizations rose. In these long and important periods (to be more exact, in the last two, since in the first one, man was "merely" happy), humanity had the clear impression of advancing by giant steps and always doing something very important, until the Lord decided to open its eyes and confine it within the narrow limits of the order of the curse (the term by which we allowed ourselves, in our previous "text" mentioned above, to call the human condition after the birth of consciousness). On these occasions, it always turned out that whatever seemed beautiful, good, and grand to man was barely tolerated by the Lord, while waiting for *His* man who was to make History change course.

It was in one of these states of expectation that the Lord found Himself when Abraham came along and rediscovered Him.

We have no reason to suppose, especially after our exercise in apologetics, that during the waiting period the Lord had particularly suffered from any anxious feelings of being in danger. If we don't really wish to exclude *ab ovo* that there may have been a moment in History when God almost felt His physical existence to be directly threatened by man, we can be sure that the moment had passed long ago, and that the Lord had taken drastic measures to keep it from being repeated. With the flood, not only had the garden of Eden and the tree of omniscience been buried for good under impenetrable layers of mud and slime, but surviving man found himself once again in a situation so dismal that any dream of a titanic recovery became out of the question. Noah's sons realized immediately that, albeit not without the help and mercy of the Lord, they would have to create for themselves and by their own efforts a new human world, one able to provide a living for their race, which had been degraded to the level of rats and dormice. The Lord had nothing more to fear from man, who, frightened to death by the trauma of the flood, deprived for good of the nourishment and now even the hope of the omniscient fruit, and endowed only with his intellect, was obliged to devote all his resources to scraping miserably along. And this man, reduced to this point, was moreover grateful to the Lord, who had spared his life, and it didn't take much for him to become fit to carry out the tasks assigned to him by Creation: to love, praise, and admire his Creator.

There is no better indication of the excellent results of security and tranquillity gained by the Lord from the flood than the surprising mildness of the covenant He concluded with Noah and his sons. If we compare this covenant with the one He had stipulated with the first humans after they had sinned (and we allow ourselves to call it a "covenant" for the same reason that, for no reason whatsoever, all the other "diktaks" tendered to man by the Lord are called covenants or pacts), we're almost tempted to say that He wanted to extend His hand to those of His creatures who had been saved from the catastrophe. Indeed, not even to Adam, when he had just been created and was still loved, did He offer as much as He offered to Noah and his sons as they knelt before the rainbow: they were even loaded with privileges! To begin with the greatest of them, we might mention that what He had revoked for fallen and sinful *man*, He guaranteed to the *human race* represented by Noah and his family: immortality—at least to the extent, and in the form of the promise, that He would not exterminate them again, at least not by water. Furthermore, He granted Noah what it had never crossed His mind to grant Adam: boundless permission to feed on all the animals, birds, and fishes on earth. By these arrangements, the Lord actually made man the master of the universe, since He guaranteed him a life without fear after the awful shock he had just suffered. Not only that, but He did not forbid Noah and his offspring anything, or at least nothing comparable in gravity to the prohibition that caused our progenitors to fail. This time He was satisfied to warn them not to kill each other, a relatively self-evident precept, and not to eat meat along with fresh blood, an almost superfluous precept, since from time immemorial meat as well as vegetables had been cooked. Hence no prohibitions, at least no onerous ones. But the thing most worthy of consideration in the whole covenant is that the Lord demanded nothing from man in exchange for so many gifts and concessions, absolutely nothing, neither sacrifice, nor devotion, nor filial love, nor gratitude, nor veneration. He didn't even ask to be remembered, except for the appearance of the rainbow, which would have recalled His more agreeable and reassuring sides. We might certainly say that the Lord had tacitly exempted Noah's progeny from the duty of caring about Him. It seems almost as though He had taken the firm decision to let Himself be forgotten, along with all the terrible memories that accompanied His image.

From all this it is clear that the Lord must then have been absolutely tranquil: it was the only way He could risk so much. He must have felt immensely secure when we stop to think that He had foreseen everything that Noah's descendants, encouraged by the mild covenant, would do. Shem, Ham, and Japheth, puffed up with a joy of living never felt before, and having lived through mortal danger, set about building the new world with exuberant energy. To toil, to sweat, to feel exhausted by fatigue were a real pleasure for them, and later when their work was over and they knew it was well done, it was more than ever a pleasure to go to bed with their young wives, who would face the pains of childbirth with courage and enthusiasm, thanks to their conviction that for their children it would be worth the trouble of coming into this world: a beautiful, safe, and constantly expanding world. Adam and Eve in Eden never knew an ecstasy comparable to that with which surviving humanity wallowed amid the puddles of mud and slime. With the passage of time, Shem, Ham, and Japheth realized that the Lord had not mentioned the old curse, and that, indeed, by urging them to be fruitful and multiply, He seemed rather to be giving free rein and a paternal blessing to a natural impulse. Nor had He said a word about work, almost as though leaving the amount and manner of it to man's judgment. The sons of the hero of the flood ended by deluding themselves that the order of the curse was about to expire, and that in any case they had been tacitly authorized to soften and blunt it by their ingenuity and shrewdness. And the truth is that what the nine generations from the times of Noah to those of Abraham created was no small achievement: in that period, the first great civilizations of History, the kingdoms of the Sumerians, Hittites, Assyrians, Babylonians, and Egyptians were born, and in part died out. The children of Japheth and Ham seemed defiantly to demonstrate that man was capable of building with his own strength and in accordance with his own taste a world far exceeding the earthly Paradise in beauty, practicality, and pleasure.

But in this new human world there was no place for the Lord, the sole true and living God. Still, it was not an atheistic world: on the contrary, gods thronged everywhere. For the sons of Noah, taking advantage of the Lord's tacit permission, thought about Him less and less, and He, by ceasing to manifest Himself either to them or their descendants, underwent in their memories a process of distortion. When distant posterity felt the need to pray to Him and express its gratitude and devotion, each person imagined Him in his or her own way, and thus inevitably different from what He had been in reality. Our ingenuous explanation of something that cannot be verified, but which perhaps vaguely mirrors the imagination of the compilers of the Bible regarding the birth of the false and lying gods, is not meant to express an acceptance of any of the theories on the origin of polytheism. We wish only to point out what a huge gap there must have been between the regime of the sole true and living God and that of the various pantheons. For the gods discovered by Noah's descendants "in place of" the Lord formed part of the human world, were inside or behind all actions and manifestations of human life, their almost palpable presence made the human atmosphere vibrant, and faced with the anger of one it was always possible to turn to another for protection. After the tyranny of the Lord, it may have seemed an advanced form of freedom to serve many masters without becoming the slave of any. Man must no longer have felt at the mercy of a single incommensurable and irrevocable force; rather he felt he was being contested by forces higher than himself, that he was almost the object and reward of the rivalry of immense but not necessarily overwhelming powers, and this constituted his hope and his dignity. These gods, despite the fact that their divine essence was superhuman, were at the same time very familiar to man, almost tangible, and in a certain way human. Men lived in close communion with them, were constantly concerned with them, offered them sacrifices, and in the course of endless festivals performed sacred rites in their honor, and in this way all of human life, from morning to night, and from the cradle to the grave, became a kind of divine service. Out of devotion, gratitude, and fear, men built temples to these gods, and represented them in sculpture and painted images to make them more present and concrete. For their part, the gods, being so well served, had nothing against men also building cities, palaces, baths, and tombs for themselves, and doing their utmost for their own tranquillity and security, their own comfort and pleasure. These gods even went so far as to allow some men not to sweat as they worked and some women to know only the pleasure of love. The overwhelming majority of humanity, however, who continued to toil by the sweat of their brows and give birth in pain, kept going along, thanks to the uninterrupted presence of the gods, in the unshakable conviction that even the bleakest life was sanctified.

There was a notable difference with respect to the order of the curse, which before the flood had hit humanity so hard, and no one could imagine that the gods, who had made human life so much easier, were nothing but simple idols. And no one could imagine that the thousands of years during which the human spirit had taken its first intoxicating flights were of so little interest to the sole true and living God. What was it that induced the Lord to grant man a little rest and allow the progress of the spirit to go off in directions that pleased Him so little? Although with the flood He had fortified Himself against any possibility of being threatened by man in His position or His person, why did He put up with His own disgraceful situation during the thousands of years in which He was forgotten and deprived of all worship? And if it is true that He had been nourished by the sacrifices offered to Him by man, why did He then condemn Himself to such a long fast? This situation, although destined for a happy ending, was no doubt diametrically opposed to the one in which He would have liked to find Himself; in any case it was unpleasant, and may also have included almost physical sufferings. All things considered, we can assume that this transition period, though fundamentally of no interest to Him, did not leave Him totally indifferent. And even though He put up with it, we can be certain that His feigned tolerance was part of His plan and an aspect of His diplomacy, to which He was committed from the moment He had accepted the rules of the game of History.

Perhaps we will not go too far wrong by supposing that the Lord intentionally gave humanity a breathing spell, and that His plan anticipated man's acquiring a taste for existence. In our previous "text," we tried to illustrate the degraded position in which man found himself as a result of the flood, having to give up once and for all the only ambition worthy of him, that of becoming truly "like" the Lord. Man in that state of mind, in other words man in the Noachian phase of his march, though unable to express himself with philosophical concepts, realized just the same—thanks to the morsel extracted from omniscience, constituting both his misery and his pride—that existence, at least human existence, would be irrevocably emptied of its meaning, and would henceforth become a macabre dance over the abyss. Man after the flood, in the "Noachian" phase of his march, realized that from now on—having been separated from the harmony of the cosmos and become critic, enemy, and reformer of Creation, rather than remaining an integral part of it—anything that he thought, desired, or did, any idea that he formed about the beauty and worth of existence, would all be only a kind of drug in order to forget his broken dream and mask the void it had left behind. Man, conscious of good and evil, in the "Noachian" phase of his maturity of spirit, for the first time asked himself—albeit without concepts that can be conveyed in words—the fatal question: *Is it worth it?* Is it worth it to consume oneself in toil while multiplying one's degenerate race in pain? And man, conscious of good and evil, was in a position to answer with either a yes or a no. In this respect, faced with the free will of His creature, the Lord was powerless. Omnipotent God would have been unable to prevent a portion of the human race from answering no. And so a portion of humanity, albeit not aloud and not even consciously, but with a rebellious stirring of that "something" that invincibly concealed the faint knowledge of chaos in the deepest layers of its soul, answered no.

After the flood, the Lord, who in His own interests had exterminated masses of people but allowed the human race to survive, all of a sudden found Himself faced with the danger that the survivors would spontaneously renounce the honor of this gift. It would have been unwise to go on raging against these frightened, desperate creatures, and striking them with further disasters—it even seemed risky to remind them of the old curse. Rather it was advisable to treat them gently, handle them with kid gloves, let them be happily, intoxicatingly ensnared by the illusions produced by their reasoning intellects, and nourish in them the joy of living, thereby silencing the voice of the void, of the vanity of existence. It was thus time to alleviate the circumstances of their lives, let them believe that their sweaty toil was no longer a punishment but an inspired flight toward self-assertion, and that not even painful childbirth was a punishment but merely an interlude in the eternity of love. Yes, it seemed like the right moment to let them forget the old curse. And it seemed like the right moment for the Lord to let Himself be forgotten as well.

Possibly this period of transition caused the Lord some inconvenience, and He may have had to fast, but nevertheless His calm was imperturbable. Thanks to the parallelism manifested in those remote times in the succession of generations, He could be sure that—just as long ago, simultaneously tenth and first, His beloved son Noah had arrived, the navigator of the flood, who had walked with Him and on whom He had been able to rely—another beloved son, also tenth and first, Terah the emigrant, would unfailingly arrive, and by his move once again radically alter humanity's position before its God. And the Lord was sure that this man's son would be Abraham, who no less than Noah would walk with Him, and in his own consciousness reinstate the image of Himself that was agreeable to Him, and which in Noah's consciousness had understandably suffered a slight distortion. And the Lord was likewise sure that just as Noah had had a frightened son named Shem, who through Eber and Terah had transmitted anguished memories of the order of the curse into the soul and blood of Abraham, so Abraham too would have a frightened son, Isaac, who this time, loudly and tirelessly, would transmit to posterity and for thousands of years to come the testimony of His incommensurable greatness.

Knowing all this, it was no trouble for Him to wait for Abraham, even if He had to fast.

VI. *Sarah laughs*

TO THE EXTENT ALLOWED BY HIS IMMENSITY AND OUR OWN
incapacity, we've arrived at a closer knowledge of the third of our
protagonists, the Lord. We should like to hope that even those
more partial to the novelistic side of our hybrid literary genre than
to the essayistic will still agree that the pursuit of such knowledge
has not been wholly in vain, since it has also brought to light
certain unexpected aspects of our two human protagonists. No
longer can we enjoy the luxury of treating the vicissitudes of the
godly tribal chieftain and his wife, the most beautiful woman in
the world, as a legend that is "almost true" or a "story with many
fairy-tale elements." What we are primarily dealing with is a
myth, and, like any myth, it mirrors the condition of humanity at
some phase of its march. In both Abraham and Sarah we must see
man at that moment in his spiritual development when the sole
true and living God made His solemn entry, or re-entry, into

human consciousness. There is no need to say how important this moment was and is for the direction of civilization and history, but it ought to be pointed out that it was a moment when myths could not fail to emerge. Although the reappearance of the Lord and of the order of the curse in human consciousness destroyed ambitions less lofty than man's titanic prediluvian dreams, and although the repercussions were not immediate and apparently involved only the leader of an insignificant tribe of shepherds rather than the whole human race, nevertheless the people chosen to preserve, cultivate, and develop its experience of God, and who ended by undermining with it the entire world that man had built for himself on his pride and the joy of life, this people understood that what had happened was comparable in its importance only to the expulsion from Eden and the flood.

If until that moment it may even have seemed that, first, orig-inal sin and, later, man's violence had taken the Lord by surprise and embittered His disappointed heart, almost forcing Him to allow everything on earth to go adrift, now, by re-emerging in the consciousness of Abraham, He gained a clear victory: less swiftly than before, but with greater certainty, He put man back in the position where He felt he belonged in view of his sin and its punishment. Once more man had to take note of the fact that following the expulsion and the flood he had become a worm in relation to the incommensurability of the Lord, and that he had no other choice but to accept His order of things. And he had to realize that should he try to exceed the limits of the human, he must not at the same time exceed the limits of that order: at most he could exalt it by glorifying in it like Enoch, while silencing in himself any awareness of one "who is not but could be."

But if one had necessarily to resign oneself to the order of the curse, and much as man with his reason had done his utmost to make it a rule of life, there remained in him that bit of repressed but indelible omniscience in everlasting revolt against the yoke; and in the depths of his soul, buried so deeply below his con-sciousness as to exclude any responsibility on his part, something kept secretly operating in him, something that sought to elude and frustrate the Lord's oppressive order and withdraw from it. This "something" buried in the human subconscious took two forms in rejecting a degraded and humiliating existence. One was to ignore the shackles of punishment, breaking them through the exaltation of the joy of living, cleansing the curse of everything in it that was truly cursed, that is to say, by reducing toil with the sweat of one's brow and the pains of childbirth to their purely instrumental value as "necessary evils," and raising to the rank of goals and proud achievements the things that man in the course of thousands of years would be able to extract from his suffering state: the excitement of progress, which made life easier, more beautiful, and more comfortable, and the excitement of love, in which giving birth was no longer the purpose, but an incident to be tolerated or eliminated. It is obvious that from the standpoint of the order of the Lord, the purposefulness and self-sufficiency of man and of sexual pleasure were among the clearest expressions of the death instinct.

The other form of the death instinct operating in man was equally clear, or rather it was rougher, cruder, and more frightening than the previous one, which had at least been masked by the life instinct. This second way of withdrawing from the order of the curse was the rejection of existence, a self-imposed death sentence on humanity by the suspension of reproduction. This doesn't mean, of course, that in one or another phase of humanity's march someone announced that he no longer cared to reproduce because he was sick and tired of the order of the curse. Likewise no one set out to build splendid civilizations with the thought of thumbing his nose at the order of the curse. What determined such attitudes was that man was subconsciously taking a stand in the face of his condition and the order imposed on him by the Lord, a *parti pris* so hidden and unsuspected that we have allowed ourselves to call it a death *instinct*.

So we can certainly say that there were moments in humanity's march when to want to live and to want to die were equally expressions of the will to self-destruction, since life was conceived in a manner contrary to the divine order and death was a way of escaping it. This statement may seem arbitrary for the moment, but if it does, the fault lies in the devious nature of the death instinct itself, which enjoys taking the most false and deceptive paths. If in its first form it had masked itself as the joy of living and the excitement of creating, manifestly dragging the human race toward destruction, in its second form, the crude one, it had cunningly donned the garments of the order of the curse, mocking and frightening the best sons of God-fearing Shem! Indeed, it was precisely those who, in accordance with their faith and best convictions, as well as the most ardent desire of their hearts, had tried to walk with the Lord, who now all of a sudden began to have a terrified feeling that things were getting increasingly difficult, and already they were losing even the hope of fulfilling what seemed to be the Lord's most simple and at the same time—thanks to its voluptuous preliminaries and its social and economic utility— most agreeable command: the command to reproduce. Yes, procreation did not occur with the same ease as it did for those to whom the Lord had not given this command, and whom every so often He unhesitatingly exterminated. Furthermore, in reproducing and multiplying themselves, it was precisely those who had been chosen by the Lord to beget a humanity that would be to His liking and direct life on earth along the path He wanted, who had botched the job. We know about Noah's stubborn and exasperating sterility, and by now we have noted Abraham's enervating problems in this regard.

In our previous "text," the hero of which was Noah, we suggested that the explanation for this strange suspension of generative forces, which occurred just before human existence had taken the new directions foreseen and desired by the Lord, could be found in the fact that "something" in man, an inner voice, the evanescent echo of omniscience, reawakened by the horror of imminent catastrophe and the subsequent degradation of humanity's position, had sounded the alarm and ordered a halt. Even today we do not see any more plausible hypothesis. At most, in keeping with our new terminology, we would now say that it was the death instinct that checked man's procreative power, so as to save him from catastrophe and a bleakly senseless existence. Noah's genealogical tree speaks clearly: the closer the moment of the flood came, when humanity would die like rats, the harder it was for man's generative forces to succeed in overcoming the instinctive inhibition, ending with a striking, and at first irrevocable, failure in the very person of Noah.

But, on the other hand, if it seems sufficiently justified to impute such an instinctive stance to the hero of the flood, that is to say, one independent of his reason and will with respect to the survival of the human race, would it likewise be justified to impute it to Abraham, who with brilliant intuition had rediscovered the sole true and living God and grasped His essence in all its irresistible clarity? Would it not be much more justified to suppose that Abraham, along with his great discovery, had also accepted *instinctively* all the unforeseeable consequences deriving from it, and, albeit unknowingly, had also submitted *instinctively* to the order established by the Lord? To counter these arguments one need only point out that the instincts, too, undergo a process of stratification, and that the most powerful ones are precisely those most deeply buried, which means that Abraham, while instinctively accepting in full the order of the curse, likewise instinctively, but with an instinct that came from a deeper layer of his soul, rejected it. If we see Abraham less as an individual than as *man* at a particular phase of his march, it is correct to suppose that in him that certain "something" in the depths of his soul was horrified by the presentiment of the further degradation of the human condition, the effects and consequences of which would be even more disastrous than those of the flood. But was this presentiment sufficient cause to inhibit the reproductive faculties of God's discoverer, who approved of reproduction not only with his reason but instinctively as well? Perhaps even this would have been enough, and yet we can detect a more immediate threat in the air, one that appeared even more frightening than a new worsening of the human condition, and like an alarm bell must have kept the death instinct awake in Abraham. We are looking for, and already we find its traces, a disaster neither imminent nor remote, but which—in the "Abrahamic" phase of human progress, in an "Abrahamically" defined ethnic and geographical setting—will rival the horror of the deluge, and make the question, destined not to become conscious, reappear in the depths of the human soul: *Is it worth the trouble?* It seems obvious to us that the catastrophe lying in wait to swallow up the new Abrahamic humanity can be identified as the four centuries of slavery in Egypt. The Lord had informed Abraham of what would befall his progeny. But, in reality, Abraham—or rather that "something" in him that in the depths of his soul was in possession of omniscience—already knew it beforehand, had known it, so to speak, since the most remote times. Noah had already known it, Shem knew it, and Eber and his descendants knew it perhaps even better than they, but it had still not set off the alarm in their subconscious since between the ages of twenty-eight and thirty they had thoughtlessly begot children. But can anyone state with equal certainty that even in the depths of Terah's soul that "something" had not already begun to stir and was raising questions about the propriety of begetting the man who was to discover the Lord? Terah, tenth of a series of generations who were masters of themselves and first of a series condemned to slavery, although no less willing than his ancestor Noah and his son Abraham, nevertheless had to live seventy years before seeing the arrival of his firstborn son. And when he finally decided on his fatal journey, he must have felt in the depths of his soul not only the anguish of uncertainty, but that of certainty as well . . .

Perhaps in Abraham, who by his discovery made the Lord win the match, that residue of omniscience no longer had any reason to warn him of the burden of his responsibility to his immediate descendants and future humanity? Of course it warned him, and the proof is the fact that Abraham, at the age of ninety-nine, had still not produced the son in whose person the stipulated covenant with the Lord would have been signed, sealed, and delivered. All this seems almost unbelievable when we remember that he had married the most beautiful woman in the world, whom he adored beyond measure, and from whom he had wanted a son even on the verge of old age. But actually no other case reveals more clearly the disguises of which the death instinct is capable, not even hesitating to hide behind the mask of the imperative imposed by the order of the curse. Since we are now more familiar with the relations between Abraham and Sarah, it would not be an uncalled-for suspicion that these relations were based much more on the instinctive desire to suspend reproduction than on the rational one to procreate: the *coup de foudre*, in their case, was not provoked by the wish to have a descendant, but was simply a trap set by the death instinct. The truth is that no woman on earth was ever less suited for the part of progenitrix, and if nevertheless Abraham, inevitably and without hesitation, chose her as his wife, he did so because he too did not wish to become the progenitor of his own offspring.

In the first years, or first decades, of their marriage, neither of the pair was alarmed by the fact that their tent was not yet gladdened by an infant's cries: on this point they were reassured by the example of old Terah. On the other hand, even if—following human custom and the voice of a superficial instinct—they had vaguely desired and in no way hindered the birth of a child, they did so unwillingly, exalted as they were by the mystical-erotic cult of the woman's beauty, whose perfection was supposed to remain unchanged. Still, the blessed event could have happened at any time, had Sarah not been barren. But the idea that she was barren was so absurd that it didn't even cross their minds, Abraham's in particular, for he was in constant contact with the Lord and kept receiving renewed guarantees and exhortations concerning unlimited proliferation. Thus Abraham, on their way to Egypt, had no reason not to hope that sooner or later Sarah would make him a father. But then Abraham, or rather the death instinct in him, hastened to provoke the stupid disgrace that would forever ruin his relations with his wife and obstruct the normal course of their already shaky marital life. When later the yawning void of her own life, past and to come, opened before Sarah, and in her heart she ardently longed for a child from her womb, it was old age taking her by surprise, an old age that fortunately was only chronological and left her youthful beauty intact, but nevertheless deprived her womanhood of completion. Considered separately, these facts appear as pure coincidences, but taken together they are disturbing indications of a single thing: the devious but firm determination not to bring children into the world. Still, this event, despite all the difficulties and complications, might always have happened had Sarah not been barren, and they both realized this from the moment that Abraham, with wholly natural simplicity and speed, succeeded in impregnating the Egyptian handmaid.

Yes, according to the testimony of the Holy Scriptures, Sarah was barren, and in no way does this fact surprise us, for in that particular phase of humanity's march *man* meant not only Abraham but Sarah as well. And this *man*, which they were, represented, and expressed, was struck by the horror of the future human condition, and more than anything perhaps by the still not imminent, yet not all that distant, misery of the four centuries of Egyptian slavery. To us it seems a mistake to saddle Abraham rather than Sarah with the responsibility for their failure to procreate—or vice-versa. It was *man*, in their persons, that put up resistance, a single resistance that at most differed by manifesting itself in male and female form. It would be a gross error to imagine that in a certain phase of the human spirit's progress Sarah was *woman* and Abraham *man*: such an idea is not only absurd but historically unjustified, because in no period of History have male and female traveled humanity's path separately. Adam and Eve together constitute *man* at the stage that takes its name from original sin, Noah and his unnamed wife are both *man* in the phase of human progress designated by the event of the flood, just as Abraham and Sarah together constitute *man* at the moment of the revelation of the sole true and living God. So if Sarah was barren, this fact is far from signifying that, simply because Abraham was not impotent, at the new turn in humanity's spiritual path the human female had put up a more stubborn resistance than the human male. Sarah's barrenness was a self-defensive maneuver by *man*, the projection and expression in female form of the same death instinct that had also acted in Abraham. It was precisely because of her barrenness that Sarah was chosen by that "something" that acted in Abraham, for the purpose of canceling his virile powers and causing them to fail.

In the light of these reflections, the fact that we know nothing about Noah's better half has little or no importance. Although it is customary to put all the responsibility for their persistent sterility on the shoulders of the patriarch, it is possible, highly possible, that Noah's wife had also been long and stubbornly barren. If we take a close look at the genealogy of Abraham, we can even say that for a certain period of time Eve herself was also barren, or rather that there was "something" in her that had difficulty in accepting the curse of childbearing; in any case, it hesitated longer than the same "something" later hesitated in the wife of her son Seth, and even in the latter the indecision lasted longer than in the wife of her son Enos. Indeed, in the course of a few generations human opposition kept diminishing, as resignation to humanity's degraded position gradually grew, only to flare up again in the last generations of the series, when the horrified "something" began to sniff the stinking slime of the flood. But neither in the slowness nor the haste can we separate the respective responsibilities of man and woman. When we think back on the part played by Eve in original sin—namely, the first step toward the achievement of omniscience—it may seem to be the female principle in the human being that gives greater expression to the death instinct, while the male principle aspires to preserve order or to re-create it when it collapses.

It is much more interesting to point out that at the dawn of Time, after the expulsion from Eden, resistance to the divine order to reproduce was relatively weak in humanity, and Adam and Eve, beaten and humiliated, quite soon adapted themselves to the order of the curse. Eve almost resignedly birth to her degraded species, but we could say she did so with practically no hesitation or delay compared to Noah's wife, who stubbornly persisted in her barrenness until the threshold of old age, even though, having reached this point, she gave up and in rapid succession delivered the future progenitors of postdiluvian humanity. Thus Noah and his wife did not hold out beyond human possibilities, and ended, though with considerable delay, by yielding to the order of the curse.

Compared to their resistance, that of our protagonists was much more dogged. If Noah's wife, for reasons unknown to us, had for a long time been incapable of bringing children into the world, Sarah was plainly barren, and tenaciously persisted in her barrenness *beyond* human possibilities of procreation—that is to say, well into old age, that state from which conception and giving birth were excluded not only by the death instinct operating in her, but already, once and for all, by nature itself. It required divine intervention, a miracle, a violation of the natural law for the Lord to be able to impose His will on humanity's latent but increasingly entrenched resistance. Except that here once again, the Lord, although it took a miracle to do it, succeeded in wrapping the affirmation of His will in human form: Isaac, when all was said and done, was begot by Abraham and delivered by Sarah. The idea doesn't seem to us at all farfetched, or the fruit of our overheated imagination, that in the next decisive clash in the exhausting struggle between God and man, humanity shifted its defenses still further ahead, and instead of the failed weapon of barrenness, used purity, inviolability, and virginity to defend itself against the hero of the new covenant that would further aggravate man's situation. And in this predicament, the Lord found Himself unable to stage some human *mise en scène* to mask the brutal assertion of His will: indeed, it would have been rather risky to entrust an earthly mortal with the task of violating a virgin's resistance. And spontaneously the question arises: If and when another decisive moment in the struggle between God and man comes, will the Lord still find a Mary ready to give birth for Him to the executor of the Third Testament? It doesn't seem to us a totally absurd idea that the next "man of God" may be the result of artificial insemination, or the product of alembics and test tubes.

Perhaps it has not been wholly pointless to recall all this before picking up the thread of our story again and watching our hero, his brain hammering and his knees quaking, totter home after the terrifying encounter. In the end, however, he clung firmly to the essential point: what the Lord desired was not only unreasonable but actually absurd, and he would make no move in that direction, if only because he wouldn't dare to make the slightest mention of such madness to Sarah. But fearing that the Lord might read his thoughts, he composed a brief sentence and murmured it over and over: "Anyway I still have three months." And he would have liked the Lord to hear it, be satisfied, and not seek to read his private thoughts. Fortunately, he had a better weapon at hand to convince the Lord that his first and major concern would be to carry out His commands: yes, the damned circumcision of himself, of Ishmael, and of all the men of his tribe, the great collective operation whose grim spectacle, accompanied by resounding cries, would attract the Lord's attention and draw it away from that other operation to whose execution he was now consciously opposed to the fullest possible extent. Oh, how much simpler it was to cut off the foreskins of all the males in his house! And how much simpler it would also be to cut off everybody's hands, feet, nose, and ears, perhaps even those of Sarah herself, rather than go to her and say that by the Lord's command they must resume their conjugal life, and moreover for the purpose of producing a son!

Next morning, with dogged zeal, he set out to perform the bloody task the announcement of which had spread terror in the tribe of peaceful shepherds. But there was no way they could protest. Abraham informed them that this was a command from the Lord, and they all obeyed, for though none of them had ever seen Him and all had doubted His actual existence, they could only agree that the mysterious Lord had treated their master well, and through him, themselves. And so, muttering and cursing, all the

men and male children submitted to the painful surgical operation. Amid the cries of the victims and the shrieks and moans of
their womenfolk, Abraham, assisted by his servant Eliezer and
with razor-sharp knives in hand, worked tirelessly from the first
hour of dawn until late at night, and at the end, his hands now
trembling with fatigue, he executed on the servant, on Ishmael,
and last of all on himself the operation that God had ordered.
Afterward it was a great relief to be able to stay in bed for a few
days with a high fever and not think of anything but his own
physical sufferings. True, before his feverish eyes, the figure of
Sarah sometimes fleetingly appeared, and her face, instead of sincere compassion, expressed scornful mistrust; on these occasions
our poor invalid found himself bathed in a cold sweat, and immediately began praying to the Lord to spare him the ambiguous
pleasure of regaining the use of that certain part of his body that
had been out of practice for some time and had now just been
mutilated. It was awful merely to think that, sooner or later, in
order to be accepted in her bed, he would have to beg this woman
who was able to look at him with such scornful mistrust, almost as
though she were trying to detect in him the incipient symptoms of
raving madness. "Anyway I still have three months," he murmured restlessly, now more for his own sake than for the Lord's.

Sarah was indeed thinking just what Abraham in his dazed and
drowsy condition had suspected her of thinking: that for her husband the fatal hour had come when the silent madness that had
always trailed behind him would suddenly be transformed into
raving lunacy. Having witnessed the frenzy with which he had
performed the bloody operation on his people and on himself, all
the while calling on the Lord, she was left without even the shadow
of a doubt. She began thinking seriously about how and with
whose help it would be possible to restrain him and render him
harmless. She did not feel the slightest compassion for him. If
hitherto she had let herself be deluded, she was now convinced that
the placid periods of their life together, in which she had been
capable of feeling toward him like a mother, sister, and friend, had

actually been nothing but a kind of "truce of God," which she had maintained at the cost of enormous efforts, but had always been ready to break at the first opportunity. These strained if idyllic periods had been less unbearable ever since Abraham had ceased pestering her as a lovesick husband; now, however, she realized that the wretched man had succeeded in gaining her indulgent tolerance, not by restraining his sensuality, but by not having mentioned for some time the name of the Lord. Now that with this disgusting butchery, the Lord's name had come forth once more, Sarah felt everything inside her boiling up again, and she couldn't wait to rain down on the old lunatic's head the long repressed flood of disgust, horror, and hatred that she nourished for him. Thanks to the miserable physical shape he was in because of his own madness, Abraham for the moment was spared this tempest of rage, which would surely have been lethal had Sarah decided to unleash it on him. The woman had to content herself with noting that she didn't feel even the slightest compassion for him, and that it wouldn't make any difference to her if he ended up croaking on his bed of senseless pain.

"It would be an excellent solution," she thought with a twinge of remorse. But actually it was not only anger that gave her this unbearable feeling of suffocation, but also a kind of grim anxiety that she had never felt before. She tried to find an explanation for it in the fact that her heart was filled with terror at the prospect of having to live with a raving lunatic. But finally she had to acknowledge, although her pride rebelled at the idea, that the reason for her profound anxiety was simply the Lord's reappearance in their lives: the Lord in whom she didn't believe because she had never seen Him, and above all because she had never wanted to believe in Him, and whom she had every reason to hate with all her heart. Indeed, even if He existed only as her husband's fixation, He was the cause of all the ills that had struck them, and whenever He reappeared, still worse things happened to them. Now here was the tribe of shepherds who several days after the cruel operation still writhed in horrible pain and battered her eardrums with their outcries. But that wasn't all. Sarah had the clear impression that things would not end here: the Lord must have even bigger surprises in store for them. Her anguish grew to such an extent as to consume her anger, and now she anxiously awaited her husband's recovery, not to heap on him the full expression of her contempt and disgust, but to seek comfort with him from her terror.

Meanwhile Abraham, to his great disappointment, kept noticing that his recovery, despite the gravity and divine importance of the operation, was fairly swift, and that the interlude he had gained by his feverish state not only had been insufficient to make a decision about the future, but had even been too short to allow him to recover from the shock of the encounter. A single comforting thought crossed his mind: that it was not unusual for children to come into the world after a pregnancy of seven months, and that therefore one shouldn't rule out the possibility that this phantom son of his could also be a seven-month baby, in which case he would not only have at his disposal almost three months but almost five in which to think about it and act! In any case, if on the one hand he could still feel calm, on the other it seemed to him that it wasn't the right moment to begin a thorough discussion with his wife about the circumcisions, which sooner or later he would have to explain. It therefore seemed to him that the only reasonable thing to do was to prolong his convalescence *ad infinitum*, and by invoking his physical and mental exhaustion, to demand for himself the treatment that any sick person has a right to. Quite soon, however, he had to realize that unfortunately he would not be able to proceed like this for long, since Sarah kept buzzing around him with disturbing frequency, and it seemed clear that she was finding it hard to restrain herself from talking to him. Still, her look no longer gave off the threatening signs of an inevitable storm. She seemed worried, more frightened than frightening. Abraham explained this change to himself by supposing that Sarah was anxious about his mental state. Since he did not want to get excited, he did nothing to reassure her: indeed, he lavished on himself all the solicitude to which any convalescent is entitled.

But never would he have imagined that his convalescence was fated to end in such an abrupt and frightful way. Only a few days had passed since he had got up from his bed, and he was comfortably stretched out in front of his tent, in the pleasing shade of the leafy terebinths, musing over certain calculations on the time he had left to think and act: he shuddered at the thought that of the three months he had been granted, two weeks more or less had already gone by, but then he was cheered by the hope that this margin might even be five months. All of a sudden, however, he felt his blood run cold. *And he lift up his eyes and looked, and, lo, three men stood by him*: they seemed almost to have sprouted out of the earth, or dropped from the sky. But it was less the unexpected apparition that scared him to death than the fact that there could be no doubts about their identity. And in the irregular beating of his heart he seemed to recognize the deafening sound of thousands of alarm bells.

He was certain that the visit boded no good. But how could such a horrible certainty be accepted in the space of a moment? A crazy idea, absurd beyond measure, flashed through his brain, and yet he clung to it convulsively: Maybe—he said to himself in desperation—maybe if I treat them as simple wayfarers, they'll behave like simple wayfarers. It was the policy of the ostrich, a miserable policy destined to failure, but all the same he felt that he would reproach himself for the rest of his life if he didn't try it. So leaping up from his convalescent's bench, *he ran to meet them . . . and bowed himself toward the ground*, then addressing the one who seemed the most distinguished of the three, he offered hospitality in polite and excited words. He promised to have water brought to wash their feet, tired and dirty from the dust of the road; he invited them to stretch out in the shade of the terebinth, and tried to put them in a good mood with the idea of a few morsels of bread. He did his utmost to put himself in their good graces and even to make them believe that this visit had no other purpose but to give them a chance to wash their feet, rest, and have a snack, before proceeding merrily on their way. But to make sure that they were aware of the duties of a respectable wayfarer, and partly also to measure the effectiveness of the ostrich policy, he added aloud: ". . . *after that ye shall pass on; for therefore are ye come to your servant."* But his soundings did not produce reassuring results. The three men, indifferent to his effusions as a generous host, listened impassively to his chatter without any expression on their wooden faces, until one of them, with an impatient gesture of his hand, interrupted him by saying: *"So do, as thou hast said."*

No, it was decidedly not a rosy situation, and those impenetrable wooden faces promised nothing good. As he went to fetch everything he had promised, it occurred to him all of a sudden that a few slices of bread would not be enough to gain the benevolence of these three. Unfortunately, the idea of fetching and hastily preparing a heifer, a goat, and a ram, each three years old, and a turtledove and a pigeon besides, was simply out of the question, but all the same he remembered that the Lord craved meat and he very much hoped that in His human form He would even be content with *a calf tender and good.* So instead of a simple snack, he decided to offer a delicious dinner, and the idea greatly pleased him, if for no other reason than with the pretext of preparing a sumptuous banquet he could be excused from entertaining his guests. So he suggested to them that the best thing they could do until mealtime was to rest in the shade of the terebinths.

Unfortunately, for a meal of some size, he needed his wife's help, since only Sarah was personally able to take *fine meal, knead it, and make cakes upon the hearth*, in a way that had sent their guests into raptures. Timidly and with a bad conscience, he entered his wife's tent. She was in a gloomy mood, and did not even notice that her husband had unexpectedly interrupted his convalescence. She had not yet begun her toilette, on which she spent several hours a day, and to Abraham she looked tired and worn out, not to say old and ugly. As he had foreseen, Sarah flew into a rage over the unexpected arrival of guests and absolutely refused to understand why any fuss should be made over three wayfarers. Abraham, who would rather have died than confess the identity of his guest, came up with some pious fib, and Sarah finally agreed to go to the kitchen. She stated, however, loud and clear, that she would not honor those people by her presence. Her refusal was so firm that Abraham did not insist; in truth, he felt relieved, for the idea of bringing Sarah face to face with the Lord struck him as so awful and absurd as to boggle the imagination. So Sarah put aside her beauty treatment, and just as she was, with her face still not made up and her hair still uncombed, put on a greasy dressing gown reserved solely for working in the kitchen. Such a garment, at least, meant there was no possibility that she would come out to greet the strangers.

Never in his life had Abraham been so anxious about the way Sarah and the servant women prepared a good meal. Every minute or so, as though he were out of his mind, he kept rushing into the kitchen tent, sticking his nose in everything, urging them to do their best and be quick about it, and even—what was really the last straw!—trying to offer advice. Furthermore, like a sheep afflicted with the staggers, he kept running all over the camp, from the storerooms to the stables and the wine cellar, and tried to take over the churn and personally supervise the preparation of fresh butter. He was completely deranged, and from Sarah's horrified gaze he knew that she now considered him a dangerous madman beyond recall. It was impossible for him to explain that all his frantic activity was simply a pretext to postpone the moment when he would have to rejoin his guests, who, rigid in their grim immobility, were taking a siesta in the shade of the terebinths.

There was something chilling in the rigid immobility and impenetrable wooden faces with which the three men were seated under the tree, close to the kitchen tent. They didn't open their mouths, and their behavior, in general, was not what one would expect of wayfarers who had been welcomed with generous hospitality: already stingy with words, they had neither a smile nor a grateful look for their host. They sat down around the table with the same grim look, silently swallowed the tender veal, and spoke not a word of praise even for Sarah's excellent pancakes, the pride and glory of her culinary art. And none of the three thought to invite the master of the house to the banquet, while he for his part had not had the courage to sit down among them, but stood there near the tree, waiting respectfully and at the same time prey to the darkest presentiments. The oppressive silence that spread around the table was so deep as to became deafening, and ended by reaching even Sarah and the servant women behind the hanging carpet that curtained the entrance to the kitchen tent.

By the time the three grim-faced men had devoured the last crumbs, Abraham was bathed in sweat, his knees began to shake so badly that he had to lean against the solid trunk of the terebinth, and at the same time he felt an irrepressible urge to yell, to yell at the top of his lungs. And he tried. Had he succeeded, he might almost have awakened from this nightmare. But he didn't succeed: instead of his voice, only a wheeze came from his throat. He would have to live the nightmare to the end. And he knew that the worst moment had arrived.

One of the three men, the one with the most majestic appearance, asked him all of a sudden, with no preamble: *"Where is Sarah thy wife?"* From that long, dull, suffocating silence, his voice burst forth like a trumpet blast, aggressive and overbearing, a voice that even as it scolded and accused, demanded a single, unequivocal answer. Abraham went red in the face. Not only had the voice been offensive, but the question itself was outrageous, insolent: the stranger had called the mistress of the house by name, but had not done so as a good friend, or an old acquaintance entitled to some familiarity, but as a great lord accustomed to treating all common mortals like servants. The first thought that terrified Abraham was that all this had also been heard and understood by Sarah, and in his mind he saw his wife's face darken. Yes, this was the end. The policy of the ostrich had failed miserably. Hemming and hawing, make-believe, and slyness no longer made sense: he realized that he would have to exercise discretion. Maybe Sarah was there behind the tent curtain, waiting for him to answer back, to teach the rude guest a lesson, or at least, in a dry or cold but dignified tone of voice, offer some trite excuse or other for her absence. But instead, scared out of his wits, like a pupil caught out by the teacher, he was unable to do anything but confess the truth in a trembling voice: *"Behold, in the tent."* And it was awful to think that Sarah had also heard his cowardly response.

Sarah had indeed heard everything. Her face went pale, then flushed red. But she had no time to nurse her wounded pride, for all of a sudden she realized who the stranger was. All of a sudden she realized that the Lord was something more than her husband's fixation. And she realized likewise that misfortune, the presentiment of which had depressed her for weeks, was on the doorstep. So she kept an ear cocked.

Meanwhile Abraham stood trembling under the tree, powerlessly awaiting the final developments. Powerless to such a point that, in singular contradiction to his own monotheism, he began to pray to the Lord who was usually in heaven to save him from the Lord who stood facing him. His trembling lips longed for the earth to open under his feet and swallow him up, or preferably swallow up the three wayfarers before they uttered another word. For he knew, with unmistakable certainty, what would now happen. But how could he throw himself on his knees before the Lord and confess that he had still said nothing to Sarah, how could he beg Him to treat the pride of his unknowing wife with more delicacy, how could he urge Him to keep in mind his pitiful marital relations—alas, how could he do all this when Sarah herself was surely eavesdropping there behind the curtain, and listening to everything in a state of extreme agitation? Oh, if only the earth would open under his feet! With his eyes closed and his shoulders hunched, he was fervently wishing that such a providential cataclysm would happen, when the Lord in a loud, tactless voice, making absolutely no decent attempt to mitigate the rudeness of what He was about to say, repeated almost word for word His absurd and needless prophecy, which was less a prophecy than the curt communication of a fact already for some time accomplished in the future. It was almost unbearable for Abraham to imagine what Sarah was feeling on hearing such words. Alas, the Lord seemed unaware of his wife's bad character! Therefore, in expectation of the worst, he glanced timidly toward the tent, ready to see the carpet pushed aside at any moment and his wife emerging like a fury, a ladle in her hand and her face contorted with rage, to assail the three undesirable guests with appropriate curse words and drive them away. Knowing Sarah, he could well imagine her at that moment putting the Lord to ignominious flight!

But for a seemingly endless moment nothing happened: the chilling silence, which shortly before had spread around the table, now seemed to emanate from inside the tent. For a seemingly endless moment it looked as though all life had been suspended in the world. Then, all of a sudden, the deadly silence inside the tent was broken by a sound of unmistakably human origin, very short and subdued, but which seemed disrespectful, almost obscene. At this point Abraham closed his eyes more tightly and hunched his shoulders even more.

It was Sarah laughing.

Actually it was not so much a laugh as a kind of snort of relief, and it was only by its contrast with the deadly silence that those outside had that disconcerting impression. What had happened was that Sarah had listened with growing terror to the Lord's statement, but when afterward during the seemingly endless moment she had been able to grasp the meaning of His words, she had felt a heavy burden lifted from her heart—and her relief was expressed in her odd little laugh. Of course, with that little laugh she was mocking herself for having been terrified, but more than herself she was mocking the one by whom she had let herself, for a moment, be foolishly terrified. Where had he been, this mysterious friend of her husband's, what had he been doing, all these last years? Had he been asleep? Had time stopped for him? Sarah remembered this one's ambitions very well, she remembered all the times he had goaded her husband, who in turn had goaded her, to have a child! But to speak of such things in the present or future was an anachronism in the worst taste. And in her throbbing heart surged a slight but malicious sense of triumph: yes, if the purpose of the Lord's visit was to deliver this communication, then the Lord was defeated!

But Abraham, outside the tent, had seen the Lord's face darken and was far from nourishing illusions. For a moment at first, he had hoped that the indecent little laugh, having been so short and subdued, had not reached the Lord's ear. But what does not reach the Lord's ear when the Lord is paying attention? He was visibly transfigured by an awful rage that made not only His face glow, but His whole body and His garments as well, while before Abraham's eyes He grew fearfully beyond the narrow limits of human form. *"Wherefore did Sarah laugh?"* He thundered threateningly in Abraham's direction, and at that moment, inside the tent, Sarah had the sensation that all the elements had been unleashed and that the earth was coming unhinged with an ominous roar. The slight feeling of triumph, which a moment before had made her heart throb, vanished into the void to give way to a fear she had never felt before. If a moment ago, still excited by the idea of her own superiority, it had flashed into her mind to make a kind of sortie outside the tent and, in the splendor of a youth and beauty that had withstood the perfidious effect of time, laugh in the face of the guest dozing in his anachronism, now she was afraid she didn't have the strength to endure her fear alone and madly wished to be at least close to her husband. And when, as a result of the Lord's last words, the tent poles began to wobble and dishes fell off the shelves with an infernal crash, while the vault of heaven and every corner of the world seemed to echo with the proud cry, *"Is any thing too hard for the Lord?,"* Sarah could stand it no longer: completely forgetting her unpresentable state, she ran out of the tent and threw herself on her husband's heaving chest. And when the Lord, perhaps somewhat appeased, confirmed that in a year she would give birth, it seemed to Sarah that with this ineffable and absurd ignominy He wanted to humiliate her pride, but also, in part, punish her for her irreverence. Wringing her hands convulsively, with a desperate movement she broke away from Abraham's chest, and taking a few wavering steps forward, raised her eyes to the guest, while her livid lips formed voiceless words, almost a sigh: "*I laughed not . . .*"

Thus she saw the Lord. With the expression on His face in which anger was gradually subsiding, with His superhuman stature and the splendor that radiated from all parts of His body and His garments, He seemed to Sarah an extraordinarily handsome and fascinating man. Her fear vanished, giving way to an astonished admiration, and she felt herself pervaded by a strange elation. Even had she wanted to, she was unable to remove her gaze from that face that emanated such supernatural strength, power, and authority. One thought, more piercing than a dagger thrust, crossed her mind: she should have met Him before . . . He would have been the man for her, worthy of her divine beauty and the incandescence of her heart, so unjustly said to be cold. The Lord seemed to have guessed her thoughts. The threatening clouds of anger disappeared entirely from His noble features, and He stared at the enraptured woman, looked her carefully up and down, examining her twice from head to foot, and then an almost imperceptible grimace appeared on His lips.

But Sarah noticed it and felt faint. She realized she was no longer young and beautiful, and remembered with horror that she was in dishabille, that she had not even begun her morning toilette; despairingly she remembered that her face was not made up, that her uncombed hair was sticking to her forehead beaded with sweat from the fumes of the kitchen, that she was wearing a greasy dressing gown, and that her pretty feet with their red toenails were shod in floppy slippers. Then her face blushed with shame and hatred. Meanwhile the barely concealed smirk with which He had expressed His judgment on the feminine merits of His antagonist vanished from the Lord's lips, and His face again expressed arrogance and enormous contempt. Finally He said with indifference, "*Nay; but thou didst laugh,*" and shrugging His shoulders, He turned to His traveling companions and set off with slow steps toward the main road.

Abraham, having witnessed the terrible scene with a clear sense of guilt toward his wife, thought it best to run after the Lord. And when, a few hours later, even more upset by the Lord's further communications and the signs of His infinite power, he returned home, he saw with alarm that Sarah, still uncombed and in her dressing gown, was sitting motionless on the bench under the terebinth. Anxiously he approached her, but all of a sudden he was thunderstruck: the person who sat there, all slumped over, was really and truly an old woman.

To this point had the Lord reduced Sarah, His most relentless adversary, the most unyielding stronghold at the disposal of the human subconscious. For a moment the thought crossed Abraham's mind that for him, too, this was a sad revenge for all the scorn and humiliation that Sarah had inflicted on him for decades and decades because of the Lord. But it was too bitter a revenge for him to feel any satisfaction. The sight of the woman who yesterday had still seemed to him the most beautiful in the world and who in a flash had become old, filled his heart with profound melancholy and dismay: the Lord's revenge struck him indirectly, canceling in a twinkling all the miraculous results of love's magic. And now there were serious worries in the offing. For although the Lord, by revealing to Sarah in no uncertain terms what would be expected of them, and in this way relieving His discoverer and faithful servant from the duty of taking the first impossible step, had in a sense smoothed the path for him toward the fulfillment of the divine plan, at the same time He had made it still more difficult. With His infinite wisdom and unlimited power, He certainly would have done better to have left a splendid young woman under the terebinth instead of a dejected old one. As happened so often, His left hand seemed not to know what His right hand was doing.

Abraham did not even think of approaching this woman, so undone in body and spirit, with the rites of love's magic: given their situation and state of mind, it was more fitting to make her share his own defeat, misery, and impotence. Now it was no trouble for him to explain to her, in simple and spontaneous words, that it was not he but the Lord who had willed all this, and that their whole life had been willed by the Lord. Then, alone and defenseless, like the poor old couple they were, they wept and moaned over this thought, hour after hour, day after day, in the shade of the leafy terebinths. The pity they felt for themselves, and for each other, created between them a consoling spiritual bond, which encouraged Abraham to tell her in detail all the things about which the bloody operations and his long convalescence had been an excuse to keep silent.

Abraham also revealed that that absurd and quite unnecessary son, who nevertheless was willed by the Lord, would have to be called Laughter, likewise by God's will. "It's because I laughed," said Sarah, shuddering. "I laughed before you did!" said Abraham, partly to claim for himself the ambiguous glory of priority, partly to relieve his wife's remorse. But they went on racking their brains trying to understand what laughter had to do with the horror with which the Lord had struck them.

As far as the divine plan was concerned, they stopped at this point. In the final analysis, what was impossible was impossible.

VII. A cry reaching heaven

SELDOM IS THE QUESTION RAISED AS TO WHY THE LORD, AFTER
dispatching whatever business there was to dispatch with Abraham
and Sarah, strode off in the direction of Sodom in order to dispatch
something urgent there as well. We learn in school that one event
followed the other, and for the rest of our lives we are satisfied
with this vague childhood memory. Accordingly it never occurs to
anyone to look for a more organic connection between the two
episodes, beyond a pure and simple chronological sequence, and
any such idea is particularly avoided by biblical scholars. True, we
have to admit that some sort of tie between the two episodes
has always been acknowledged, even constantly exploited, especially by preachers, for the edification of the faithful: the connect-
ing link is the person of Abraham himself, who, it will be recalled,
entered a plea of mercy with the Lord on behalf of the two corrupt
cities, warning Him that He risked destroying the innocent along

with the evildoers. But in these sermons the whole episode tends to serve merely to illustrate the great patriarch's kind heart and sense of justice. Such a formulation may well be enough for those who consider the Bible to be an anthology of moralistic tales.

To many of those who think of the Bible as a history book, it seems obvious instead that the Lord had combined His two actions in time, since finding Himself on earth, He might as well kill two birds with one stone: after all, it was only a hop, skip, and a jump from the oak grove of Mamre to the city of Sodom. But you have only to glance at a map and this inviting hypothesis is demolished. Actually the distance is not all that short and takes more than a hop, skip, and a jump: even as the crow flies it comes to about eighty kilometers. So it is not a distance that a wayfarer, or rather three wayfarers, would be able to cover between afternoon and evening, even if they hurried. Unless the Lord and His angels flew, which obviously would have presented no difficulty, either to Him or to them. But, in that case, we cannot help observing that it would have been much easier for the Lord to "pop down" directly from heaven than to fly or take a cross-country hike from Hebron to Sodom. In our opinion, He could have postponed this brief visit to Sodom, or paid it earlier, had it been simply a matter of distances and means of locomotion.

It would therefore be a good idea to discard without delay the hypothesis that the Lord's moves were dictated by convenience, as well as the other one according to which the tradition, for the sake of simplicity, would have combined and condensed two historical events fairly close to each other in time. Such things may happen in chronicles, but never in a mythological story, of which even details that may not seem pertinent form an integral part. Finally, if we keep in mind that there is a close link between the mournful vicissitudes of Sodom and the story of Lot, Abraham's closest relative, it quickly becomes clear that we have no reason or right to neglect the interrelations among the three episodes; on the contrary, it is incumbent upon us to discover the logical connection that brought them together in time, both in the biblical story and in the Lord's intentions.

Today, when we want to stigmatize an environment addicted to libertinage, or an attitude inspired by it, we use the expression "Sodom and Gomorrah." Memories of the religious lessons of our school years survive in this way of summing up our moral indignation: indeed, it was precisely to keep our imaginations from setting out on unedifying paths that we children were taught *ad usum Delphini* that the two destroyed biblical cities had been living in grave sin and immorality, thus provoking the wrath of God. And, from the pedagogical standpoint, it was an exceedingly laudable idea to stay with generalities and imprecision, although in this case one understood less than one might have had things been spelled out more exactly. Actually the Bible makes no secret of it: the sin whose cry reached heaven and so troubled the Lord that He descended to earth was homosexuality, still called "sodomy" even by its model practitioners. Thus men and women, however perverse their relations may be with the opposite sex, have every right to feel outraged when excited preachers of morality dig up for them the sin of Sodom and Gomorrah. There is no doubt that the sin of the two biblical cities was homosexuality, and to be exact, sexual relations between men, since there is no evidence that their poor neglected women sought consolation in lesbian pleasures.

To anyone who keeps all this in mind from the start, it seems quite natural that the Lord destroyed the two cities because of the sexual perversion of their male population. And to anyone who limits the field of his or her interests to the opposite sex, the hypothesis would seem to need no revision: it is obvious to such a person that the Lord experienced deep revulsion at the sight of such immorality, and in a fit of rage wiped from the face of the earth the two cities where homosexuals practiced their revolting traffic, not secretly and with a bad conscience, but publicly and with self-assurance, elevating perversion to the dignity of the norm. Although Abraham had already taken Him for a primarily spiritual Being, and theology has since demonstrated that in essence He was, and is, an absolutely spiritual Being, the Lord always behaved one hundred percent like a man, appeared before His chosen in male form, and finally even produced a son by an earthly woman. So it is no wonder that such a God let Himself be guided, indeed carried away, by a deep revulsion when He decided on His radical gesture.

Having reached this point, the author seizes the opportunity to put in writing, and immortalize, his immense, untiring, and incorrigible enthusiasm for the weaker sex. Although he is aware of the implacable verdict of science according to which we are all homosexuals—some consciously, some unconsciously, some latently, some manifestly, but in any case, in one way or another, all without exception, including therefore the author himself—he is pleased that his homosexual inclinations are as latent as they can possibly be, so latent that he is unable to fathom the phenomenon of homosexuality, and at the sight of a pederast is overcome by the same uneasiness mixed with fear that he feels in the presence of a drunkard, a madman, or any other person incapable of following "normal" human patterns of emotion and thought. The author does not deny that this totally negative attitude of his is a bit morbid, and may even be a clear sign of his latent homosexuality: nevertheless, though himself the opposite of a bloodthirsty type, in his physical horror at the intimate practices of homosexuals, he would almost be able to understand and appreciate the divine nausea—were it not for the fact that he knows a good deal more about matters of God than about the pleasures of homosexual love.

Without wishing to overestimate whatever modest success we have attained so far in a better knowledge of the Almighty, we have surely made it abundantly clear that it is never permissible to assume that some human motive, such as anger or indignation, nor even some higher human virtue, such as goodness and justice, lies behind manifestations of divine will, or in general, behind divine acts. The Lord's reactions are presumably planned, and, to be sure, are always good and wise, but divinely so, and it is only their sudden and improvised character, astounding and sensational, that makes them look like a violent explosion of elemental force. Without wasting any more words on the subject, we can state with utter certainty that the destruction of Sodom and Gomorrah was in no way a manifestation of divine nausea over the sodomitic perversion. Our task is to find out what place was assigned in the divine plan to the suppression of the two biblical cities, and why it was chronologically linked with the story of Abraham and Sarah.

The fact that along with Sodom and Gomorrah the Lord did not suppress homosexuality itself (which has flourished all over the world and in every age, and according to statistical data, still flourishes today, to a much higher degree than one would have thought) shows that this was not one of His intentions, and perhaps not even in His power. Actually all the Lord did was to suppress a bunch of pederasts: the "sinners" but not the sin. And His action is also troublesome because of the fact that He not only exterminated the sinners, namely, the male homosexuals, but the entire population of the two cities, including the poor neglected women, who had suffered a good deal more than He through the sexual perversion of their menfolk, and also the innocent children, who still knew nothing about anything, at least those who at the moment were still babes in arms. Such a decision by the Lord aroused the greatest indignation in the pious Abraham. The discoverer had another opportunity to modify the idea he had formed of his discovery. As we know, in Abraham's experience the Lord's character was not devoid of disconcerting and unwelcome features. Not to mention the dirty tricks He had played on him in the past, He was now plotting a new one, tormenting His follower with impossible and useless demands, and treating a fair lady discourteously. All the same, Abraham would never have suspected Him of wanting to suppress whole cities just to punish certain perversions, revolting to be sure, but still insignificant, and he remained particularly shaken by the fact that the Lord had decided to exterminate the innocent along with the so-called sinners. He could not swallow such an awful idea; miserable and powerless, driven by a deep emotion that was wholly human, he warned the Lord against committing a act so cruel and unworthy of Him: *"That be far from thee to do after this manner, to slay the righteous with the wicked . . . that be far from thee: Shall not the Judge of all the earth do right?"* The Lord resigned Himself grudgingly to Abraham's haggling, and anyway it did not make Him change His mind. He destroyed the two cities all the same, thereby showing that there were not ten "innocents" even among the babes in arms. Abraham came to the conclusion, not without regret, that with the discovery of the sole true and living God, he had placed the whole world at the mercy of a blind and deaf will, and probably more than once the thought crossed his mind that it would have been preferable not to have to connect all the horrors with which life was afflicted to the name of the Lord, but to leave them stuck to the false and lying idols.

This is how Abraham, God's discoverer, having neither experience nor a particularly keen mind, might have reasoned. Believers who at all costs and contrary to all the evidence want a good, wise, and just Lord may turn a blind eye to divine cruelty and injustice; but we who, among other things, have taken on the task of clearing the Lord of the accusations and excuses with which He has been besmirched in the course of the centuries certainly cannot pass over the regrettable episode. How can we allow Him to be accused of treachery and considered an uncouth butcher of innocents? Would it not be more fitting to recall the supreme divine justice that has nothing to do with our ethical convictions, but which guarantees instead the unfolding of the divine plan: the justice that through Adam's sin cursed the whole human race and that through the hubris of Cain's descendants exterminated even the children of Seth? The destruction of Sodom and Gomorrah inevitably reminds us of the great collective tragedy of the flood, and despite the fact that one affected all of humanity, while the other involved only the population of two cities, we cannot dismiss the thought that once again—although now in a historical period and a specific ethnic and geographical setting, and thus on a more limited scale—the same thing happened that had happened in Noachian prehistory. And this all the more since, on a limited scale, Abraham was also a kind of Noah and Shem, at a decisive turn in the destinies of the human race. It was not therefore sinners and innocents that succumbed, but an inferior human material, which in some way, and for some reason still to be clarified, would have been out of keeping with the impending new era.

To show that our idea is more substantial than a mere fantasy, we have only to lay on the table that *specificum* common to these two essential moments in humanity's march that provoked the Lord's direct intervention. The Bible comes immediately to our aid by explicitly singling out the compelling motive by the expression "the wickedness of man." *"The wickedness of man was great"* in the times of Noah; *"the cry of Sodom and Gomorrah is great, and . . . their sin is very grievous."* By now we know what kind of situations are indicated in the Bible by these terms, so simple and simplistic as to be deceptive. By now we are too far along to be able to delude ourselves that the biblical words conceal instances of puerile disobedience or naughty behavior or venial peccadilloes, since we have already seen how it has always been a question of the major conquests by which man has made himself both great and unhappy, and by which he has confronted the Creator with new tasks, foreseen in advance, to be sure, from the beginning of time, but nevertheless in need of solution. By his original sin, we repeat, man attained omniscience—i.e., awareness of the possible and the capacity to know it—and free will; in the times just before the flood he was thus, at least potentially, on the point of reconquering the lost Paradise. The biblical terms "sin," "wickedness," and "violence" correspond to equally decisive facts: the reawakening of consciousness, freedom of will and choice, the capacity to think and criticize, the revolt against the deadly perfection of the universe, the revolt against the vital and vivifying principles of the order of the curse. Now it remains to be seen whether we have any reason or right to suppose that the "wickedness" of Sodom and Gomorrah constituted as grave a problem, albeit on a reduced scale, for the decisive new turn in humanity's march as did the consequences of original sin or titanic violence. In other words, is there a point of view from which homosexuality may appear alongside the reawakening of consciousness, the knowledge of good and evil, and the use of reason and the critical faculty?

Surprising as it may seem at first sight, our answer is yes. We should even add that, in this decisive moment in the struggle between God and man, the sin of Sodom loomed more threateningly than any other previous effort by man to frustrate or obstruct the divine plan. As we have seen, God had been able to parry all the dangers coming from man, and theoretically had been able—as He still can—"to hope" that sinful man, or rather conscious man reaching out to the loftiest heights of the intellect and spirit, by making good use of his knowledge of good and evil would end at a certain point in History by spontaneously accepting His order. But what would happen if all of a sudden humanity were to realize that homosexual love could be a path of salvation—the way out of the vale of tears? No doubt about it, the divine plan would be emptied of its object and purpose. No less than sterility, homosexual love is also a form of suicide by the human species.

Well, at the "Abrahamic moment" in the struggle between God and man, the Lord found Himself faced with Sarah's barrenness and the Sodomites' negation of life. Never had the death instinct raged more furiously and more impudently in man than at this particular historical moment, which foreshadowed the overwhelming victory of the Lord and the restoration of the order of the curse. And if we care to accept the divine point of view, according to which the sterile conjugal life of Abraham and Sarah and the sexual perversion of the Sodomites were simply two aspects of the stubborn resistance put up by humanity in the face of a more humiliating future, then all our preliminary qualms about the logical and chronological links between the two biblical episodes vanish, and henceforth they appear as two scenes in a grandiose fresco, completed at the end by the addition of the sad story of Lot and his daughters.

In short, at that "Abrahamic moment" in the struggle between

God and man, nothing less than the preservation of the human species was at stake. Now in our mind's eye we see an expression of mistrust and discontent spreading over the faces of most of our kind readers; many make a gesture of impatience, some curse and slam the book shut, and quite a few would be ready to hurl themselves at us and wring our necks in retaliation for the naïve nonsense that we're asking them to swallow. We can almost hear the indignant accusations by which they seek to put us in our place, recalling our attention to the fact that Sodom and Gomorrah were a very insignificant point on the planet; that not all humanity, not even the wicked part of it, was destroyed along with the two cities; that not even the hated sin was destroyed; that the significance of it all was too closely tied to a specific place and setting to be generalized and universalized, and finally that the Lord could have found a way to reveal Himself at another point in the world and at a time more favorable for the easier execution of His plan . . . But let's settle this question for good. The kind reader shouldn't speak to us this way, for the very reason that he or she has stayed with us to this point. One has only to think back on the energy with which the Lord committed Himself at that decisive moment in History, and of the enormously important decisions He took, even overturning the order of nature, to bring about the birth of little Isaac. Yes, everything that happened in those times at a dot on the map of Palestine may have seemed *then* of only local importance, but no longer today, to us who know the universal consequences of those events. Let the kind reader reflect on the fact that nowadays the Lord has half a billion followers precisely as a result of those events that were tied to such a circumscribed setting. It is useful to repeat, for the benefit of those who think it so obvious that "it all might have turned out differently," useful to repeat that perhaps it is precisely for God that everything had to proceed, and has to proceed, as it did and does. The Lord knew, better than fanatical believers in His omnipotence, that at the "Abrahamic moment" in History, He would win or lose everything. And He would indeed have lost everything if instead of fully committing Himself, He had entrusted His fortunes exclusively to Abraham, i.e., to Man: He might have lost the battle, if not forever, at least for a long time, until a new "Abrahamic moment" had emerged somewhere else in the world to tip the scales in His favor (and we can certainly concede that much to His omnipotence). But since the Lord had foreseen this particular "Abrahamic moment," and even knew it to be fulfilled in His plan, it would have been unreasonable even for an omnipotent God to let it go by without seizing it. He therefore acted without delay and with the utmost determination.

The new humanity was to be born from Abraham and Sarah: the already existing humanity and the one that would emerge from it in other regions of Palestine or the earth, in Mesopotamia, say, or at the North Pole or in South America, was for the moment of little or no interest to the Lord. All that mattered to Him at that particular moment was Abraham: *"For I know him, that he will command his children and his household after him, and they shall keep the way of the Lord, to do justice and judgment,"* as He remarked on His way to Sodom. And naturally Sodom and Gomorrah mattered to Him, too, those two highly civilized cities that by standing there, in close proximity to Abraham and his future children, seemed to announce proudly and provocatively to the people under God's yoke that only a life built in opposition to the order of the curse was beautiful and worthy of man. For Abraham, and for his future descendants, the destruction of Sodom and Gomorrah meant many things: it was first of all a sign of the Lord's unlimited power, it was simultaneously a warning to those who might be tempted to transgress the limits imposed by the Lord, and it was also a move to intimidate people yet unborn, who, chosen by the divine plan, were now destined to follow and perpetuate the Lord's law more than His order. Yes, in all probability the destruction of the two cities also pursued pedagogical aims for the benefit of Abraham and his family, a clamorous demonstration that, compared to the grandeur of God, everything that man had built without Him or against Him was vain and fragile stuff . . . Even so, the Bible leaves no doubt that the Lord, by His clamorous gesture, wanted chiefly to settle accounts with the sin whose cry had reached Heaven.

Nowadays this sin no longer disturbs the Lord's ears with its cries, no longer does He rain brimstone and fire on males who flirt with each other, and besides, even in those remote times He was indifferent to the fact that homosexual love was thriving in all other parts of the world. He could not, however, turn a blind eye, or rather a deaf ear, to the cry that rose to Heaven from Sodom and Gomorrah, close to the cradle of the chosen people. We ought not to forget something that from a practical standpoint may have carried considerable weight in the Lord's decision: along with the two corrupt cities, He also caused a bad example to disappear from the horizons of a small population destined to multiply, but that tended instinctively to cut off its existence *ab imis* by not being born. As we see, there were plenty of reasons for the terrible divine intervention, and they furnish a sufficient explanation for it. Still, we cannot fail to recognize in it something more significant, more grandiose, almost more solemn, which transcends its practical and immediate purpose.

We must not lose sight of the fact that what we are witnessing is the restoration of the order of the curse, which was founded on the two pillars of sweaty toil and painful childbirth. Thanks to our now by no means negligible knowledge of the divine character, we must surely admit that the Lord had judged such a punishment as the most fitting for man's sin, or, to put it more precisely, as the most appropriate precaution against the dangerousness of man. The Darwinian formula of the *struggle for life** is, in the final analysis, a travesty of the words of the divine curse, which indissolubly linked self-preservation and the preservation of the species to struggle and suffering. As punishment, the curse was a clever idea, but it was certainly no less a precautionary measure: man became too burdened with worries to be able to devote himself to his divine aspirations.

* In English in original.

The human position changed radically not only with respect to the Lord, but also with respect to previous conditions.

The fact that the divine curse installed a new order in human life requires a few words on our part about the order that preceded it. Our progenitors, before sinning, lived in Eden under conditions that we can certainly call "paradisiacal," and of which we all have, rather than precise ideas, a vague and yet indelible impression. We have already alluded here and there to certain characteristics of Edenic man, and it is enough to point out only one to realize the abysmal difference between the paradisiacal state and our present conditions: before committing sin, man was immortal—or at least he was destined for immortality—and this is clearly shown by the fact that the Lord's first countermeasure was precisely to institute mortality, from which the other two basic punishments in the order of the curse derived. In this connection, the double version of the cosmogonic tradition preserved in the Book of Genesis, and its disconnected, confused, and contradictory explanation of the facts, have produced in the heads of believers mistaken ideas and unmotivated fantasies that, to tell the truth, not even official theology has been able to dispel, much less correct. That there could have existed a phase of the Creation in which man was immortal, or destined for immortality, already seemed incredible to the compilers of the Bible, but obviously it had also seemed that way to a much older tradition, which for this very reason had conceived a tree of immortality next to the tree of omniscience. According to this somewhat rationalistic variant, the Lord expelled our progenitors from the garden of Eden chiefly to prevent them from *acquiring* immortality too. Indeed, *the Lord God said, Behold, the man is become as one of us, to know good and evil: and now, lest he put forth his hand, and take also of the tree of life, and eat, and live forever.* . . . All this is in clear contradiction with the famous prohibition by which the Lord threatened man with death if he ate the fruit of the tree of good and evil: such a threat would have made no sense if man had not been predestined for immortality.

That it was not simply a matter of Adam as a person, but of Man as first and only exemplar of his kind, is also shown by the fact that the divine threat did not come true literally. Adam and Eve by no means died on the day when they ate the forbidden fruit, but went on living for hundreds and hundreds of years: instead the human race became mortal. Besides, universal mythology is in agreement that man was immortal in the "paradisiacal" phase of his existence. All this shows that some verses of the Book of Genesis reflect traditions from much later times, which were no longer capable of forming an idea of human immortality.

Actually not even we can conceive the immortality of an individual man, and perhaps immortality conceived in this manner is in itself inconceivable. Or could it be that the Lord, with the creation of the earthly Paradise, was dreaming of setting up a stable and everlasting zoological park, whose most precious specimens would be the first (and only) humans, namely Adam and Eve? To be exact, we should specify that originally only Adam was chosen for this decorous role, since Eve was created, or rather made, from his rib only as an afterthought, almost by caprice, or in any case, as the result of an idea that suddenly emerged with the motivation: *"It is not good that the man should be alone; I will make him an help meet for him."* And if we keep in mind that both of them were destined for immortality, it is truly hard to find a different motivation for the creation of woman, since immortality precludes the reproduction of the species, as well as the struggle for self-preservation. The famous verse from the Book of Genesis, considered to be irrefutable proof of the divine origin of the institution of marriage, contradicts the idea of human immortality and obviously reflects post-Edenic conditions, since it orders man to leave his father and mother and cleave unto his wife, thereby adopting concepts as yet not conceived and inconceivable, and thus absurd in the primordial state of Paradise. Altogether it seems to have been the Creator's idea—as is shown unmistakably by the words with which He decides to "make" the woman—for Eve to be a companion, an assistant, a secretary, but in no way a wife for Adam in the garden of Eden.

Now it is not only interesting but proper to raise the question:

What was the position in Paradise of the fishes in the sea, the birds in the sky, and the animals that "walked" or "crept" over the earth? As specimens in the permanent zoological garden of Eden, they too would have had no reason nor way to know the post-Edenic need for the preservation of the species, and therefore we have the sacrosanct right to imagine that God from the rib of each male animal ("after his kind," and insofar as they had ribs) had made a female, and certainly not for any different reason or purpose than in the case of man: to give it a proper assistant. For the immortal animal, "the preservation of the species" would have been just as much an absurdity as it was for immortal man. We should not, however, forget that in the whole story of the Creation there is not the slightest mention of the individual immortality of animals, and so it seems to us more justified to concede that in the garden of Eden, and around man who was destined for immortality, the fauna and flora were in a state of eternal change, and that unlike man, the animals felt the need for procreation, as well as its pains and delights. That this is how it must have been from the dawn of life on earth is proved not only by the order to *"be fruitful and multiply"* by which the Lord accompanied the act of creation (but the expression could be the result of superimposing a later tradition, as in the case of the first man), but also by the negative fact that the animals were not forbidden the tree of omniscience, whose fruit also contained the secret of sex.

The superimposing of the two variants of tradition reported by the Book of Genesis, as well as the contradictory conclusions that can be drawn from them, make it impossible, in this case, to accept the biblical text "word for word," as would be the first duty of every self-respecting Christian, and no catechism has bothered to give him any valid help in resolving his doubts. And yet there would be a possibility—we might call it the only possibility—to which, however, official theology still shows an understandable repugnance: the mythological interpretation, in which the two contradictory versions are not mutually exclusive, but rather complete and complement each other. Indeed, no sooner do we decide to approach the problem of human immortality, as set forth in the Bible, with the same confident simplicity with which we confront all the other myths of immortality in world mythology, than all the tortuous and troublesome problems, justified as they are despite their obvious naïveté, automatically disappear. Such as, for example: Why and how should anyone who is immortal preserve his species? Why should anyone who has to remain in life perpetually by divine will have to work, when actually he wouldn't even have to feed himself? Why was an assistant given to someone who had absolutely no need of one? Why was this assistant given in the form of a woman, when the man had no need to reproduce his kind? And so on.

When a myth of immortality speaks of individual immortality (and actually all mythologies speak of this form of immortality), it does not occur to anyone to suppose that an initial stage of phylogeny had ever existed, or a phase of human existence in which man, already clothed in a so to speak "anthropomorphic" psychophysical form (we might say: in the "Adamic" phase of his march), would have been immortal. Today we know that with their myths of immortality the various peoples, in different ways, grasped and expressed a true stage of human evolution in man's long and wearisome march, a very remote—we might say pre-initial—phase, that has always lain outside his experience and memory, but which both did and had to exist, and of which the experience and memory still firmly survived in the subconscious, crystallizing in the idea of immortality. Clearly this idea or image does not mean individual immortality—rather it means a condition that preceded the birth of human life and foreshadowed the awakening of consciousness; it means a prehuman phase of evolution, in which all men were the *first man*, one man and many men, one generation and all generations, those deceased and those to come: dead and as yet unborn, all and together, they constituted the first man, who was thereby immortal like the animals and no more conscious of death than animals are. Man became mortal, mortal in the biblical sense and in the ordinary sense of the word, when he ate the forbidden fruit and acquired consciousness.

In this interpretation of the Edenic and post-Edenic binomial death-immortality (and certainly one cannot and should not give any other) all the apparent contradictions between the two biblical versions, which because of the problem of death seemed jarring, disappear or are reconciled. There is no longer any doubt that, under his "Edenic" conditions, the human male had to work—if gathering and protecting food and the female can be called work—just as it is also obvious that the human female had to give birth. According to this interpretation, and only according to it, theologians are right when they say that the essence of the divine curse consisted in the forms and not in the facts in themselves: in the sweat of toil and not in toil itself, in the pain of childbirth and not in childbirth itself. Truly, not even an animal's life is so easy as to be exempt from hardships and suffering: this despite the fact that animals bear the weight of existence with greater assurance, and confront its risks and difficulties with complete naturalness, while their more robust organisms, their less complex nervous systems, and their psyches, unenlightened by consciousness, keep them from having some idea of the real crudeness, or cruelty, of the struggle for life, and from suffering with the greatest intensity the physical and psychic tortures that this struggle involves. All this formed a structural part of the "management"* of nature and likewise protected the human being during that immensely long period in which the events of life, repeating themselves in an endless, uninterrupted, monotonous sequence, still had no name and no memory; in which birth, coupling, and death were not preceded by expectation and anxiety, nor accompanied by celebration; in which immortal man, no differently from the ape procreating the ape and the ant procreating the ant, always and unchangeably brought the first man into the world. And this state of things lasted until man tasted the fruit of the forbidden tree, when through his reason, enlightened by consciousness, ev-

* In English in original.

erything that had hitherto seemed to him "natural" became terrible and terribly oppressive—and after the first man the second man was born.

As a result of sin, the order of Eden, agreeable to God and agreeable to man, was followed by a completely different order, one that we are pleased to call the order of the curse, but which was by no means pleasing for the Lord, and even less for man. That the eviction from Eden signified the decisive moment in humanity's march, the one when man detached himself from nature and turned against it, has today become such a commonplace that it no longer evokes the meaning and seriousness inherent in it. True, it's not a bad idea to stress that man detached himself from the order of nature, but still it was the result of an eviction, forced on him by the pressure of external circumstances: when, that is, thanks to his now conscious reason, the fact was revealed to him that for him the conditions of Paradise were no longer so paradisiacal. Obviously the Edenic order all of a sudden became dangerous for man, or rather man, with the awakening of his consciousness, perceived its threat, and then, not wishing to succumb like so many other animal species, with a stupendous effort and a heroic gesture, gave up immortality in exchange for survival. Under the threat of being crushed at any moment, he courageously set about introducing changes in the divine Creation: yes, thanks to the forbidden fruit, he knew what good and evil were from the moral standpoint; but now he was also able to distinguish good from evil in Creation. To survive, he needed heat and light, also in winter and at night, and he discovered fire; he had to be able to hit birds on the wing, and he invented the bow and arrow; he needed the physical strength of the mammoth, and he invented the wheel. By necessity, he had to become omnipotent like God, and complete like Nature, and little by little he invented everything: without realizing it, he created for himself a frankly human order within the framework of the order of the curse. This new order, which he constructed for himself with purely human intentions, keeping in sight exclusively human interests, was inevitably organized within the order of the curse, and

thus man's toil became harder and woman's labor pains more atrocious. And then everyone had to die: everyone, individually, and
not without having experienced the fear of death.

Once having sinned, man gradually took account of all the huge
difficulties and worries that had been foisted on him in exchange for
omniscience, but also of certain marvelous aspects of existence of
which hitherto he had not had even the vaguest idea. Usually not
enough importance is given to a fact that in the biblical story takes
on dramatic overtones: the fact that along with death, man also discovered love; indeed, for an intoxicating moment, he knew love before knowing death. After the great adventure of the forbidden fruit,
Adam and Eve, almost drugged by an elixir of love, in the rapture
and anxiety of the first moments of their rebirth, could not see or feel
anything but the fact that they were naked. No one will suppose that
as a result of the marvelous fruit they felt chilly: they donned fig
leaves not to cover their back, but their sexual organs. And this is
what it was all about: in their nakedness they discovered sex.

It is a long time since we were so naïve as to imagine that in the
earthly Paradise the relations between Adam and Eve were "fra-
ternal," that is to say, devoid of sexuality. On the contrary, we
know very well that the first human couple brought the first man
into the world in an infinite series. "*And they were both naked, the
man and his wife, and were not ashamed,*" and the reason they weren't
ashamed is because they could not even imagine a different condition. For most of the year, each of the two attended to his or her
own affairs, and at night, or if circumstances allowed, even during
the day, tired from their exertions or satiated with food, they lay
down beside each other to take a nap, just like other animals, in
the coolness of a cave or the shade of a tree, and with the greatest
mutual indifference. Only at certain periods of the year, especially
in spring, did they take a curious interest in each other. Adam
could not breathe the intoxicating odor that emanated from Eve's
body without getting excited, while Eve discovered an ineffable
delight in rubbing herself against Adam's hairiness. Then they
remembered—or "something" in them remembered—how they

were accustomed to discharge the enormous tension of their senses: the organs, in fact, that at other times of the year served exclusively to relieve them of the annoyance of an excess accumulation of liquid in their bodies, in spring and in the other periods of sexual stimulation also became appropriate for uniting them in one flesh, as foreseen and ordained by God. Eve crouched face down on the ground, and emitting strange sounds, between furious howls and voluptuous moans, raised her buttocks, and Adam, having walked around her several times and become sufficiently intoxicated by the aroma emanating from her, finally stopped behind her, raised himself on both feet, and with a mournful and voluptuous gasp, mounted her. Besides being a sweet and irresistible need, this game was a magnificent spring pastime: the torment of desire and the pleasure of satisfaction conditioned and complemented each other like appetite and eating. But after a while, this period of rut passed, as unexpectedly as it had come, perhaps because Eve no longer gave off that strong exciting odor, and everything that hitherto had been so stimulating for Adam's senses now left him indifferent. Then, after another short time, Eve's body began to show the signs of a strange deformation: for absolutely inconceivable reasons her belly and then her breasts swelled, until finally, all of sudden, from inside her emerged a strange little four-legged creature, one, sometimes two or even three, whom she held underneath her to keep them warm, nursing them for months and years with the white secretion from her turgid breasts.

When Adam and Eve ate the fruit of the forbidden tree, it was obviously not spring, and Eve was not giving off that strong stimulating odor, but nevertheless Adam desired Eve and Eve desired Adam. At that precise moment, human love, which is independent of odors and seasons, was born, as was the first sexual perversion, the position of human intercourse. And, having overcome the first period of fear, Adam and Eve agreed in thinking that "sinning" was worth the trouble. And since it still took them a long time to grasp the close connection between the sexual act and procreation, they considered love to be a great achievement whose value was absolute. In the new order, therefore, although the shadow of death and the weight of the curse had made it bitter, there was yet a concrete pleasure, an incomparable delight that was always at hand, a great ecstasy and an end in itself, and which even today is our supreme good, even today when we have no more doubts that sex is another of the many traps set for us by the Lord.

This trap functioned impeccably, and by fulfilling its purpose, constituted the guarantee of the whole order of the curse, since it is the direct cause of painful childbirth and the indirect one of sweaty toil. There were times, however, when the divine trap exceeded its functions: with its agreeable sweetness, it appeared so inviting that man, who fell into it and always enjoyed falling into it, never wanted to get out. Man increasingly esteemed his first, fundamental, and most pleasant discovery, love independent of periodicity, and in it he concentrated all his memories of Eden. In the ecstasy of love he was able to discard his personality, and in each sexual act he relived the happy tragedy of death and resur-rection, re-evoking in his mind Edenic immortality. Love became a kind of supreme good for which it was worth the trouble of being born, living, and sometimes almost even dying.

This overestimation of love, although certainly disliked by the Lord, did not interfere with the divine plan so long as it guaranteed sweaty toil and painful childbirth, but it took on the appearance of a problem and became disturbing when it began to alleviate the gravity of the curse and to occupy a central place in human life. Love, which "moves everything," went beyond the limits of sex and rose to the rank of a universal principle. As eroticism and libido, it penetrated all forms of human life and all of man's activities. The hardships of toil almost vanished in creative inspi-ration, and man was transported in an almost erotic fever toward glory, success, magnificence, luxury, while the restricted field of sexual love also became increasingly enlarged, with physical and spiritual pleasure exalted to the detriment of procreation, consid-ered a kind of by-product and essentially extraneous to it. Among the sons of Noah, Shem and his descendants had conformed to the order of the curse, and Eber and his descendants in particular had respected marriage and family life as institutions sanctified by God, and had confined love within this framework; on the other hand, the children of Japheth and Ham, who along with some of the more emancipated children of Shem had produced high civilizations, reserved an eminent place in their lives for extramarital love, which not only did not have the reproduction of the species as its goal, but even abhorred it. Prostitution, unchecked by any divine prescription in that post-Noachian world, was not only tolerated as an institution, but in some parts of the earth even became a sacred one. And homosexuality not only spread everywhere, but was even considered a higher form of love. But while it might happen to a prostitute to succumb to the divine curse, and by becoming pregnant, to have to give birth with unspeakable pains, what could the Lord have thought about pederasts and lesbians? Indeed, it is impossible to conceive a form of love more constitutionally contrary to divine intentions than homosexuality, which is perfect sensual pleasure as an end in itself, and by its nature categorically precludes any possibility of procreation. Much as—as we have already mentioned—this form of love may repel us, we are forced to admit, or perhaps rather to be the first ones in the world to state, that homosexuality is the greatest achievement that the human species has ever come up with in its opposition to the order of the curse ordained by God. It is a clear triumph of the death instinct, and humanity's most sensual form of self-destruction.

If hitherto the Lord could allow Himself to turn a blind eye—as He can also allow Himself to do today—to the spread of this magnificent human invention, lust as an end in itself certainly constituted a mortal threat to His plan, and thereby to His existence, at that Abrahamic moment of the struggle with man and in that setting where the decisive moment had taken shape. If we add once more that the very man to whom He had revealed and entrusted Himself was likewise possessed by the death instinct, having exclusively pursued the pleasures of the flesh in his barren marriage to the most beautiful woman in the world, we can easily see that to the Lord a direct and personal intervention not only seemed necessary, but this intervention must also be both clamorous and terrifying in an exemplary way. Sodom and Gomorrah had of course to perish so that what would persist for Abraham's future descendants would not be the temptation of the two nearby sinful cities, but rather the frightful memory of their destruction at the hands of the Lord.

But, as we said, there was something more in the divine gesture, something that by its solemnity surpassed the merely punitive and pedagogic character of the intervention. In our opinion, the Lord's grandiose demonstration of omnipotence was at the same time a declaration, made not in words but by a gesture, about conception and the divine rules concerning human love. The Lord rejected sterile lust, that first and fundamental and magnificent human self-affirmation against the order of the curse, striking it dead before the terrified eyes of those who had been chosen to drag along the burden of sweaty toil and painful childbirth, and demonstrating that human needs and viewpoints have no right to exist when it comes to observing God's law. With a single gesture, the Lord swept away the symbol of sterile pleasure barely a moment after having enjoined two old people to unite in a humiliating embrace for the procreation of a son. What a difference between the refined colloquies of the Sodomites and the forced carnal union of the two oldsters, whose thoughts, instead of evoking lustful images and ideas, filled them with terror and dread! At this point we believe we have grasped the close connection between the story of Abraham and that of the two sinful cities, and in support of our thesis, we have the famous and infamous episode of Lot and his daughters: another example of forced insemination that, far from provoking voluptuous images in the minds of the protagonists, was strictly subordinated to the divine plan. What a difference between the heedless pleasures of homosexuals and the squalid incest of two respectable girls, whose descendants, however, were always treated with particular consideration by the Lord! A sense of guilt, remorse, and almost intolerable anguish formed the honor guard to their humiliating intercourse with the father whom they had deliberately made drunk, incestuous intercourse that nevertheless respected the divine order to "be fruitful and multiply"—in extreme cases, even in extreme ways. For the Lord does not know disgust and He does not know sin: He just knows His own plan.

The central theme of this mythical cycle is the clash, in its most radical forms, of the two conflicting conceptions formed by God and man about the function of love in human life; but it is just this almost absurd polarity of forms that reveals how man, at a particular phase of his march, tried to grasp something essential in the mysteries of his existence. The human tendency toward eroticism as an end in itself finds still another expression in the Bible, in the notorious, but seldom critically examined episode of the sons of Judah. Er and Onan, foreseeing or in order to forestall the insemination of Tamar, had gained sexual pleasure in the pure state in their conjugal life, i.e., within the very framework of the order of the curse, and both died a horrible death by direct intervention of the Lord, not unlike the profligates of Sodom and Gomorrah; while the sequel to the story eloquently illustrates the divine principle of "be fruitful and multiply," thanks to the romantic adventure of Judah and Tamar, in which the father-in-law impregnates the daughter-in-law, certainly without knowing it and without wishing to, but still not in that state of unconsciousness that absolves Lot, father of his own grandchildren (this time, too, the initiative had come from the woman: Tamar, like Lot's daughters, had courageously applied the saying "for extreme evils extreme remedies," and had been shrewd enough to distinguish the spirit from the letter of the law, even the divine law).

We don't think we are wrong in stating that the appalling story of Judah's sons, in the perspective of the "Jacobian" moment in the deadly struggle between God and man—although reduced to still more limited geographical and ethnic dimensions, i.e., to a family setting—is equivalent to, and for its universal importance even goes beyond, the biblical episode of the "sin whose cry reached Heaven," so that it, too, is only a reproduction, or restatement in a minor key, of the myth of the deluge; while the passing intrigue between Judah and Tamar, which transgressed the natural and divine law, but was fruitful and of essential importance for the purposes of the Lord's plan, calls to mind the carnal union of the two old people, and that of the father with his daughters. The Lord dealt harshly, as He had never done before and does not do even today, with the simple sexual enjoyment of two young husbands, because at that particular moment it was intolerable, while he gave free rein to an act of incest, which He had hitherto punished and would punish in the future, under the Mosaic law, by death, only because at that particular moment it was useful, even indispensable, to His plans.

We have been pleased to call our readers' attention to the radical nature of the language of myth, also because the central theme to which it refers is closely connected with what is still a burning issue today: sexual relations between spouses and birth control. Certainly people today would not venture to interpret the divine plan in such a way as to feel authorized to commit incest, as did Lot's daughters and the resourceful Tamar; on the other hand, the terrible fate of Sodom and Gomorrah and that of Er and Onan will not deter any sensible man from satisfying his healthy homosexual instincts if he prefers men to women, and, above all, will not convince husbands and wives to consider their marriage bed a baby factory. For the mentality of civilized nations today, preventing, limiting, postponing, or even eliminating the birth of children is no longer a question of religious and moral conscience, but an eminently social and economic problem, and it is certainly not the divine precept, but instinct and inattention that lead to blessed events. For the moment, even the Church, by accepting a "natu-ral" Malthusian system, seems no longer to insist on unlimited proliferation as the supreme goal of every conjugal union, and thus, implicitly and involuntarily, authorizes and blesses not only calculatedly barren embraces, but even an entire calculatedly bar-ren married life. One gets the clear impression that the basic principle of creation, "be fruitful and multiply," is about to collapse, or at any rate is prone to transgressions and infractions, its observance being subject to man's judgment or will. This suggests that for the Lord, from the standpoint of His plan, in this phase of His struggle with now unfettered man, the prolificacy of marriage has become a matter of indifference, no less than homosexual love and the lustful acts that every so often sweeten even the forced concubinage of wives and husbands.

This is how the situation looks today, and only the most narrow-minded obscurantism refuses to recognize it. Those who make it almost their profession to be scandalized will be scandalized; as will those who take satisfaction in being more Catholic than the pope; those who confuse, usually on purpose and in bad faith, morality with traditional or conventional forms that have become devoid of meaning today; and, of course, also those who in good faith conceive the divine plan not as a dynamic stratagem, but as a rigid system of ethical principles, built on vague concepts of infinite divine wisdom, goodness, and justice. But for them we have reserved a word of consolation and enlightenment.

Without casting doubt on the universal validity of the principle "be fruitful and multiply," we should stress that, according to the testimony of the Bible itself, the Lord only rarely insisted on the demographic increase of humanity: in the case of Adam and Eve, when it was a question of perpetuating the illustrious species uniquely destined to bear within it the idea of God; in the case of Noah, when the human race, reduced to himself and his family, had to start repopulating the earth; in the case of Abraham, because his descendants were destined to sustain and consolidate the idea and the law of the sole true and living God; and finally, in the case of the chosen people, whose numbers were supposed to equal those of the stars and the grains of dust on the earth. From these testimonies we would even go so far as to argue that unchecked and unlimited proliferation, even promoted by miracles, extramarital adventures, and incest, interested the Lord only at particular moments and in circumscribed ethnic and geographical settings. Some might object that the order to "be fruitful and multiply" was universal and concerned all living beings, meaning the whole of humanity inhabiting the terrestrial globe. The fact is, however, that the Lord was urging only the ancestors of the Jewish people, while demonstrating toward the rest of humanity the most solemn lack of interest. The Bible itself offers us an abundance of data showing how the Lord considered the lives of individuals and of whole populations irrelevant. In order to promote His chosen people, He judged the existence of others not only unimportant and useless but even pernicious, and with a wave of His hand eliminated from the face of the earth those who, in the final analysis, owed their lives to the fact of having been reproduced and multiplied. And, as we know, not even the innocent found favor in His sight. How many times did the Lord order Moses' people to exterminate their enemies ruthlessly? For the massacre of how many women and how many children is the Lord directly responsible? We could almost say that great human multitudes excite His aggressive instincts, as happened in the times of the deluge and the destruction of Sodom and Gomorrah. And if we take into account that today we number three and a half billion and that our relations with the Lord have once again reached a rather delicate phase, it truly gives one pause . . .

Anyway, you believers in good faith and you moralists in bad faith, disabuse yourselves: the Lord doesn't give a hoot about your prolificacy, and it doesn't occur to Him to demand that you rush to overpopulate this poor, already overcrowded globe. For the Lord the life of one individual or the lives of many count for no more than that of a blade of grass. What counts instead is the life of some, as in those remote times the life of Isaac was important to Him. If you are destined to bring an Isaac into the world, rest assured that the Lord will provide: you can take every precaution, and you will still procreate, by miracle, by incest, even with your homosexual partner. Don't worry about the Lord: He would rather have a new Noah today than four billion people tomorrow, He would rather have an Abraham who is not on the point of leaving for the moon but of lighting the sacrificial pyre.

As always, however, He must wait patiently for the advent of His man . . .

But at the "Abrahamic moment" in humanity's march, His man was already there, and destined to proliferate at all costs: he was to beget the phantom son who would reinstate and perpetuate the order of the curse.

And now, after this long digression, let us return to our Abraham, who, panting along after the three wayfarers, in search of an answer to his most pressing personal problems, involuntarily became a witness of the Lord's destructive intentions toward Sodom and Gomorrah, and incidentally the defense attorney for the population condemned to such a horrible fate.

Absorbed in his own dreadful problem and under the spell of the terrible scene that had taken place shortly before in front of his tent, Abraham was incapable of appreciating in all its horror the divine announcement about the impending end of the two thriving cities. This is not to say that he wasn't shocked by such a divine intention, but still, compared to his personal problems, everything else seemed to him of secondary importance. A single question revolved ceaselessly in his brain: how to arrive with Sarah at the unimaginable moment when he would have to take some initiative to beget the phantom son. True, the Lord, albeit in a crude, unmannerly way, had informed Sarah of the task, thus freeing him from taking the first and most difficult step; on the other hand, Abraham, who at that moment had no idea that Sarah had suffered a collapse, had reason to fear that her reaction to the humiliation she had received would be manifested in a furious rage and a still more stubborn resistance, which instead of bringing the divine plan closer to realization and himself to the goal, would irrevocably separate them even further. He therefore listened with bitterness, indeed, with hostile feelings, to the Lord's proposal to destroy Sodom and Gomorrah: he certainly hadn't run after Him to hear this, but to get a few suggestions on how to persuade his wife to cooperate.

Anyone who wants suggestions at all costs usually ends up finding one, and thus a very plausible idea flashed through Abraham's mind. He suddenly remembered those distant times when, making a heroic effort to overcome his congenital cowardice, he had descended onto the battlefield and rescued Lot with his family and possessions from the hands of the enemy. God alone knew that he hadn't had the slightest wish to lift even his little finger on behalf of that odious rascal, and if nevertheless he had exposed himself to the enemy's arrows and lances, he had done it for the love of Sarah. For Sarah was fond of her unworthy kinsman, while he wanted only to please her so as to ingratiate himself. She had indeed rejoiced in the deliverance of her loved ones, although, to tell the truth, her gratitude has been short-lived: she had accepted him once in her bed with sensible resignation, and even a second time after stubborn resistance, but a third time she hadn't accepted him at all, and couldn't have cared less that the man beseeching her had been her brother's heroic savior.

But the fact remained that twice in the past, Sara had put up with him in the marriage bed on account of Lot: wasn't it perhaps possible that, on account of Lot, she would put up with him again, at least once? All of a sudden, the idea that had flashed through his mind seemed wonderful, and he seized on it with great excitement: he was being offered another opportunity to save Lot and his family! Of course, he couldn't ask this of the Lord as a personal favor, having learned from experience that the Lord always left him in the lurch when in his own interests he turned to Him for help, or at least advice. Although when it came to knowledge of the Lord, he was still a beginner, Abraham had already had some experience in dealing with Him and therefore resorted to cunning. He preferred to remind the Lord of the divine virtues that he had naïvely attributed to Him in the past, and with which the Lord moreover had always been pleased. How could the Lord reject his plea, when Abraham brought up that famous justice, of which actually he had never in his life seen any indication, but which the Lord cared so much about? In his excited state of mind, Abraham felt he could prevail on the Lord by taking advantage of His vanity. He therefore shrewdly appealed to His magnanimity and generosity: *"Peradventure there be fifty righteous within the city: wilt thou also destroy and not spare the place for the fifty righteous that are therein?"* he began. The Lord was taken aback: He found Himself in a trap and could not help listening to His follower. But He did so lightheartedly, knowing full well that there were not fifty righteous men in all of Sodom. Abraham, on the other hand, didn't know whether there were or not, and actually didn't much care: what mattered to him was that there be a wide enough margin to save Lot and his family.

The dispute between the Lord and Abraham was already bewildering to us in our childhood, and we have never been able to understand why Abraham, if he seriously meant to save Sodom and Gomorrah, did not behave with greater firmness and dare to demand of the Lord that the sinners be spared even by the presence of a single innocent. Once he had reached the number ten, why didn't he go down to five, to four, to three? Let us go ahead and suppose that he really wanted to save Lot and his family, and that this was all he had in mind: so why didn't he have the guts to reduce the limit of the "righteous" to four, that being the number of persons in his kinsman's immediate family? Abraham had no way of knowing whether there were ten righteous people in Sodom or not, but he was sure that Lot, his wife, and his two daughters were "righteous" in that they were not homosexuals, and obviously this was what it was all about. Only recently have we learned, thanks to a legend preserved and handed down in the rabbinical writings, that, according to the tradition, Lot had two married daughters in addition to the two notorious ones, which means that the family contingent, with the latter and their fiancés and the husbands of the other two, came precisely to ten. In the light of this information, we thus see that Abraham was by no means being compliant. Aware of his own purpose, he did not yield to his congenital cowardice but played his cards shrewdly. Not without a certain naïveté, he presumed with certainty that there were ten "sexually" righteous persons in the city of Sodom, and to tell the truth, he was not proposing to save Sodom because of them, but trying to save these ten persons while incidentally saving the city itself.

As we know—and next morning Abraham learned it too—things did not go exactly as he had imagined. The Lord did not judge Lot's two other daughters and their respective husbands to be righteous, nor the two future sons-in-law who had cohabited with him, and not even did Lot's wife (a pure-blooded Sodomite besides) turn out to be completely righteous, and Sodom perished and Gomorrah perished. But in taking leave of the Lord, Abraham, although upset by the ugly turn that things were about to take in both his private life and that of others, could at least set out for home with the clear conscience of one who has done the best he could. As he walked along, he certainly did not delude himself about the immediate effects of the good news he would tell his wife. But he had reason to think that in some way she would appreciate his loyalty.

That in the meantime, however, the beautiful Sarah had been transformed into an old hag, he would never have imagined!

And never had the Lord's will seemed further from being fulfilled!

VIII. Honeymoon in Gerar

READING THE STORY OF ABRAHAM AND SARAH IN THE BIBLE, one can't help feeling a certain annoyance on coming to the episode of Abimelech. One gets a clear impression that it is a poor copy of the adventure in Egypt, and moreover the episode reappears once more, reproduced almost literally, in the story of the son who was called Laughter. And while the ignominious Egyptian adventure marks the turning point for Abraham's further career, the Gerar episode may seem unimportant for our hero's future vicissitudes: clearly the thousand pieces of silver that the hapless king would later pay to Abraham to cover up the scandal were worth less to the latter than the price of a single one of the camels he had received from Pharaoh when he was in the direst poverty. Because of its moralizing interpretation, the Gerar episode is the umpteenth testimony of the protection God extends to His chosen people in delicate situations. But any reader endowed with good sense and good taste immediately retorts that there wasn't all that much to protect: in Egypt, yes, Sarah had been a young woman of extraordinary beauty, but by the time she came to Gerar, she had already reached the age of ninety, and even by our reckoning of the years would be considered a rather elderly lady, so that the episode, already pointless in itself, seems regrettably disgusting and almost absurd.

It may even be unnecessary to say that our opinion on the subject is diametrically the opposite, and not only because we systematically uphold the reliability of our single source, but also and primarily because, in our judgment, the Abimelech episode forms an integral part of our protagonists' story: indeed, without it, it would be hard to arrive at the birth of the phantom son. But *honni soit qui mal y pense!* We, who swear by the reliability of the Bible on this point as well, insist that Abimelech did not touch Sarah and Isaac was truly sired by Abraham, as God had announced.

We would really be perplexed by a scholar who in his work granted his imagination only a tenth of the scope that we, from time to time, grant entirely. But if we hadn't given free rein to our imagination, we would have found it hard to detect the structural connection among the three episodes of Abraham, Sodom, and Lot, a connection that cannot fail to interest the humanistic sciences. We are much less presumptuous about the adventure in Gerar, and are far from stating that scholars might find it useful to recognize its close connection with the story of Abraham and Sarah. Certainly, however, it won't do them any harm, nor make them lose their tempers, if they would be kind enough to take it as we do—as a necessary link between two episodes in our story. All of them will undoubtedly agree with us in recognizing that there is an enormous gap between the desperation of the two dejected old people sitting in the shade of the terebinth tree and the birth of little Isaac, and that this gap must somehow be bridged. What seems to us rather strange is that it hasn't occurred to anyone to see in the Abimelech episode the only psychological bridge capable of joining the two sides of the abyss.

With the same naturalness with which the Bible tells it, we note the fact that *Abraham journeyed from thence toward the south country, and dwelled between Kadesh and Shur, and sojourned in Gerar.* But if we think it over carefully and keep in mind that Abraham had lived in the grove of Mamre, at Hebron, for almost twenty-five years, in ever increasing comfort and a relative quiet that bordered on a kind of happiness, his sudden departure really ought not to seem so natural, and we feel compelled to ask why.

In reporting the movements and displacements of Abraham and his people, the biblical text always gives or suggests the reasons: the departure from the Mamre oak grove is the only case where the Bible gives no explanation, and we cannot think of any legend that might be of help to us. To depart in such a great hurry from a place where one has lived comfortably for almost a quarter of a century seems, for our historical sources, to be an absolutely normal and peaceful event, not requiring any further clarification. But if we reflect a moment on our specific case, all of a sudden the terseness of the biblical text no longer seems so strange. Had we been in Abraham's shoes, wouldn't we ourselves have resorted perhaps to the expedient of travel? After what had recently happened among the terebinths of Mamre, it had become psychologically impossible to stay there.

The Mamre grove harbored the human order that Abraham had established piece by piece, at the cost of painful sacrifice, bitterness, and humiliation, and from the dense foliage of the terebinths a great harmony seemed to emanate, the melancholy harmony of permanence, which just missed being happiness. It was there that Abraham hoped to spend the remaining decades of his life, increasing his wealth, instructing Ishmael to receive and carry on the duties of his office, and enjoying, above all, the fond relations that had been created between him and his still beautiful and youthful Sarah, and where, in exchange for his renunciation of amorous passion, he could find the lukewarm languor of her sentiments as mother, sister, and friend. For this he showed her his gratitude by an assiduous and gallant courtship, well aware that only by love's magic, albeit in a minor key, was it possible to preserve the woman's youth and beauty beyond the limits of old age. And he showed her his gratitude with gifts, quite conscious that elegant new clothes and rare and costly jewels constituted a more effective beauty treatment than fine words. But, in reality, it was not merely a question of gratitude, much less of disinterested behavior, for he still felt an overwhelming spiritual need to adore this unattainable woman, and in the depths of his soul he never ceased to hope that sooner or later the hour would come when Sarah— realizing finally that the miracle of her youth and beauty was due exclusively to her husband's loving magic—would grant him her love in return. He did not let himself be discouraged even by the thought that implacable nature would gradually overcome his mild sorcery, being convinced that in his woman even real old age would take the appearance of a subtle withering and would thus preserve for him a sufficient erotic fascination. He therefore summoned all his patience, and he may not have been entirely mistaken in his calculations in hoping that she, who had succeeded in simultaneously becoming mother, sister, and friend, would at some time or another, with a resigned gesture of gratitude and pity, or rather with an elegant gesture of understanding and wisdom, also succeed in becoming a wife. Abraham never stopped dreaming that sooner or later the time would come when Sarah would look on him with new eyes; the hint of a mischievous and virginal smile would appear on her splendid lips; then, shrugging her shoulders, she would approach him, and putting one hand on his arm, say: "You deserve it, my poor friend, it's time I finally started treating you better. If you don't disdain my faded charms, from now on I'll be a good wife to you." Whereupon he, beside himself with joy, would protest and show his love and desire for her more than ever. At that moment true happiness would begin for them.

But the Lord rudely destroyed the dreams of the Mamre oak grove. On the night when the doom of Sodom and Gomorrah was about to be sealed, Abraham wept and cried out to Heaven: "Why have you done this, O Lord? I always wanted her to get old, only not as the result of your anger, but protected by the magic of my love and adoration! I always wanted to have her back as a wife, but glowing with youth and beauty preserved by my sorcery, and not prostrated by old age! I kept dreaming constantly of lying in bed with her, but as a result of my persistent and polite courtship and her touching consent, and not by your brutal command! In my religious sensuality I never stopped cherishing voluptuous images of physical love, but I never thought I'd still have to worry about procreating and forcing her to give birth. Why have you done this, O Lord, when everything has been going fine because of Ishmael? Why have you done this to me, and since you've done it, why don't you tell me what to do now?"

Actually there was nothing to be done. Or rather, if anything could be done, it was to cast out as far as possible the upsetting memory of the most terrible day in their lives. Like two prisoners condemned to death, they dragged out their days under the nightmare of the approaching fatal hour. Sarah shut herself up in her tent, without emerging even for meals, and she covered with a scarf the gold mirror she had received as a gift from Pharaoh, never wanting to look at herself again. And Abraham preferred to disturb as little as possible the tormented solitude of her collapse. One by one the weeks went by, and he no longer had three months at his disposal in which to fulfill the Lord's will, nor even two—indeed, all of a sudden he realized that more than half of the allotted time had passed. Alas, for some time he had given up deluding himself that instead of three months he had been granted as many as five! He had more reason than ever to fear that the Lord would lose patience. And he imagined the Lord springing up out of the earth or dropping from the sky to appear suddenly before His faithful, but at the same time listless and—it must be admitted—rebellious, servant. And he realized how He would be capable of resorting to force to see His will executed, thus with the risk of another humiliation for himself and Sarah. He thought of this repugnant possibility with growing frequency and terror, and no longer dared sit in his favorite spot in the shade of the terebinths, thus feeling displaced in his own little kingdom. His residence for a quarter of a century, to which he had become fondly accustomed, had turned overnight into a den of threatening specters, where he ventured to move from one tent to another, almost stealthily, only after cautiously looking inside and quelling unspeakable fears. Life had become simply unbearable.

In these circumstances he had the revolutionary idea of moving. Ever since his disgrace in Egypt, he had always had a holy terror of any change of residence, but now it seemed to him that this was all that could save them. Save them from what? Certainly Abraham would have been ashamed to admit it, but—though not completely convinced—he hoped somehow that if he changed his address, not even the Lord would be able to find him.

Beyond this absurd but fundamental hope, he also expected other results from his idea: first of all, it would do his wife a world of good. Sarah, seeing her husband come in with a solemn look, had been seized by an insane fear, convinced that he was about to speak of "that horrible thing." When Abraham informed her of his plan, she felt relieved, and in a few minutes was rejuvenated by several years. "No words ever sounded sweeter to my ears, my poor friend!" she said, and a faint blush tinged her face, ravaged by much weeping. And Abraham, himself flushed with emotion, went on: "O my lady, I won't let you pine away all alone in the darkness of your tent! That is no fate for you, my goddess! You were born to shine and dazzle with your beauty and youth! A change of climate, new surroundings, new faces will be a balm to your body and spirit. We'll go somewhere more civilized, my love . . ." Sarah looked at him in astonishment, but all of a sudden her beautiful brows darkened, almost as though under the shadow of a cloud: "It's no use, my poor friend. I'll never recover, as long as the threat of that horrible thing hangs over my head!" Abraham, his face now flaming, vehemently seized his wife's hand. "Stop thinking about that threat!" he cried impetuously. "Stop worrying about some frightful dream. Nothing is going to happen, my little princess. The will of the Lord will always be strong enough to prevail over man's, but it is helpless before non-will, human passivity. From nothing is born nothing, my darling, and for me it's more important to see your youth and beauty bloom again than to spoil them by threatening you with something that I don't even want myself. We won't talk about this whole business anymore, and we won't even think about it!" "Oh, Abraham!" cried Sarah, and while two joyful tears shone in her eyes, she stroked her husband's hand with timid gratitude. And when that bony, freckled hand touched him, Abraham felt that he had never loved and desired his wife so much.

News of the unexpected departure aroused no little excitement in the tribe of shepherds, and the whole encampment looked like a scurrying anthill: it was no small matter to strike the tents after having been settled there for twenty-five years! If the idea of moving at first aroused a few worries in some, this soon changed into general euphoria, due simply to the unusual, but all the more cheering, spectacle offered by the patriarch and his wife. Overnight they had shed the gloomy air that had hitherto ravaged their appearance and now busied themselves with fresh youthfulness, with a mischievous smile on their lips, visibly enthusiastic about their coming departure. From all these factors, the good shepherds concluded that their master and mistress had a good reason for being cheerful, and they accordingly expected a further increase in prosperity from the imminent move. Meanwhile, with extraordinary intuition, they saw a connection between the unexpected uprooting of the camp and the events of the memorable days a few months earlier: the painful and humiliating surgical operation, the visit of the three mysterious wayfarers, who had plunged the whole tribe into an atmosphere of the macabre, and especially the frightful tragedy of Sodom and Gomorrah: although from Hebron, it took a little over half a day on foot to reach the two incinerated cities, they were still close enough to raise fears of a similar disaster in minds prone to anxiety. In the final analysis, the whole tribe instinctively shared their leader's sentiments: it would be a good idea to put the greatest possible distance between themselves and the site of these bad memories. And if the good mood of the master and mistress infused them with feverish excitement, this in its turn fed the enthusiasm of the patriarch, who almost ended by persuading himself that he couldn't have made a better decision.

The most valid and heartening proof of this conviction was the fact that Sarah was regaining her normal appearance. Which is putting it mildly: rather she was like someone recovering from a long and grave illness, who turns again toward life, and full of confidence and a longing for health absorbs the revitalizing energies of existence with every pore of her body and soul. The vague smile that never left her lips imparted an adolescent charm to her mellowed state, which this time we might more rightly call a reflowering of youth. On the road they met other nomadic tribes, received people in their encampment, and paid visits to other tribal chieftains, and Sarah had ample opportunity to shine, to show off her expensive clothes and precious jewels, and above all to make experiments, in which she noted that all the women still envied her and that the men still gave her appraising sidelong glances of the kind they usually didn't waste on women who were out of the running. Compared to the happy times when all men had looked at her with eyes turbid with bestial desire, this may not have been much, but still it was satisfying for the moment, after having descended into the hell of old age. The day after such experiments she would gaze attentively at herself for a long time in her mirror, until one day, though it made her feel rather ashamed, she could not help wondering if in her rejuvenation treatment she would ever reach the point of again being ardently desired by some man other than Abraham.

She was reborn: she hoped, trembled, and dreamed, while her beauty bloomed anew, clothed in the golden colors of an autumn sunset. The journey across the broad plains was a real triumph for Abraham. His gaze, more satisfied from one day to the next, fed on the magnificent sight of his wife, who because of him had returned from the underworld. Never could a therapy have proved more effective! So much so that when they arrived at the borders of

Gerar, Abraham found himself in the grip of an unexpected anxiety that he himself called exaggerated. But the truth is the truth: he was tempted to ask Sarah to hide in the basket!

Ah, the basket! During their preparations for the journey, it had reappeared on the scene, stirring up the most rankling memories to such a degree that for a moment they both feared the unseemly collapse of their flimsily based euphoria. But Sarah, almost as though following a medical prescription warning against disagreeable emotions, saved the situation. Casting a rather acid smile at her husband, who was now prepared for the worst, she remarked resignedly, "I don't think we'll need that basket anymore." Abraham went red up to the ears and lowered his eyes. "So long as Sarah is the most beautiful woman in the world, we'll always need the basket," he replied courteously with a fine compliment, and at first his wife didn't know whether to laugh or cry. "Never again will anyone want to kill Abraham because of Sarah, my poor dear friend!" she said finally with a deep sigh. "But even if it should happen, the basket is no use, as we saw the last time. It would make much better sense, as it would have before, if you'd just say I'm your wife."

Abraham always felt cut to the quick whenever Sarah reminded him of the historical gaffe by which he had managed to ruin their married life. But, in essence, Sarah was perfectly right: if a Pharaoh would not have abducted the wife of a tribal leader to whom he had offered hospitality, even when the woman in question was the beautiful Sarah, she would not be abducted by the king of Gerar, all the more since Sarah was no longer all that beautiful. Nevertheless, having reached the outskirts of the city of Gerar, Abraham fell prey to the old anxiety, which suggested to him that, as a temporary solution, he conceal his wife in the basket. And no amount of reason and good sense could overcome his uneasiness: what if Abimelech, despite it all, sent people to carry off Sarah?

He was angry with himself, called himself an old fool, and screwed up his courage by repeating to himself that he was no longer a starving beggar but a powerful and respected lord. And yet his nervousness, instead of passing, grew by the hour. Still he did not have the nerve to ask Sarah to shut herself up in the basket, if only for those few hours needed to put up their tents: indeed, he himself found the idea extremely ridiculous and humiliating, and repeatedly rejected it with anger. But neither could he sit with his hands folded, because while his people were setting up camp on the meadows bordering the city, a crowd of townsfolk came out to watch them, and Abraham's suspicious eyes made out a number of suspect characters who without a shadow of a doubt had to be scouts whose job it was to supply the harems of the king and the court dignitaries with beautiful foreign women. And, damn it, Sarah was somehow always in full view, and, damn it, to Abraham it seemed ages since she'd looked so fresh, youthful, exciting, and provocative! The patriarch, though he had his hands full with other matters, first admonished her, then scolded her, and finally ordered her not to show herself, but to retire into the tent. Sarah at first was amused, then she teased him: "What's the matter with you, my poor friend? Do you seriously believe that all eyes are still dazzled by my irresistible beauty and that tomorrow the king's men will come to take me away?" But Abraham was in no mood for joking: "Get in the tent!" he said in a sharp and irrevocable tone. And Sarah, obeying the order, was visibly irritated.

Before nightfall, Abraham had to overcome another irrational fixation from the ugly Egyptian past. For days he had been bothered by the fear of neglecting a timely measure of prudence by not convoking his people and reminding them of that certain *whole* truth according to which Sarah was not only his wife, but also his sister, sister at least of Haran's daughter Milcah, who in her turn was the sister of Milcah's father's daughter, namely Iscah: unfortunately, not even he remembered exactly how he had once managed to construct in such a masterly fashion that deceptive "whole" truth for the purpose of showing that Sarah was so much the sister of some and of many as to render the already evanescent fact that she was also his wife insignificant, improbable, and impossible. But here too he ended by getting angry with himself. For even had a lunatic or blind man turned up who wanted to abduct Sarah, the surest protection would have been to let it be known as best he could that she was his wife.

Next morning, he had occasion to be convinced that it would be superfluous, tragically ridiculous, to take any measures of precaution: Sarah herself was her own best protection. For on entering his wife's tent, he found her looking peaked and down in the mouth, as though all the beneficial effects of the journey had come to nothing. His first impulse was to say a few kind and comforting words to her, but it took only one grim look on his wife's part to dampen his courage and also his good will. In his irritation, he took his revenge by toying with the idea that all he had to do as a precaution would be to persuade Sarah to let herself be seen up close by the king's emissaries, and to invite his people to trumpet far and wide that this surly and slovenly old woman was their leader's wife. But Abraham was too soft-hearted to act on such malignant thoughts, and besides he was tired, very tired.

Still, in spite of it all, it wouldn't hurt to be a little prudent. It would never have occurred to Abraham that legend was much stronger, more real and vital, than even tangible facts, and by becoming a constituent element of a people's spiritual patrimony, remains unchanged by the passage of time. In vain had many decades gone by since the sojourn in Egypt, in vain had the tribe of shepherds witnessed their lady's slow but inexorable withering, in vain had the patriarch revealed to them the essential truth as compared to the whole truth: the legend had been established for good from the moment it was born and had no wish to adapt itself to time's swift passage. Abraham had no idea that while he, fortified in his judgment by obvious facts, had seen that any measure of precaution was pointless, his people were conversing with their inquisitive visitors, and between hints and whispers that gave their gossip a tone of importance and mystery, letting everyone know that the most beautiful woman in the world was hidden in their leader's tent. And when the inquisitive visitors, their curiosity aroused, inquired how this marvelous creature kept under lock and key was related to their leader, they—after some hemming and hawing, but unanimously—declared that she was his sister!

Abraham, unaware of all this, had completely succumbed to his sadness over the failure of his therapy, which during the journey across the plain had promised astonishing results and instead had ended with Sarah in greater disarray, looking uglier and more run-down than she had ever been since the moment of the Lord's visit. This unforeseen result of the treatment was so painful to him that he seriously began to consider the possibility of giving it all up, of relinquishing for good the desperate struggle by which he had tried to restore at least a pale reflection of his wife's former youth and beauty, and resigning himself to defeat. That absurd and pointless wish of the Lord's, of which nothing more had been said, and which he now thought of only rarely and almost with an attitude of idle curiosity, came back to him the way it had seemed at the moment when it was first communicated to him: as absolutely ridiculous and nothing more. And Abraham couldn't help letting forth a bitter little laugh, not devoid of a certain sarcasm, in the Lord's direction. So not even He could do everything.

But it is hard to relinquish for good something that is more or less the meaning and purpose of our existence. Abraham, now driven only by a kind of humanitarian sentiment, decided to make one more attempt to boost his wife's morale. But he was equally determined not to lose his temper. He was careful to announce his visit in advance in order to give Sarah time to perform her toilette. Thus she received him decently dressed, but for all that no better disposed toward him; indeed, she gave the poor devil a sullen look as though he'd come on purpose to torment her. Abraham had only to see her to feel all his nerves trembling and his brain becoming clouded from great hot waves of blood. He responded to her hostile gaze with an equally hostile glare of his own and found he had no urge to soothe or caress this living statue of desperation. It may have been because he judged his undertaking doomed from the start that for the first time in his life, he spoke to his wife harshly, but he also knew that if he tried to control himself, he would have an apoplectic fit. For a few moments he stood there motionless, staring almost in astonishment at this intractable and disagreeable woman, now old and ugly besides, who had soured his whole existence, and finally he followed the dictates of the rage that had been accumulating all his life in the depths of his soul. He struck his fist on the palm of his other hand and started shouting: "Enough! Stop it, for God's sake! I'm sick and tired of seeing that awful martyred look on your face! What's the matter with you anyway? I tell you once more that you have nothing to fear: what happened once isn't going to happen again. Or maybe"—and now he went red in the face because he felt he was on the point of saying something horrible—"or maybe that's just why you're worried, because this time you can't expect the king's messengers, like you did Pharaoh's?"

He fell immediately silent, fearing that his wife would jump to her feet and give him a well-deserved slap. But Sarah, who from the beginning had listened in surprise, and then almost in amusement had scrutinized her husband in this state of mind so unusual for him, did not jump to her feet with the expected indignation. Becoming no less red in the face than he, she put her hands to her head and with a convulsed gesture rubbed her forehead. Then she raised her eyes, burning with a strange flame, and murmured: "You've guessed it. That's why I'm suffering. It hurts me . . ."

Abraham went, if possible, still redder in the face, and took a step backward, terrified like someone seeing the devil. He was totally unprepared for such a shameless reply, by which Sarah had managed in a single moment to sully his honor as a husband, his masculine self-esteem, the sanctity of his love, and the meaning of his whole life. Another surge of blood rose to his head, further darkening his reason. "So that's it!" he cried, in a voice that wavered between pain and contempt. "So that's what this is all about! You still have such thoughts in your head! A fine thing, I must say . . . For years I've tried to accept the idea that you didn't want my love, but I was fool enough to think that you didn't want the love of other men either! And I would certainly never have imagined that you were capable of letting me know it with such indecent frankness!"

Sarah, both astonished and amused, but with growing gaiety, observed her husband's rage, and finally, with a gesture full of compassion, reached out her hands and interrupted him in a soft, serene voice: "You misunderstand me, my poor Abraham, you completely misunderstand me. All the gods, including your Lord, can see into my heart, and they know that it holds no shameful desires or sinful dreams. They know, and they are my witnesses, that not even in thought do I long for a man's embrace, and that I'd be the most desperate creature in the world if the king were to have me transported to his harem, where at my age and with the way I look, I'd cut a poor figure. It's a question . . ." "Enough!" shouted Abraham and his purple face was contorted with pain and rage. "Enough! Now you've given yourself away! The only reason you're frightened of a romantic adventure is because you're afraid of cutting a poor figure! If you thought you were younger and more beautiful, your heart would be throbbing with desire and excitement, and you'd be the happiest woman in the world. You wouldn't even think of what I'd have to suffer, and the ignominy I'd have to endure! No matter how much time goes by, no one's nature can change." And driven by an irresistible impulse, he took a step toward his wife, and bringing his face, contorted with indignation, close to her astonished eyes, he shouted in a hoarse but ringing voice: "Slut!"

But meanwhile Sarah, who was staring with growing stupor at her husband in the grip of this absolutely unheard-of state of mind, underwent a surprising transformation. Just as some three months earlier the Lord's scornful words had made her age, now the word "slut," almost as though it were a magical formula, in a few moments gave her back her youth and beauty. Her face brightened, her complexion took on a youthful freshness, her eyes shone with a flirtatious sparkle, the hint of a blissful smile appeared on her lips, and her whole figure, with almost imperceptible flexibility, straightened up—and this marvelous transformation was so striking that Abraham's bitter contempt dissolved on the spot. He could not decide whether it was his own eyes deceiving him, or if a miracle had taken place, but once again Sarah was young and beautiful, as she had been before the Lord's visit. Or rather, she had become much younger and much more beautiful than before, as she had been perhaps at the time of the visit to Egypt.

And now this reborn Sarah, with a fond and spontaneous gesture, which re-evoked in Abraham's mind memories of the first weeks of their marriage, grasped her husband's trembling hands, and while a blissful and beatifying smile shone on her face, spoke these words: "Oh, you crazy fool! I should really get angry for the way you insulted me, but I understand and appreciate the feelings that drove you to it—oh, how I appreciate them! But, I repeat, you misunderstand me, my dear friend. Believe me, I don't even think of what would happen in the king's harem if I were taken there, or how it would happen. I not only don't think about it with desire, but not even with horror, simply because my thoughts don't get that far. My thoughts don't even get to the threshold of the royal harem, they stop at the threshold of my own tent. And if you wouldn't let yourself be carried away in such a touching way by mistaken jealousy, but were to try lovingly to understand my state of mind, then you'd understand what hurts me without feeling sullied in your pride and vanity as a man and husband. Because I'd be lying if I denied that it hurts me: it truly hurts me that nobody now thinks to abduct me from my tent, because that means that no one looks on me as a woman anymore, but just an old carcass that it's not worth the trouble to abduct. Which also means that even in my tent they leave an old carcass."

For all the casual elegance with which she expressed herself, trying to maintain an impersonal detachment from her own feelings, at the end two tears appeared in her eyes and all the beauty and youth that, at the miraculous touch of the magic word "slut," had come back to her from one moment to the next now began to dissolve with visible rapidity. Abraham, again moved to the depths of his heart and ashamed of his unusual behavior, kept his eyes lowered, while he racked his brain to find another magical word with which to arrest the fearful process of re-aging. But he was too upset at first to think of any useful idea; it was much easier to yield to the suggestion of his deeply moved heart. He let himself fall to his knees before the adored woman, encircled her waist with his arms, and pressing his face against her abdomen, he murmured with conviction: "It's better this way . . ." Then Sarah, distractedly tracing a line with her middle finger on her husband's bald skull, gave a long sigh: "That may be, but I don't know for what . . ." "For you," exclaimed Abraham passionately, "to preserve yourself for me, who loves you with constant fidelity and growing love, and in whose eyes you'll always remain young, beautiful, and alluring!" Now Sarah, partly from irritation, partly from affection, gave a little tug to the beard of the man kneeling before her, and shook her head in discouragement. "That's just what I can't believe, my dear old Abraham," she said with another long sigh. "I know very well that your fine words, your kind compliments, your endless courtship are only meant to keep up my morale and convince me of the reality of an illusion in which I'd gladly believe but unfortunately can't. This you must understand, my dear friend! If for once I could hear your expressions of enthusiasm and adoration from the lips of another man, perhaps I'd even find it easier to believe you. But . . . your old Sarah isn't tempting anymore to any man," she concluded with ill-concealed bitterness, again grazing her husband's bald head with her finger. At this gesture Abraham exclaimed pathetically, "But I want you until my last breath!" and pressed his face against his wife's abdomen.

At that moment, a kind of perplexed cough came from the entrance to the tent, and the venerable couple turned to see old Eliezer almost rigid with shame for having witnessed such an intimate scene between his master and mistress. Sarah, making vague gestures to adjust her hair, retired to the back of the tent, while Abraham, relinquishing any attempt at dignity, tried with the help of his hands to get back on his feet, his eyes darting bolts of anger at the old servant. Eliezer, disconsolately spreading his arms wide, hastened to justify his undesired presence by announcing nothing less than the arrival of messengers from King Abimelech of Gerar. At this unexpected news, Abraham was seized by such agitation that his anger went up in smoke. He would have bet that the king's men were bringing him a negative reply to his request to be allowed to stay, a request that he had not failed to accompany with proper gifts. At the prospect of having to spend the night taking down the tents that had just been put up, he grimaced, stroked his beard, and gave a sigh: "Let's get it over with. Send them in."

The idea that they might have come for Sarah didn't even cross his mind. He never even dreamed that his shepherds had divulged the legend instead of the facts, and even less that this legend had piqued the fancy of King Abimelech.

The king's emissaries, charged with scouting for women, though unable to give an exact report on the nomad tribe and its chieftain, had painted in lively colors certain disconnected details about the patriarch, said to be protected by a mysterious and invisible God, and about his extraordinarily beautiful sister, once a favorite of Pharaoh's. The petty desert king, who, unlike the divine sovereign of Egypt, felt like a nonentity, but on the other hand, shared the snobbish opinion of many that a woman's worth is in direct proportion to the social position of her lovers, welcomed the news with lively interest, and excitedly urged his men to tell him more about this marvelous creature. They didn't have the nerve to confess that they hadn't yet seen the marvel in question, but having lent credence to the gossip they had collected, they now laid it on thicker. "Bring her to me," ordered the king, without further hesitation, and he also commanded them to offer a suitable dowry to the foreign tribal leader. But in the end, almost by divine inspiration, he wanted to be reassured about a delicate particular: "Are you sure she's the chieftain's sister, and not his wife?" Like the Egyptian sovereign before him, he raised this question out of mere prudence and was surprised to see the puzzled expressions on the faces of his men; they looked at each other and began to whisper among themselves. Truly, up until now, they all could have sworn that the legendary woman was the chieftain's sister, except that when they were asked directly, they began to remember the hemming and hawing of the shepherds, and much as the version they had reported seemed more probable to them, other words began to buzz maddeningly in their ears, according to which somebody in that complicated family was somebody's wife, and thinking back on it, they felt their blood run cold at the possibility, conceded but not admitted, that it was the beautiful woman who was that somebody's wife. Finally Abimelech, having eyed them in a way that boded nothing good, rebuked them and gave them these instructions: "The question needs to be clarified. So go to the chieftain himself and ask him personally. If the woman turns out to be his wife, leave her in peace. I like matters to be clear."

But his liking for clarity was not enough to ward off the troubles and fears lying in wait. By ordering his men to clarify the situation with a simple question—"What is this woman to you?"—King Abimelech, even had he been endowed with an exceptional imagination, could have had no idea of the hornet's nest of complex and painful problems he was about to stir up in the souls of the venerable couple. After the usual preliminary salaams, which were especially warm and encouraged Abraham's hope that at least he would not be driven away from one hour to the next, the messengers' question was delivered and terrified him like a bolt of lightning. He went pale, his sight grew dim, it seemed to him that everything around him was beginning to whirl, and all of a sudden he had the precise impression that an immense danger was hanging over his life and that of the whole tribe. His lips began to tremble, and trembled so shamefully that he was completely unable to utter the short sentence that was ready on the tip of his tongue: *She is my sister.*

But fortunately the effect of the lightning bolt did not last more than a moment, the terror vanished, and in Abraham's mind a beneficent light shone: now he felt quite content that his trembling lips had not been able to whisper the old lie. Uttered now, it would have been nothing but a mechanical, and in any case irrational, repetition of the fatal one long ago. Everything he had thought and pondered in recent years came back to his mind in a flash, and the line of conduct to follow presented itself clearly. Yes, it's true, it would have been enough to state it simply—*She is my wife*—and the king's messengers would have gone away, disappointed perhaps, but reassured by his response. To eliminate from their minds the slightest remaining doubt, Abraham could have answered in a more detailed way, saying: "She has been my wife now for over forty years—I'm about to turn one hundred and she is the respectable age of ninety." But wishing to dispel not only doubt in the king's messengers, but even the wish to commit some rash act, Abraham decided it would be more appropriate, before speaking, to turn around with an intentionally dignified air, take a few slow and majestic steps toward his wife, then with a gallant and affectionate gesture take her arm and lead her, with the same slow and majestic steps, before the king's messengers, so that the lamp hanging in the entrance might illuminate her face. Just by imagining all this he felt remarkably relieved, and an imperceptible smile, both crafty and tender, appeared on his lips. "Sister or wife, it's all the same now," he thought, comforted and also deeply moved.

From the majestic old man's behavior, the messengers realized that he was preparing himself for some great scenic effect, and so they waited with a certain curiosity to see what would happen. But a sudden backward step by the patriarch, who, having turned around, had moved slowly and solemnly toward the figure of a woman hidden in the shadows at the back of the tent, completely disconcerted them. The king's messengers could not see that the crafty, tender smile on Abraham's lips was giving way to an expression of the utmost stupor. They could not understand that what they were expecting as the most natural thing in the world would so astound Abraham as to make him take a wavering step back. They could not know that for years and years Sarah had never been so young and beautiful as she had become once more at the moment of their entrance, or to be exact, at the moment when they had asked the question: "What is this woman to you?"

Only to Abraham was it obvious that a miracle had occurred: this splendid young woman whose slender figure stood, motionless and yet vibrant in every fiber of its flesh, in the shadows in the back of the tent, looked more like his daughter than his sister. It was a true miracle, which astonished, overwhelmed, and arrested both thought and breath. How could he approach this portent, take her arm and lead her forward, announcing with a solemn gesture: "She is my wife"? Time had stopped for an immeasurable interval, and Abraham did not know how long he stood there, rigid, admiring Sarah in mystical rapture. Perhaps it was for only a few seconds, perhaps a long minute, but in the end it seemed to Abraham that endless time had gone by before he realized that the slim adolescent figure was trembling all over and that in her eyes flashed the sparks of someone who was anticipating the ecstasy of love. Only then did the first thought make headway in Abraham's dazed mind: he understood that it was not so much a question of a divine miracle, as of the apotheosis of the tireless and unremitting magic of his love. And at that moment, like an illumination, he realized that Sarah would not be sorry to leave, and he also realized that it was his duty to let her go.

Almost in a state of drunkenness, he acted with the clear sensation that all his gestures were directed by an outside force. Contrary to his plan, he did not take Sarah's arm, but with a decisive motion took her by the hand, and like a father presenting his daughter for the first time to a group of suitors, led her solemnly forward into the well-lighted part of the tent. For a long moment he stood motionless beside her likewise motionless figure, and eyed the effect with secret excitement; finally he slightly raised the arm with which he held his wife's hand, and in a low but firm voice declared: *"She is my sister!"* From that moment on, everything happened as in the distant past, with monotonous similarity: the king's messengers expressed their lord's respectful wishes, and conveyed his greetings and his promises regarding a long and peaceful sojourn and numerous rich gifts. Compared to the past, there was only one difference, but a striking one: this time Sarah, as she was about to be led away, did not dart him a look full of contempt and open hatred, but like a nubile maiden, modestly lowered her eyes and before crossing the threshold of the tent, seized her husband's hand with a convulsive gesture and kissed it.

The drunken stupor of the miracle continued to possess him even when he was left alone in the tent. In the dark silence that quickly followed, Abraham could almost hear the cold dismay that had fallen on his people outside, but he did not stop smiling blissfully. He was completely content. *"Then,"* he pondered half-aloud, "I behaved like a disgusting worm, *now* I've been great." Then another thought came to him: *"Then* I lost Sarah, *now* I've regained her." Finally, with an air of triumph, he concluded: *"Now* at last I understand how much I love her!"

Unfortunately, this state of ecstasy vanished all too soon, and Abraham, again reduced to his normal miserable proportions, not only could not tolerate, but could not even understand the magnificence of that moment of illumination. It took him only a few minutes to become once more a husband consumed by jealousy. He constantly had before his eyes the image that husbands never succeed in dispelling in similar cases, and the consolation of having acted reasonably does nothing to relieve their sufferings. During his first sleepless night he began to hope what his good sense rejected with horror: that King Abimelech would judge his adored Sarah as too old and send her away. But at the same time, he realized that this would mean the end of everything. Yes, of course, Sarah would come back to him . . . but Abraham had not forgotten the words that his wife had uttered in this regard: "It may be better this way, but I don't know for what . . ."

The critical morning had already passed without the king sending Sarah back, and from this fact Abraham concluded that his wife had found favor in Abimelech's eyes and that therefore the miracle had worked. Sarah's image had been fixed in his mind in the halo of that magical moment, dazzling with beauty, modestly trembling, with a gleam of excitement in her eyes, so that his fantasies, which in his imagination of a lovesick husband had been unleashed in an orgiastic turmoil, became more and more unbearable.

Then the whole day passed, the night passed, another day and night passed, and our hero, not even restored by sleep, understood that the magnificent impulse of that moment of ecstasy had ruined his life no less than what he had pusillanimously done at the time of the Egyptian adventure. By now he was convinced that Sarah had preserved her youth and beauty, that they had even been increased by amorous ardor in the arms of that young lover, and that she would not soon come back to him, unless . . . as the result of a new miracle, she were not suddenly aged again, or if the Lord should decide to intervene as He had done in Egypt. In his affliction, he turned his thoughts once more to the Lord, and although in recent months he had done his utmost to drive Him out of his mind, now he ardently evoked Him so that He would be close by. Not even this time did he ask for anything but to have Sarah back, at any price, in any condition, even unimaginably old and ugly; to him it now seemed only just that the Lord should help him by punishing him, by destroying his dream of love.

At that moment, almost as though to increase his sufferings to the limit, he was reminded of someone whom he not only preferred not to mention, but not even to remember: the phantom son who was supposed to be born to him from Sarah's womb. Now, to his utter consternation, it seemed to him that the term he had been granted to take the necessary measures to bring about the blessed event had lapsed beyond recall. Thus Abraham spent a great part of his third night of solitude in feverish computations, realizing at the end the gravity of his act of rebellion and all the horrible consequences that might result from it. In the pangs of that sleepless night the nightmare of a hellish punishment loomed before him, and it would have been even more unbearable than Sarah's loss. He could no longer recall the precise words with which the Lord had foretold the birth of that absurd and unnecessary son, but he remembered clearly that the Lord, in announcing the birth of

Ishmael, had stressed that his firstborn would be born from *his* loins. Did the same thing apply to the son who would have to be called "Laughter"? The Lord had only said (this he remembered) that his wife Sarah would have a son. But, alas, did the sentence mean that this son would be born from *his* loins? God, without even contradicting Himself, might diabolically punish His servant by eventually restoring his wife, ugly, old, and miraculously pregnant with the son of King Abimelech to boot . . .

At that moment Abraham would never have imagined that the Lord had already made a decision, and that on that night King Abimelech in his palace hadn't closed his eyes either—and not because he had sacrificed the hours reserved for sleep to the pleasures of the new concubine, but because he, too, had had the good fortune to make the acquaintance of the sole true and living God. All that the worthy Abraham knew was that in the early hours of the morning some of the king's men burst into his tent, and giving him hardly enough time to get dressed, had hustled him into a chariot and driven him to the city. Still half dazed, he suddenly found himself before the sovereign of Gerar, from whose furious words he managed to make out that his lie—albeit inspired this time by magnanimity and not cowardice—had been discovered because of the Lord, and that this event, on this occasion as well, would be to his enormous advantage. Indeed, after the inevitable tirade, not only was Sarah restored to him and not only was he paid *a thousand pieces of silver* as compensation, but behind the chariot that drove him back to his camp the king's men led sheep, oxen, menservants, and maidservants. And at the moment of their arrival, a high court official repeated to him words from the king that Abraham, in all the confusion, found hard to believe: *"Behold, my land is before thee: dwell where it pleaseth thee."*

This all happened so quickly, almost in the twinkling of an eye, that Abraham didn't even have time to recover from his initial shock and ensuing amazement. Amid his people, who came thronging around him in jubilation, he watched dazed as his many new possessions were unloaded and arranged, and it took a little time before he finally found himself *tête-à-tête* with his wife. Actually, in all that confusion, it was only this moment that mattered to him, and it was almost intolerable not to be able to give her his attention. Seeing her now once more in his tent, seated on the edge of the couch with what was simultaneously the virginal look of a maiden and the knowing look of a mature woman, with both an anxious and a detached bearing, and enveloped in that indefinable aroma of a slowly withering exotic flower, Abraham felt his heart overflow with bitterness and happiness. With a leap he was beside her, he threw himself on his knees, and while tears flowed in great abundance from his eyes, his lips murmured the same words of twenty-five years ago in Egypt: "Oh, Sarah, how I've suffered for you." But this time Sarah did not reject him as she had done twenty-five years before, but looked at him fondly, while her lips shaped a timid smile. "Take heart, my friend," she said, "the Lord saved me." But Abraham shook his head in despair: "Of course, my lady, my love, light of my life, of course, the Lord saved you *then* too, but not from everything . . ." Sarah, visibly embarrassed, turned her gaze slightly and swallowed. "But this time," she said, "the Lord intervened in time."

At this answer the sorely tried old man raised himself vehemently on his stiff knees, and his eyes scrutinized the woman's adored face. "What did you say?" he asked, dazed. "Despite the fear and amazement of this morning, I seemed to understand that the Lord enlightened Abimelech's mind only in the final hours of the night. But you . . . you spent three nights with him, in his bed." At this point Sarah slowly turned her head; on her face the bashful smile of a maiden reappeared, then extending her arm, she took a tuft of her husband's beard between two fingers, and began twisting it gently. "Calm down, my friend," she said. "I wasn't in his bed. I spent the days and nights in the women's quarters, among the other concubines. The king didn't touch me."

For a moment Abraham looked her up and down with incredulous eyes, then with his two hands he seized the freckled hand that was playing with his beard. "How is it possible?" he whispered, full of suspicion. "There's no need, my dear, for you to deceive me out of delicacy or gratitude. For me all that was settled the moment I gave you the highest token of my love. And yet is it possible . . ." and he went pale like someone suddenly conscious of a grave insult, "is it possible that he didn't appreciate your charms?" His eyes, which had suddenly become fierce, kept scrutinizing the woman, in search of something that might not be pleasing to a man. Sarah was beautiful, beautiful even at that moment, but she had been incomparably more beautiful three days earlier when the king's men had taken her away! "And yet you were magnificently beautiful that evening!" he cried in pain. "Is that man blind?"

Then Sarah broke into a ringing little laugh, and her half-open mouth with its white row of teeth gave her a look of childish coquetry; straightening herself slightly, she put her free hand on both of Abraham's, which were holding her other one prisoner in a convulsive grip. "I can't tell you how sweet and touching you are, my friend! But things went differently. He thought I was beautiful, very beautiful, in fact. He led me personally to his bed, he undressed me with his own hands, and as each garment came off he said something in praise of my beauty. Then . . ." "Never mind the details," grunted Abraham, "just tell me why . . ." At that moment Sarah removed her hand from those of her husband and with an impatient, almost furious gesture, shook her fist in the empty air. "Because at that moment what in me had *ceased to be after the manner of women* came back . . ."

That was all it took for Abraham, who until then had been kneeling by the couch, to find himself lying flat on the ground. Torrents of feelings and emotions were raging in his heart, and his brain threatened to explode under the pressure of his thoughts. But this was surely not the moment to think and draw conclusions. It was solely the moment to lead the two aged lovers, after this eventful kind of honeymoon journey, to a well-deserved first night, and the fact that it was not night but a bright morning of sunshine made no difference. In the atmosphere of the divine miracle the barriers of inhibition and reluctance fell, and intoxicated with happiness and astonishment, unmindful of themselves and everything else, Abraham and Sarah were joined in a holy embrace. In the exaltation of their senses and feelings, they were unaware of old Eliezer, who came in hurriedly on some urgent business but retreated just as hastily before becoming a wonderstruck stone statue. And above all, it did not cross their minds that this was the last day on which they would have been able to execute the Lord's command.

On that day Sarah's revived womb conceived the phantom son.

IX. *The Lord laughs (Epilogue)*

WE HOPE WE'VE SUCCEEDED IN CONVINCING THE KIND READER not only that the Abimelech episode is not a pointless and unpleasant repetition of the adventure in Egypt, but that without it the mythical story of Abraham and Sarah would be incomplete, not to say incomprehensible. Obviously we have allowed our imagination a good deal of freedom in reworking the scant biblical facts, and we are prompt to admit that the course of events could also have been reconstructed some other way, perhaps with more convincing verisimilitude; but, we repeat, the novelistic element in our "text" is of secondary importance, and if this time too we have given it free rein, it was really to entertain our readers a little and ourselves as well. We have moreover kept in mind that people today are very sensitive to psychology, the only thing to which they lend a trusting ear, so it may have been somewhat of a cheap trick on our part to use it to bind what happened in Gerar to the body of the story. Besides, myth is not necessarily a-psychological; in fact, it isn't so at all, it's just that by its nature it tolerates gaps, which it is precisely the writer's job to fill. In the final analysis, we have not tried to do more, or with less right, than Homer and the Greek tragedians, but they, among other advantages, had abundant data.

Our suspicion about the essential importance of the Gerar episode was aroused precisely by the fact that it is apparently so pointless and unpleasant, and that in the monumental Abrahamic mythologema, which—as we have seen—also embraces and assimilates the tragedy of Sodom and Gomorrah, and even the distressing carnal union between Lot and his daughters, it seems to represent a jarring note, offensive to the ear and to common sense. But being firmly convinced that, in the sacred texts in general and in Genesis in particular, not one word should be overlooked, and even the most trifling as well as the most repellent elements of the biblical story should be taken seriously, we could not close our eyes to this apparently insignificant episode, if for no other reason than the fact of having been alerted by the circumstance that our heroine's twilight adventure had to take place, for chronological reasons, more or less at the end of the three months preceding the conception of the son foretold and ordained by God.

Perhaps what seems to us the fruit of our imagination, however inspired, was also Abraham's motive in reality when, after twenty-five years of residence among the terebinths of Mamre, he folded his tents and set out to wander with his people on the plains of the land promised to his, likewise promised, descendants. As he made his way toward the shores of the Mediterranean, he perhaps could not help feeling in his heart that he was attempting a strange, late, second honeymoon journey in search of a strange, much desired, and quite absurd second wedding night, in order to have the undesired and equally absurd son promised by the Lord and wanted by Him alone. And we would like to hope, in the interests of our hero, that the way we have suggested that the miracle came to pass was truly the one corresponding to reality, and that Abraham himself realized that it had come to pass in the best of ways. For while he had deliberately refrained from coming to the Lord's help, consciously denying Him any cooperation, he had been convinced from the beginning that if He seriously wanted to, the Lord would carry out His own will at all costs: in his moments of greatest discouragement, Abraham had not ruled out the idea that the Lord might finally reappear, His patience exhausted, and violently force him and his aged spouse into a miserable and humiliating embrace. This time, however, the Lord had given him a wonderfully pleasant surprise, for the simple reason that His miracle, contrary to what Abraham had expected on the basis of previous experience, was not devoid of human logic. The good patriarch, in his boundless faith in divine omnipotence, considered it quite admissible that even an old woman with a dried-up womb might give birth by the will of the Lord; but his imagination would never have ventured to the point of supposing that the Lord, by so ordaining, could make sure that an old woman would again become, at least temporarily, an attractive young one, in full possession of her female capacities, which meant that instead of a forced and humiliating embrace, a spontaneous, joyous, intoxicating—and despite all its sacrality—happy one again became possible. And all this was due to the Almighty's agreeable idea of having His most tumultuous miracle preceded by a prologue!

The new experience, however, did not greatly modify the idea that Abraham, in the course of a long life, had formed for himself about the Lord. To the surprisingly pleasant solutions that the Almighty, when He wanted to, could improvise to bring the most desperate human problems to a happy ending, the patriarch contrasted the sufferings and anxieties, the humiliations and dissatisfactions, the efforts and horrors that he had been forced to endure since the beginning of their covenant. But he was already too old, and now very tired, to be able to feel deeply unhappy. The many and frequent signs of divine omnipotence had taught him the harsh lesson that human life was merely an instrument in the hands of the Lord, an instrument at the service of mysterious ends, and that

214 / THE HOLY EMBRACE

man had to content himself with that bit of his life that was of no use or no importance to the Lord. These glimpses of existence in which man had the illusion of acting freely were rare and brief, and obviously badly spent—by now he knew it!—since the Lord was always in a hurry to change their course for the worse. For the worse, of course, according to Abraham's ideas and tastes, but presumably for the better according to the Lord's. Perhaps no one, from those remote times to today, was ever less capable than the discoverer of God of distinguishing between good and evil. In order to steer a middle course, get by, and navigate between the rocks of moral uncertainties, he ended by accepting an apparently infallible practical rule. While he was always rather relectant to accept as good even the most obvious and palpable good, he never hesitated to recognize as good the worst difficulties and saddest misfortunes that befell him, since these things undoubtedly came from the Lord, and the worse they were, the more surely they expressed His will. Worn out and resigned as he was, incapable of rebelling, protesting, or formulating critical judgments, he was the first to utter the great philosophical theorem that has since been treasured for thousands of years: All's well, no matter how bad things are, since it is the will of God!

It is a curious thing that fatigue and resignation often lead to such an accomodating optimism, instead of to despair or pessimism, which—strange to say—presuppose a combative spirit and a good dose of vitality. The road to such ultimate wisdom as "All's well since everything is the will of God" is paved more with suffering and defeat than with intellectual efforts and the thirst for knowledge. And the man who is in possession of this ultimate wisdom not only succeeds in not understanding anything about anything, but also in giving up: it's enough that God knows and is content.

Thus our Abraham died without understanding the deeper meaning of Isaac's birth. Once in a while his wandering thoughts tried to focus on the problem of why the Lord had preferred to overturn the order of nature with an astounding miracle rather than intervening thirty, twenty, or even only ten years earlier, when Sarah was young and beautiful not by a miracle but by virtue of the order of nature. But that was as far as he got, his mind refused to work further, and heavy iron shutters came down to block his horizon. In the same way he was never able to understand why his son should be called "Laughter."

Ever since the divine announcement of his birth, the innocent little monster was a source of sadness for our hero, who at most was thereby helped in solidifying the foundations of his optimistic wisdom. Even the unforgettable second "wedding night" in Gerar turned into tragedy. The haughty Sarah was humiliated by her late pregnancy and felt she would go out of her mind when she realized that the repetition of the Egyptian adventure was nothing but a trap set by the Lord. Needless to say, the miracle that made her able to conceive a child in her womb, give birth to him, and nurse him at her own breast, was not enough to preserve for long the youth and beauty that had come back to her for a fixed occasion and purpose, and even less to dispel her frigidity and innate scruples. The holy embrace of the Gerar honeymoon was and remained unique, and from that moment on Sarah wanted to hear no more about it from Abraham, who—according to her—by this despicable gesture of his had provided a worthy conclusion to the long series of base and cowardly acts with which he had besmirched their whole married life. She felt so humiliated that she no longer left her tent, not wishing to see the amused or compassionate smiles of her people; she even sent to Gerar for a midwife to attend the birth, and did not allow anyone to see her nursing her baby. Abraham, too, was excluded from this spectacle, though—as we recall—he had always dreamed of it, weaving around it poetically voluptuous images. But, as usual, he tenderly respected his wife's moods.

Still, he had to realize that all this secrecy brought with it considerable dangers for the reputation, and even the authenticity, of his sole heir. Whispered rumors came to his ears, according to which it had not been Sarah who gave birth to little Isaac, but they had secretly bought him from a caravan, and she had not been the one to nurse him, but a wet-nurse whom they kept hidden in her tent. So the tribe of shepherds suspected that their venerable leader was throwing dust in everyone's eyes to assist his wife in the maneuver by which she was seeking to dislodge Ishmael. Abraham discovered with painful astonishment that his people sided with Hagar and her son, while he had nothing on hand to prove that little Isaac was his son and Sarah's, given to them *in extremis*— indeed, quite beyond the extreme limit of any possibility—by the Lord Himself.

It is to a situation of this kind that a few passages in the Bible seem to allude. *"Who would have said unto Abraham, that Sarah should have given children suck? for I have born him a son in his old age,"* exclaims the elderly Sarah after the delivery. And the sacred text adds: *"And the child grew, and was weaned; and Abraham made a great feast the same day that Isaac was weaned."* This passage is particularly striking and raises the following issue: either the weaning, being a critical moment in a child's life, was a traditional occasion for feasting among the Jews (as indeed it was), and so why emphasize the fact that Isaac's weaning was *also* celebrated with a proper banquet, while nothing of the kind is recorded in the Bible for any of its other important figures; or else the weaning of little Isaac (i.e, the "great feast" itself) had a particular importance, but in that case why not say so explicitly? The inattentive reader of the Holy Scriptures (exegetes included) does not linger over this excess of zeal by the compilers of the canon, which to us, however, seems less like loquacity than the now unintelligible residue of an abundance of ancient legends that once circulated around Isaac's weaning feast, but for one reason or another, were no longer to figure in the canonical text. In this connection, we recall a similar phenomenon in the case of the mysterious name of Iscah.

The seemingly gratuitous mention of a "great feast" seems to us wholly justified by the painful situation in which, according to our reconstruction, Abraham had come to find himself in the eyes of the world and his own incredulous people, a situation that can also be glimpsed in the biblical sentence preceding the one about the feast and which torturously begins: "Who would have said unto Abraham . . . ?" Yes, indeed, who would have said it? And who did say it? But in defining the importance and meaning of the great feast, the legends speak more clearly than biblical allusions and our intuition: it was Abraham's intention for it to be an emphatic demonstration of Sarah's maternity, and accordingly of the legitimacy of Isaac's rights of succession. Sarah, on this occasion, certainly behaved in such a way as to leave no doubt in anyone's mind and heart about her status as a recent mother and her regenerated capacity as a woman. Older and uglier than ever since the time of her meeting with the Lord, beside herself with shame, the humiliation she had endured, and also with rage, she bared her milk-swollen breasts before the assembled guests, and to everyone's penitent consternation, stuck her nipple in little Isaac's mouth to give him one final taste of mother's milk. But as though this weren't enough, and not satisfied with the brilliant proof, she made the rounds of the table with her naked breasts still exposed to the perplexed gaze of the onlookers, and offered milk to all the infants whom their young mothers had brought to the banquet. So it wasn't a trick! Everyone was left speechless and with the firm conviction that never in their lives had they seen a mother so well supplied with milk.

We leave it to the kind reader to imagine what a blow such an exhibition was to Sarah's pride and refinement. On the other hand, by this blatant demonstration of her maternity, not only did she regain the love and respect of the tribe of shepherds, but the suggestion of the supernatural that accompanied all these events made the halo of legend that had enveloped her since her youth shine even more brightly. If once the tribe had boasted of its lady's extraordinary beauty and imperishable youth, now it gloried in her advanced age. Proud of their future patriarch, they attributed to Sarah a morbid, almost fierce attachment to the son who had been born to her against all hope and against all desire. The legend, in some of its variants, even has her die heartbroken at the alarming news of Isaac's sacrifice.

Who can say what the relations between Sarah and Isaac were, and what sentiments she really felt for the son on whose birth she commented in words that—by virtue of the meaning of the name Isaac—turn out to be rather mysterious. *"God hath made me to laugh,"* she said, *"so that all that hear will laugh with me."* The reader who has been kind enough to follow us in our efforts will be somewhat hesitant to accept these words as the pure expression of maternal happiness. In the present case (as happens not seldom), the translation of the Hebrew text is itself an interpretation. Indeed, we have encountered versions, exemplary in every respect, that give the passage this meaning: *God has brought me laughter, those who hear of it will laugh at me*, and we fear this translation may be the correct one. In plain words and in a translation faithful to the letter and spirit of the original, Sarah may well have been commenting on the monstrous event as follows: *God has brought me Isaac* (laughter) *and for this I will become the laughingstock of the world.*

Anyway, since God had brought him to her, Sarah made Isaac her badge of honor, and on this point she always remained sensitive and vulnerable. Since she must have felt ridiculous, she did not allow anyone to make fun of her, and once Isaac had come into the world, her pride would not tolerate any diminution in the rights and dignity of her child. Her pride had given her the strength to endure the astonishing and humiliating exhibition at the weaning banquet, the high dramatic tension of which had cut short any smiles that appeared on the lips of the guests. And this same pride, not as a mother but as a "princess," which had induced her to present herself publicly in the role of a formidable wet-nurse, led her all the more easily to a cruel step that satisfied rather than humiliating her *amour propre*. With her reputation and prestige re-established, Sarah could no longer endure the presence of the Egyptian bondwoman, whom she was unable to forgive for her worthy performance in Abraham's bed, and still less for having been the cause, albeit involuntarily, of the gossip that had forced

on her the humiliating exhibition at the weaning feast. Hagar
must go, along with her young son, of whom Sarah had ceased to
be fond since Isaac's birth and soon began to hate as a possible
threat to the position of her child. The pretext for expelling them
was supplied by the unfortunate youth Ishmael, who, falling victim to the contagious laughter that little Isaac inevitably provoked, allowed himself to make fun of Sarah's child and play tricks
on him. She demanded that mother and son be instantly and
forever cast out. But what Abraham, for love of his wife, the most
beautiful woman in the world, had done thirteen years before with
a light heart and total irresponsibility (since Ishmael had seemed to
him to be the son promised by the Lord) today proved *very grievous
in Abraham's sight because of his son.* Abraham loved his firstborn
and in thirteen years had got used to thinking of him as his heir
and successor. For him Ishmael was and remained the son foretold
by God, and he would never have admitted that he had misunderstood the Lord's words. For him it had been the Lord who had
abruptly changed His mind, and he therefore considered Isaac
almost an intruder. It was the fault of the son who was to be called
"Laughter" that his ephemeral, melancholy happiness had collapsed; his fault that Sarah in a flash had lost her youth and beauty,
and he himself that fondness of mother, sister, and friend with
which Sarah had made him happy; and now, because of this intruder, he was to lose his favorite son. This last was an enormous
blow: it was all that was needed to complete the edifice of Abraham's resigned optimism, the supreme wisdom of "All's well, no
matter how bad things are," and the boundless sadness of God's
chosen people.

We have the feeling that Abraham was not particularly upset when
later the Lord expressed the unexpected and astonishing wish to
witness the sacrifice of the phantom son for whose birth He had
turned the order of nature upside down. Hardened by now to all
the divine absurdities and unshakeable in the optimism of his
sadness, he was left puzzled at most. The biblical account, dry,

laconic, without a mention of our hero's state of mind, does not contradict, but rather tacitly confirms the picture we have tried to draw of Abraham at this period in his long life. The Bible shows us a majestic old man who sets out, with superhuman phlegm, without a word of protest, with the apathy of a robot, to obey the divine command; he preserves his impassiveness to the end, and his hand is ready to strike the victim without a tremor. We would like to suppose that in his heart of hearts, he was profoundly convinced that the Lord did not seriously want this holocaust. On the other hand, in his optimistic wisdom, he completely entrusted himself to the Lord's will: it was God who committed crazy acts, and it was up to Him to find the remedy for them.

Certainly, with a protagonist like our Abraham, the whole biblical episode that goes by the name "sacrifice of Isaac" becomes drained of the meaning that has been assigned to it for thousands of years. To try a man already so sorely tried, and now almost eager to undergo more trials to corroborate his own philosophical optimism, would have been a sadistic game even on the part of the Lord, so poor a judge of the human soul. He could be sure of the result from the beginning: Abraham would have sacrificed Isaac to Him.

The test, however, took place. And if we think less of the resignation or filial obedience of Abraham as a well-defined historical personage, and more of *man*, whom he represents and signifies in this decisive phase of humanity's march, we can easily see how at this moment *man* was ready to offer a human sacrifice to the sole true and living God. In other words, the Lord found in the patriarch the person who would offer Him the only consubstantial sacrifice worthy of Him. Here is the essence of the famous episode, and if there was a test, it was a double-edged one. For the Lord was strongly tempted to taste the food that ever since His anthropomorphization would have been for Him the most delicious: human flesh . . .

Historians of religion have observed that the gods not only "get hungry," but nourish themselves with foods made preferably, so to speak, *in their image, according to their likeness*, and not even Yahweh has been an exception to this rule. He had spent a large portion of His existence in close connection with sheep, and in pre-Abrahamic times had fed on ewes and rams. Abel had quite naturally sacrificed to Him the firstlings of his flocks, and by accepting them and unceremoniously rejecting Cain's cereals, the Lord had explicitly demonstrated that His tastes were not vegetarian but carnivorous, and that He preferred lamb to all other dishes. When later, by revealing Himself to Abraham, He was able to achieve the rank of absolute Being—in essence and *par excellence*—and pure spirit, His appetite for the firstlings of the human race, until that moment carefully held in check, was aroused, since among all His creatures, it was precisely the human being who resembled Him most closely, and He had perhaps deliberately created him that way to make him more appealing to His palate. Perhaps—who would dare rule it out?—He only wanted Abraham's progeny to become infinite like the dust of the earth and the stars in the sky so as to have a livestock farm and never have to suffer the lack of this one truly worthy and exquisite dish. But, as we have seen, the human opposition of His discoverer temporarily scuttled the divine plans, and the Lord not only had to repress His gourmet aspirations, but actually resort to a miracle to bring the progenitor of the immense future human flock into the world. In the first pact that He concluded with His discoverer and first follower, when Abraham still had no offspring, the Lord had to be satisfied with merely enriching his habitual menu, but even on this occasion He did not give up mutton, the main dish in His diet. And with what did He replace Isaac after having overcome the great temptation? Once again with a ram, which He Himself had sent to the site of the sacrifice. We don't mind pointing out another indication of His predilection for sheep in the fact that in His heart, when the time came, He was to prefer Rachel to Leah, whose name is etymologically akin to cow, while the name Rachel means ewe. And finally did not the Lord call His son, Jesus Christ on the cross, by the sensual euphemism of "lamb"?

Anyway the Lord was able to withstand the giddy temptation to make a sacrificial meal of Isaac. In our opinion, He had never seriously intended, even for a moment, to remove from circulation the person on whom He had based the further unfolding of His plan, and for whose birth He had had to set off miracles against nature. By the expression of His surprising and unreasonable wish, the Lord, in addition to experiencing the thrill of temptation, wanted above all to let Abraham know that this kind of sacrifice was His due, and thus ratify His right to human firstlings. That the firstborn of the human race would be His due as a sacrificial meal, He would later expressly tell Moses—and oddly enough, man's ransom on that occasion would also be a lamb!

Finally, by not eating Isaac, the Lord may have had another thought besides that of not compromising the carefully foreseen course of History. At this delicate moment in His incipient relations with humanity, it would not have been a good idea to create superfluous obstacles in His own path. Men, at that moment in their history, not only had at their disposal a rich and varied pantheon at which to direct their worship, but almost as though they weren't yet satisfied by such an abundance of gods, were avidly searching for new ones, and creating every species and subspecies of them, demigods, heroes, and demons. It sufficed for man himself to have a glorious life, or one out of the ordinary, preferably concluded with a death extraordinary enough to strike the imagination, to have the possibility of being raised to the ranks of the immortals, with all the rights of worship due to supernatural beings. For the Lord there was therefore the danger that the human victim, who to Him was nothing but an ordinary meal, would end by rising among the immortals to increase the number of false and lying gods against whom He, in those very times, was engaged in what He foresaw would be a long and hard struggle. The sole true and living God could not yet allow Himself the luxury of consuming the food worthy of Him. The experience of several centuries later, His first and only experience as far as human flesh is concerned, must have convinced Him that He had acted properly in not accepting the sacrifice of Isaac. The tender flesh of Jephthah's daughter was an exquisite meal and worthy of a god, but around the tomb of the slain virgin who had been sacrificed to Him a cult had emerged with annual celebrations and appropriate lamentations, a cult identical with those bestowed on the hero and heroine victims of the false and lying gods. We can therefore assume that Abraham's sacrificed son would have made even more spectacular progress than the maiden of Gilead toward immortality and in the veneration of the people.

Abraham, long reluctant to accumulate new notions or consciously perfect his ideas about the God he had discovered, this time could not help noting that the Lord was also anthropophagous, or at least had cannibalistic tastes that only with difficulty were held in check. The patriarch, who by a strange vaingloriousness would never have admitted that it had been God who through him had revealed Himself to the world, but insisted that he had been the one to reveal Him, bitterly regretted his great discovery. The unquestionable clarity and infallible intuition on which his great discovery had been based had disappointed and mocked him. Frankly, he would have preferred not to have discovered such a god, but one who, in his absolute spirituality, would be just but understanding, powerful but good, the lord of his creatures to be sure, but also their friend, and above all the generous ally of his discoverer. Instead of all this, he had loosed on the world an abusive tyrant, under whose crushing weight man was not even allowed to breathe . . . Don't resist and carry out the Lord's will— such was the condition for not having to deal with Him until new orders were issued, and not having anything to do with Him was man's only possibility of peace and rest. In these periods of truce, man was finally free to make amends and try to redress the evil he had committed to the detriment of his neighbor by carrying out the divine will.

As grave punishment for his deceitful clarity and cursed intuition, Abraham was still left for a few decades with that living statue of reproach, his wife, Sarah, whose extraordinary beauty and unfading youth, miraculously preserved by the magic of his love, had vanished in moments at the hands of the Lord. The death of Sarah, whom he loved tenderly all the way to the grave, believing her to be the Lord's victim, and thus in a certain sense his as well, was a melancholy relief to him.

As we bid our heroine farewell, let us also take leave of the hero of our story. He had long since fulfilled the great mission with which he had been entrusted in the divine plan and in man's history, and there was nothing important left for him to do but hand on his experiences and knowledge, concerning the Lord he had discovered, to his heir and to the numerous offspring born to him by his second wife. As we gaze fondly after the tottering figure of old Abraham, who is about to depart the scene, we take comfort in the thought that many serene years still lay ahead of him and that he did not die without knowing the reciprocated love that he had vainly sought at the side of the most beautiful woman in the world. Keturah may not have been a great beauty, but her mind and heart were in the right place, and she knew instinctively what a man expects from a woman and wife. Young and romantic, she fell madly in love with the powerful, wise, and sorely tried old man, and she devoted herself wholeheartedly to showing him what was meant by true love. Her great merit lay precisely in having divined and singled out the patriarch's innermost psychological needs: she lavished tenderness and veneration on the man who had hitherto squandered himself in adoration of another, she offered physical and emotional pleasures to the man who hitherto had had to beg for them, and she gave plenty of sons to the "father of a multitude of peoples" who hitherto had thought himself unable to procreate without supernatural prompting and intervention. But what was most important about her was her sweetness of character and ready abnegation: she was content to make her lord content. The Abraham of cheerful mind, appreciative of the ordinary pleasures of this earth, and decidedly opposed to anything that might disturb his senile peace and quiet, was certainly Keturah's handiwork, and—we daresay—all to her credit.

*   *   *

As we part from our protagonists for good, let us still say a few
words about their son, who had been given the name "Laughter,"
and about Him who made them give him this name. In our
account of the historical laughter of Abraham and Sarah, Isaac
himself represents the third laugh. But whose laugh? To the kind
reader, victim of his or her own kindness, who has stuck with us
to the end, it will surely be obvious by now that the two old
parents' long discussions on the subject were a lot of idle chatter,
a pitiful waste of time. It would have been too great an honor for
our hero and heroine had the Lord, even out of mere spite, chosen
to erect a commemorative monument to the irreverent laughter of
either one of them by so naming the phantom son. Isaac was
simply and beyond any doubt the laughter of the Lord Himself.
And that this is the way it must have been is confirmed not only
by the Hebrew etymology according to which the name *Yitshach*
(laughter) is a shortened form of the original name *Yitshachel*
(laughter of the Lord), but by the very fact, much more important
than any kind of scientific contribution, that at that decisive moment in History, only the Lord had reason to laugh.

It must have been this way because, as we have seen, Abraham's
and Sarah's laughter had been premature, in absolute misappre-
hension of the true relations of strength. We might also add that
neither did Isaac have anything in his character, life, or destiny to
match his luminous name. On the contrary, we must say in all
sincerity that never in history or myths or fairy tales do we find an
individual so at odds with his own name. This observation, however, in no way contradicts the fact that laughter, almost like an
ironical and irreverent musical accompaniment, makes its appearance, in one form or another, in every phase of his life. Besides the
two famous laughs of his parents, we would like to mention the
general hilarity that greeted his birth and to which Sarah herself
alluded; and we also recall that his half-brother Ishmael found
something irresistibly ridiculous about him. He himself, "Laughter," with all the laughter that rose spontaneously around him, was

incapable of laughing with it. Shall we go on? The adventure at the court of King Abimelech—which had given the Lord the opportunity to produce His most amazing miracle and had led Abraham and Sarah to their holy embrace—ended in farce when repeated in Isaac's life. And did not his wife, Rebecca, laugh behind his back when she took advantage of her old husband's blindness and by a cheap trick extorted from him the blessing for Jacob?

The many laughs that, from being a prelude to his birth, went on to accompany all the notable phases of his life made Isaac a timid, hesitant man, oppressed by mysterious anxieties. No important or memorable gesture is attached to his name; he was good only at keeping agreements, living in the fear of the Lord, and making His greatness feared. Certainly this was just what the Lord Himself had wanted. The Lord had wanted him not to be born under normal circumstances like other ordinary mortals; the Lord had wanted him to have a weak character and weak eyesight, so that the derisive and humiliating laughter of those around him would drive him more closely toward Himself. At that moment in the relations between God and man, the Lord needed a follower to whom He could appear as the epitome of overwhelming force and infinite goodness. It was to this end that He had cleverly organized the failed sacrifice of Isaac. If this was a proof of extreme resignation on Abraham's part, and a proof of laudable self-discipline on the part of the Lord, for the youth himself the episode turned into a horrible joke. The fact that in the end the Lord spared his life remained for Isaac the unshakable basis for his faith in His extreme goodness. But Isaac, ridiculed, timid, suffering from persecution mania since his birth, had also had occasion on the pyre to make the acquaintance of terror, and from this he was never able to recover. From that moment on, the image of the Lord and the image of terror were superimposed and identified with each other in his soul. This statement is not, as it may seem, a figment of our imagination; we have in mind certain passages in our sacred text. Indeed, there is a kind of formula for taking an oath that often recurs in the Bible, and which is not limited to invoking the Lord simply by name, but is concerned to remind Him that He should consider Himself the exclusive property of the family of His elect. Thus we see the appearance of the God of Abraham, the God of Nahor, the God of Jacob. But rarely do we find the God of Isaac. In this case, instead of the name of God, the word *Terror* generally appears! For the patriarch who was called "Laughter," the Lord was called "Terror." It sounds like a figment of our imagination, and yet it is not.

We have come a long way from the memories of our religious lessons in childhood, during which we were taught that the name Isaac expressed the immense joy of the aged parents at the birth of an heir for whom they had given up hope, or the fond joy felt by Creator and creature in the happy union of their new covenant! Now we know that in his name Isaac bore the laughter of the Lord, the laughter of the God of Isaac, the laugh of terror . . . It may seem to the kind reader that once again we have arrived at a play on words, at pure illusionism, which fascinates the writer no less than the conjuror. But no, we have instead arrived at another curious fact.

How does the Lord laugh? Everyone perhaps has a vague idea of the Lord's laughter. Many may imagine divine laughter in the image and likeness of their own. Others, perhaps, supposing that God's laughter must be qualitatively better than the common laughter of mortals, are inclined to imagine on the lips of the Almighty an indulgent smile. But all ideas on the subject are idle speculation for which no one makes serious claims. The catechism does not enlighten us on this question, which for theology and the faithful does not exist. As far as the Church is concerned, we are free to form our own ideas about God's laughter. But what about the Bible?

The God of the Bible does not seem like someone who wants to laugh or is able to, and indeed we must read many thousands of verses to find a few that speak of the Lord's laughter. But there are some, and when we read them we feel the blood run cold in our veins and the hair stand up on our heads. According to these accounts, the Lord's laughter sounded anything but paternally good-natured and indulgent to the ears of those who had to hear it. In the sacred text, there is a single epithet for God's laughter, and it recurs regularly: *terrible*. We must resign ourselves to the fact that Isaac *was the terrible laughter of the Lord*!

Because of His Isaac, the Lord will have laughed heartily, and we cannot help mentioning the old adage that he who laughs last laughs best. A common interpretation of the name Isaac runs as follows: God laughs for the victory won over His adversaries. A simpleton might think that with such a high-sounding name, Isaac would have become a famous military leader, or at least that his descendants would have annihilated the Assyrians, Babylonians, Egyptians, and all other nations that worshipped false and lying gods instead of the sole true and living One. But all this does not correspond to the facts. What happened later in this sense already belongs to the story of another covenant between God and humanity, the one in the New Testament. The name Isaac obviously referred to a more immediate, more tangible victory. But at that historical moment, who was the Lord's adversary, an adversary much more dangerous than idols? The answer, on the last page of our story, now comes easily: the only adversary who counted for the Lord was *man* himself, who in the mythical characters of Abraham and Sarah had resisted Him to the bitter end. In the mythical character of Isaac, this *man* ended by laying down his arms and bending his neck under the divine yoke, fully accepting the old covenant. And at that moment the triumphant laughter of the Lord was heard for the first time! With the name of the son called "Laughter," God erected a monument—and by its frightfulness also a *memento*—to His own victory over man.

With Isaac, in whose ears this frightful divine laughter resounded all the way to the grave, the Lord laid the solid foundations of His victory, which would for a long time guarantee Him a position of crushing superiority over man, who so far had never ceased rebelling against Him. With Isaac, He began His triumphal career in the history of humanity, a career that should not have encountered any obstacles, if man's desperation had not prevailed over his terror. The chosen people, whose shoulders He had saddled with the weight of His destiny, began to rebel against the order of the curse, thus demonstrating that they were not prepared to carry on His lofty mission. Since, oddly enough, obstacles of this kind always turn out not to have been anticipated by divine omniscience, the Lord, taken by surprise, felt His laugh of triumph become muffled in His throat. In search of comfort and hope, He then had recourse to His prescience and steeled Himself with wise patience to await the next opportune moment to send *His man* into the world.

This man was born on earth under miraculous circumstances, some two thousand years after the likewise miraculous birth of our Isaac. And after his sacrifice, which simultaneously offered god, man, and lamb to the Lord, the terrible laughter exploded again.

The terrible laughter, which—perhaps—now in our own time, is starting to fade on His lips . . .